# WHEN IN ROME

# WHEN IN ROME

A HEART OF THE CITY NOVEL

# C.J. DUGGAN

hachette
AUSTRALIA

hachette
AUSTRALIA

Published in Australia and New Zealand in 2017
by Hachette Australia
(an imprint of Hachette Australia Pty Limited)
Level 17, 207 Kent Street, Sydney NSW 2000
www.hachette.com.au

National Library of Australia
Cataloguing-in-Publication data:

Duggan, C.J., author.
When in Rome/C.J. Duggan.

ISBN: 978 0 7336 3954 8 (pbk)

Series: Duggan, C.J. Heart of the city.
Romance fiction.
Rome (Italy) – Fiction.

Cover design by Keary Taylor
Cover photographs courtesy of Shutterstock
Author photograph by Craig Peihopa
Text design by Bookhouse, Sydney
Typeset in 11/16 pt Minion Pro by Bookhouse, Sydney
Printed and bound in Great Britain by Clays Ltd, St Ives plc

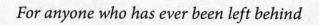

*For anyone who has ever been left behind*

# Chapter One

It struck me as a wondrous talent that Jan was able to type anything on her keyboard with her manicured hot-pink talons. Her entire focus was on her computer screen; her short coiffed hairstyle partially blocking the palm tree–lined beach backdrop. Dressed in a stiff navy jacket and cravat and wearing heavy eye make-up, Jan prided herself on looking the part, though I desperately wanted to reach out and blend her foundation line into her neck. John and Jan Buzzo's travel agency looked like the place where airline staff who couldn't quite pass the test came to live out their days, fulfilling their own crushed dreams by living vicariously through other people's travels. At the back of the room, just before the curtained alcove that didn't quite hide the view of the kettle and cup-a-soups, John Buzzo banged on the top of the printer and swore under his breath at the paper jam.

'Stupid piece of—'

'Here you go!'

A stapler punching paper drew my attention back to Jan, who, with much care, folded the stapled sheets and slid them into a complimentary faux leather binder embossed with the company's motto.

*No regrets.*

'You're all set!' Jan beamed, handing over the blue pouch with a silent fist pump for her commission earned.

I stared at her outreached hand for a long time, blinking as if I was having an out-of-body experience. I took it from her gingerly, barely believing what I had done. In an attempt to escape another one of my mother's lectures about what I was doing with my life, accompanied by the drone of the vacuum cleaner as she sucked up wayward chip crumbs from under my feet, I had gone out for some much-needed fresh air and sunshine. Now it seemed I would be basking in Italian sunshine, thanks to the budget 'Bellissimo' tour that I had just booked.

Like, seriously, I had only been making an enquiry, right? Walking past the travel agency, I entered on a whim, thinking only to ask a couple of quick questions, and maybe grab a brochure to take away. But as I opened up the travel pouch as if I was standing on a grand stage readying myself to announce 'and the winner is', there it was in bold print:

Shorten/Samantha Miss
Economy
Boarding Pass
Melbourne–Rome

*Oh, God.*

I felt all the blood drain from my face, the horror registering as I mentally began to calculate how many days I had until I would actually be scanning this very ticket.

*What have I done?*

Jan leant on her elbows and looked at me across her desk. 'Sammi, you are going to have the best time.'

I blinked, double-checking the date on the ticket against the calendar on Jan's desk, then looked up to her kohl-rimmed sparkling blue eyes.

'Remember,' she said, reaching out and tapping one long fingernail on the binder. 'No regrets.' Tap-tap.

Then why did I want to vomit into her wastepaper basket?

~

'Rome?!' My mother's predictable tirade echoed in the kitchen. 'That money was meant to be for a car, or a deposit on a house! Bill, talk some sense into her.'

Dad sighed, rubbing his hand over his beard, weary from the conversation already. 'Give her a break, love. You told her you wanted her to go out, so she went out.'

'I didn't expect her to book a ticket on some binge-drinking, orgy party-bus to Rome.'

'That's not what the brochure says, is it?' I quickly flicked through the booklet. 'Oh, yes, that's right, binge drinking day one. But to be fair, according to the itinerary, the orgy doesn't commence until day three.'

I slid the booklet over to Dad, who played along, nodding his head with interest. 'Well, you have to get settled in first,' he added.

Mum snatched the brochure away from us. 'I am so glad you two think this is funny. Have you given any thought to how you're going to prepare for this? Monday, Sammi. You fly out next Monday. You have no Euros, no travel adapters; what season is it over there? Are there travel bans in place? I bet you know nothing of all of this.'

Truth be known, I hadn't given a single thought to any of those things—I was busy trying not to freak out about what I had just done. But as I watched Mum look over the travel documents in horror, it occurred to me that this was as much about proving to my family that I could indeed make adult decisions as it was an attractive escape route. It all seemed so impossibly grown up, to book a trip away on the other side of the world. I didn't do these kinds of things; I was the baby, the homebody, strictly anti-change. Unlike my sister, Claire, the globe-trotter, I was happy staying at home. I sat on the stool next to Dad at the kitchen island, my attention drifting between my parents. Was it really such a shock that I could do something like this? That I, Sammi Shorten, could be so spontaneous and whimsical as to book a European adventure? They clearly didn't think I'd go through with it; I could see it in their eyes.

Mum squinted at the documents at arm's length, struggling to see without her reading glasses. 'You must be able to get your money back somehow . . . surely there's something in the fine print.'

Something inside me shifted, a feeling that drew my weight down onto my elbows as I leant on the kitchen countertop. 'Mum.'

'There must be some kind of cooling-off period . . .'

I sighed. 'Mum.'

'Surely a special circumstance where they can refund your money or . . .'

'MUM!'

Mum snapped up from the documents, blinking, then looked at me closely as if seeing me for the very first time. 'What?'

I smiled, small and sad, seeing everything that lay behind her eyes. In her gaze I saw her pleading for me to stay; that I could binge-watch all the TV I wanted, eat out of the fridge, make a mess, leave the hall lights on all night if I wanted—*just please don't go*.

I slid off my stool, rounded the kitchen counter and wrapped my arms around my mum; she seemed so small and fragile against my towering frame. I wasn't sure where my height came from, but it certainly wasn't from Mum.

I kissed the top of her head as she slowly, and somewhat reluctantly, put her arms around me; in 'Mum-logic', hugging me back meant admitting defeat.

'I won't even be gone that long—it'll be a whirlwind trip. I'll be home and leaving crumbs on the carpet before you know it.'

Mum pulled away. 'Yes, well, that's what your sister said.'

My smile dimmed, thinking of Claire, who had ended up in Paris, madly in love and shacked up with a gorgeous Frenchman.

I laughed. 'Ah, I don't think you have to worry about me following in her footsteps.'

'Really?' Mum looked dubious.

I grabbed my mother's shoulders and looked her square in the eyes. 'I may not know anything about anything, but the one thing I do know is that I will not be falling for some gorgeous Italian man on my trip.'

Dad folded his arms across his chest, looking ever so stern.

'Seriously, this trip is about me, not about finding love.'

Mum looked at Dad, defeated but still resolute in her worry as she mumbled, 'Famous last words.'

# Chapter Two

Jan had failed to point out in her sales pitch that my trip of a lifetime would begin with me standing in the sweltering reception of a flea-bitten hotel, sweaty and jet-lagged, waiting for the tour guide for a meet-and-greet. My parents needn't have worried; there was no chance of me finding love in a place like this.

At first I thought that there had been some mistake. I had stared at the catalogue long enough to memorise the glossy snapshots of smiling, tanned, carefree twenty-somethings with sunglasses and perfect white teeth having the time of their lives. Alongside these images was a picture of a quaint cobblestone street nestled in the heart of the city, indicating where our accommodation was: it said nothing about it being a hole in the wall with dodgy signage. I know I wasn't exactly well travelled, but when a murderous scream echoes from the top floor, followed by what sounds like a brawl, causing the house clerk to scream up at the guests, one isn't exactly filled with warm, fuzzy feelings. I half expected to find police tape and chalk outlines of bodies upstairs. For the past week I had dreamt of a concierge flanked by marble pillars floating behind the front desk welcoming me to Rome; there would be 1000-threadcount Egyptian cotton sheets, and a fluffy white robe and minibar. But there was no floating welcome; in fact, as yet I was unable to book in as a man and woman argued over the computer screen. I had no idea what they were saying, but I hoped they couldn't find me on the system because there had been some mistake, and I was about to be accommodated at a more upmarket establishment.

No such luck.

I was instead given a welcome drink, an unexpected inclusion which was sickly sweet. Not wanting to look ungrateful, I took a second sip, and then reminded myself that accepting drinks from a winking stranger probably wasn't a great idea, despite the official-looking, faded gold name badge.

'Please, sit. It won't be long.' He gestured toward the lounge area, where a cracked brown leather wingback chair had my name on it. I smiled gratefully at Gabriello (at least, that's what I thought I read on the man's name badge).

Arriving in the dark of night, the city had seemed beautiful and electric. My initial excitement was subdued as soon as I entered the taxi, the fear of certain death soaking my already dampened clothes as the driver darted, weaved and honked through city streets. It had been a complete miracle that we had arrived in one piece, and I wanted to kiss the filthy stone floor of the foyer.

The hotel was a narrow, faded building that looked more like a boarding house for ex-cons than the opulence I had been promised. My desperate thoughts were interrupted by the clicking of heels as a group of English girls strode in off the street and headed for the stairs, the elevator cordoned off with crime scene tape. I watched them linking arms, laughing, seemingly uncaring that they were about to spend the night on stained, grubby mattresses. Maybe that's why they were drunk? Loaded up to forget their regret of having booked into such a place. But then I had a thought: maybe they were part of another tour group, on an empowering girls' night out, bonding while enjoying the city sights. Maybe there was hope yet? The tour guide would soon make him or herself known, and with a friendly smile and an enchanting accent, he/she would lead me onto an exotic balcony where all the other travellers waited, making lifelong friends whilst supping on delicious antipasti and toasting the beginning of a grand adventure.

Or maybe not.

I pulled my suitcase closer to me in the lounge, waiting for someone else who looked just as dishevelled and lost as I did. Instead I saw the back of a man's shoulders, square and broad in a well-cut navy jacket. He wasn't a bewildered foreigner like me—there was certainly nothing dishevelled about him. Even without seeing his face I could tell he was at ease. As I took in the tall, lean man, all the way down to his expensive Italian leather shoes, I realised he stood out for all the wrong reasons. He didn't belong here at all. What was a man like him doing in a place like this? Again, I let fantasy get the better of me; maybe this was my travel guide? The tall, dark, gorgeous Fabrizio would soon walk over to me to confess that I was the only person who had booked the tour so I would have my own personal guide. I smiled to myself, my imagination giving respite from my squalid circumstances. Or maybe he was a spy? Bond. Gino Bond. Checking into the neighbouring room with a sniper rifle, waiting to catch out a sleazy con. Rather disturbing that the latter scenario seemed more plausible.

I groaned, rubbing my eyes, never knowing such tired-ness. I was hot, gritty, exhausted, hungry: was this what jet lag felt like? I had never travelled further than interstate before, so I'd never experienced it. I was way out of my comfort zone for so many reasons and I could feel the panic rise up in me.

*What have I done? What was I thinking?*

I had checked the itinerary a thousand times. Right date, right hotel, right time: where was everybody? Why was I stuck here in this hotel jail all alone? I dragged my hands through the darkened, messy curls of my wayward hair, fighting back tears of fatigue and hopelessness. It was then that I realised I wasn't exactly alone. Lifting my face up from my hands, I took in a deep, steadying breath as I glanced upwards and stilled. For a long moment that was more than just deliriousness or fantasy I locked eyes with the tour guide/spy. He was no longer turned away from me, but looking—no, make that staring—at me. I turned around, thinking maybe there was some mistake, that there was a beautiful, leggy blonde woman in a mink coat and diamonds standing right behind me, but after a quick glance over my shoulder, I realised this was not the case and once more my eyes locked with the man's.

In my fantasies, the spy guide would summon a waiter from nowhere and, before our eye contact broke, an exotic cocktail would arrive 'with compliments from the man at the front desk', as he acknowledged me with a cheeky little wink. I, of course, would clutch my pearls (that I didn't own) and send back a coy message of thanks and a request to join me.

But this was reality, and there was no drink, no invitation, there was just a long, lingering stare from both of us that bordered on the ridiculous, as if neither one of us wished to break the contact out of fear of defeat. The strangeness of the situation was apparent to us both; the man's mouth tugged a little, and my brows furrowed with a 'What are you looking at?' scowl. I decided to be the bigger person, lifting my chin and turning away as I nestled back into my wingback chair, feeling vaguely superior as I imagined him looking on with an amused and impressed expression. The exchange with the sexy stranger had been the highlight of my day so far. I breathed out a laugh, crossing my feet at my ankles and feeling so utterly smug—until I looked up.

'Oh, Christ.'

There before me, a full-length reflection near the fireplace mirrored my gaping face. My eyes stared wide at my mussed halo of hair, a knotted-up curl protruding from the top of my head like the crest of a cockatoo.

Oh, my God—how long had I been walking around like this? From the plane? In the taxi? Sitting here for how many hours? I clawed at the mess, fighting against the frizz in an effort to tame the horror, thinking back to how the beautiful stranger had stared at me. He wasn't going to send me a drink: he was going to send me some hair product. I wanted to die. I pushed myself way back into my chair, my hands on my head with my eyes closed, hoping against hope that he wasn't watching me now. *Oh, dear Lord, please make him be gone, let my humiliation die*. I slowly peeled my eyes open thinking I could spy his reflection in the mirror, but the angle was all wrong and I couldn't see the reception desk.

No big deal—he was there or he wasn't; what did it matter what some stranger thought, some sexy-sexy, tall, dark stranger. I would never see him again. We were just two people in a shitty hotel, never to be known to each other. There was an upside to being in Rome: no one knew me, or my story; I was a complete enigma. I could be whoever I wanted to be and no one would be any the wiser. I could simply float under the radar and lose myself in this city. At this point in time, losing myself sounded like a bloody lovely idea.

I inhaled a deep breath, calming myself. Yes, that's what I would do: I would simply lose myself. I felt better already, calmed by my own logic. *Wow, I am so grown up*, I thought to myself with a nod. *This trip has matured me already.*

'Samantha Shorten?'

I stiffened in my seat, as if someone had poured ice water down the back of my shirt.

'Is there a Samantha Shorten here?'

I slowly peered around the corner of my chair towards the voice, dread heavy in my stomach.

I was no longer anonymous.

# Chapter Three

'Ciao, Samantha, *come stai?*'

There was no time to react, no time to run through my mental archive of Year Eleven Italian lessons to gather a response to the woman who approached me, a smiling vision in canary yellow as she took my hand and shook it vigorously. Instead, I blurted out the usual reaction to hearing my full name.

'Please, call me Sammi,' I said, taking in the petite, attractive brunette with the high-wattage smile and twinkle in her eyes. I felt like a bag lady next to her.

'Welcome to Rome, Sammi. *Mi chiamo* Maria. Is this your first time?'

Looking at my scruffy, creased clothes and weary, clammy disposition, it wouldn't be hard to gather that I wasn't a high-class traveller. Still, it was a polite icebreaker.

'I've never been anywhere,' I confessed, glancing up, relieved to see the man was no longer at reception. I was safe to be as tragic as I wanted. Not that I cared what he thought, I lied to myself.

'Ah, well, you are in good hands then; Bellissimo Tours is the best way to start your Italian journey, embracing the local attractions, culture, food and people.'

The fact that Maria had left out the word 'budget' was not lost on me. I could imagine her repeating this speech a fair few times, but she had it down pat, even if I did see her eyes glaze over a bit as she rattled off the details for probably the hundredth time that night.

'Sounds great. So where is everybody else?' I asked, hoping against hope that I had, in fact, arrived at the wrong hotel, and that everyone was waiting for me across the road, in a vine-covered four-and-a-half star oasis, getting drunk on wine and eating pizza while dangling their legs into a fountain. But I should have known better than to let my imagination run away with me.

'Oh, they are all out in the courtyard; there are two entrances into the hotel.'

'And I just happened to take this one,' I said, glowering at the reception.

'Never mind—you are here and that is all that matters.' Maria clapped her hands together as if something truly amazing was about to begin. Maybe I had entered into the bad side of the hotel. Everything has a good and a bad side—even I had a bad side. It just so happened that of all the entrances in the world that I could have walked into with my matted, curly Mohawk, I had to choose the same entrance as the smiling, Italian sex god from across the way. Still, he was a distant memory now, and my night was about to kick off finally. With newfound energy, I grabbed for my suitcase, only to be waved away from my handle by Maria.

'No, no, Sammi—let the porters take care of that for you.'

My brows rose. From my experiences thus far, I couldn't help the reaction: I guessed the man lingering out the front, laughing and smoking with the doorman, was the porter. Nothing had inspired any confidence until Maria had emerged like a sun from behind a cloud, quite literally; her bright yellow sundress was almost as blinding as her smile. That smile was now absent as she made short, determined steps in her heels towards the front desk. Gone was her warm, carefree, welcoming air and reborn was Maria, Roman warrior, breathing fire in loud and quick Italian at the staff. Italian was such a romantic, beautiful language, even in such a tirade.

I was tempted to slink off into the night, cringing at the thought that I might have got them into trouble. I mean, I probably could have been a bit more inquisitive, looked around, asked more questions from more people, tried my luck with my fragments of remembered Italian. But all I had the energy to do was slump into the well-worn, yet very comfy chair in the lounge area and hope against hope that the answer would come my way—and it had, in the form of Hurricane Maria. An impressive little pocket rocket, she didn't appear much older than me, and yet she seemed infinitely more streetwise.

Now action began all around me: the smoking porter quickly extinguished his cigarette and hopped into action, and the flustered man behind the desk, who until now had been struggling between flailing through paperwork and skimming over wall keys, was aided by the young receptionist, who handed him the correct key. His face plum red, he handed the key to Maria with what seemed to be a thousand apologies, apologies that Maria turned her back on. Facing me, she smiled brightly, and there again was the flawless professional tour guide; it was as if I had imagined her fiery outburst, though the ringing of my ears told me otherwise.

'Sammi, why don't you freshen up and come meet everyone in the courtyard?'

I didn't know if it was the warmth of her accent or the notion of freshening up, but I immediately felt better. A nice hot shower to wash away the plane grime, and lathering of conditioner to sort out the curly mess on my head. That Claire had inherited Mum's non-offensive waves and I had been stuck with Dad's mop of dark curls was another way Mother Nature had conspired against me. I should have thought to ask Jan how a Roman summer would affect my hair. You know, along with all the other important things like tourist visas, airport transfers and luggage allowances.

My attention snapped to the smoke fumes emanating from the porter as he skimmed past me with my suitcase, motioning me to follow. I glanced at a reassuring Maria, whose smile seemed to magically appear anytime my confidence was flagging; she was programmed so well. 'When you are ready, just head down past the bar and out the back to the courtyard. You cannot miss it, there is a sign with "Bellissimo Tours"—it's a private function.'

I felt like such an idiot; a mere wander and I could have found them myself instead of sitting in reception like a bag lady getting laughed at. Still, at least I hadn't wandered into the courtyard looking like a rooster to a group of strangers. I guess I had to be thankful for that, but, following the skinny porter up the narrow, rusty, winding staircase, I couldn't help thinking back to those eyes, sparkling and amused, and it made me wonder. Perhaps I would have preferred the eyes of a thousand strangers, instead of that very vivid pair I couldn't quite shake.

# Chapter Four

With Maria's sunny presence infusing me with optimism, I readied myself to see my room. If a woman of Maria's calibre saw fit to do business with the hotel, surely my room would be alright? I soon had my answer. I turned into a long, dirty hallway where the peeling, smoke-stained wallpaper was nothing like what was advertised in my brochure; no, the reality was significantly more terrifying. It was like an opening to a horror movie; you know, where the lone woman is making her way through an abandoned, creepy house and you're screaming at her, 'Get out! Get out, you idiot!' I followed the porter down a long hall that I hoped would never end, afraid to see what awaited me. But after eight flights of stairs, rising heat and no air conditioning in sight, I was suddenly praying for the next door to be mine.

Finally the porter stopped and I doubled over behind him, hands on knees, taking in lungfuls of stuffy, humid air, realising how unfit I was—and I wasn't the poor soul who had carried my suitcase up eight floors! Looking up at the skinny-jeans-wearing young man who hadn't even broken a sweat, it occurred to me that after a solid five minutes of climbing, I didn't even know his name.

'*Mi chiamo* Sammi,' I said breathlessly, thinking to prompt introduction. But instead of a response, he simply turned the door handle, no key necessary, and dragged my suitcase into the darkened room. Not one to follow strange men into dark places, I ran my hand along the inside of the doorway, scrambling for the light switch. The fluorescent bulb flicked to a dull hum, illuminating the space. Only then did I wish I had left it off.

The room was occupied by three sets of bunk beds, pressed up against the walls to afford the feeling of space, but all it did was clear a section on the grubby, broken tile floor, drawing attention to the clothes that were strewn all over the place. Black wire cages that slid under the bunk beds were kindly provided to house and lock belongings, although only one person had deemed their possessions worthy of protection. The room, stifling hot, smelt like a locker room, and judging by the size-eleven runner that was lying on its side, this was a co-ed living situation. There was shoestring, and then there was whatever this was. *Hotel Luce del Sole* translated as Hotel Sunshine, but there was nothing sunshiny about this.

The porter may not have wanted to part with his name, but I sure as hell was going to part with my feelings.

'I'm sorry, but this just won't do,' I said, shaking my head, half expecting Maria to burst through and yell at the man for taking me to the wrong room. That my private quarters were elsewhere, waiting for me with my clean sheets and fluffy robe. The man looked at me for perhaps the first time. I wasn't sure if he understood what I was saying, but reading my face he got my meaning, yet still he seemed confused.

'There has to be some mistake,' I said, quickly rummaging through my papers, looking for my booking confirmation that showed beautiful, delightful pictures of a clean double bed, a room with a view and a delightful write-up about hotel amenities including a typical Italian breakfast, with milk, coffee or tea, plumcakes, small tarts, biscottate slices, toasted bread, jam, marmalade, honey, nuts and Nutella.

*Please tell me the freakin' Nutella wasn't a lie.*

The man took the paper from me, his brows stitched together as his dark eyes scanned over it. He then shook his head, handing the page back to me.

'*Bellissimo? Maria?*' he asked.

'*Si, si,* Bellissimo with Maria,' I said urgently, feeling relief surge inside me, as I felt a possible connection forming with the no-name bag man. Until he started to laugh, laugh so loud and shake his head, like I had just told him the most hilarious joke he had ever heard.

'What? What's so funny?' I demanded.

Again he did not respond, he simply wiped away a stray tear as he walked past me to the door, trying to contain himself before stilling and looking back at me, only to burst out laughing once more before he turned and walked away.

Now I was mad as hell. I was hot, tired, hungry and filthy. A filthy mood, a filthy body and standing in, for all intents and purposes, a filthy room. I stood with my hands on my hips, turning around in the chaos before something even more unsettling hit me.

*Oh, no!*

I dived out of the doorway, skidding sideways to yell at the retreating, laughing man before he turned the corner of the stairs.

'Hey, wait!'

To my surprise he actually did, pausing at the top of the stairs and turning expectantly to me.

'Luciano,' he said.

*Finally, a name.*

'Luciano, where's the bathroom? Ah, *il bagno*?'

Recognition lined his face before he nodded, pointing to a door halfway down the hall.

'Oh, please, no-no-no-no.' I knocked gently then slowly turned the handle, closing my eyes before opening the door and instinctively reaching for a light switch to click on. Only then did I open my eyes to reveal my worst nightmare.

A communal bathroom.

Yep, I was officially in hell.

~

I sat on my bed; at least, I thought it was my bed. I wasn't quite sure, but I really didn't care. There was a groan of the springs as I sank slightly, my weighted, tired body slumped in defeat as tears failed to well in my eyes, no doubt due to dehydration caused by the excess perspiration that misted over my body. By now I had imagined that I would be long checked in, showered and enjoying complimentary bruschetta and limoncello with my fellow travellers. Instead I was in hotel hell, all alone, thirsty, hungry and shit-scared about where I was, and what I had done. This was by far the worst mistake of my life. I had dreamed of Rome, the culture, the people, the history, the romance. I didn't expect anything like this; oh, if only my parents could see me now. I wiped my cheek with the back of my hand.

'Come on, Sammi, pull it together.' I squared my shoulders; the image of Mum with arms crossed and an 'I told you so' expression sobered me a little. It couldn't be all that bad; heck, if it was good enough for the five other strangers in this room then surely I wasn't so prim and proper to think myself above it. This was an adventure, a dirty, grimy . . . oh, God, was that mould on the ceiling? *No, don't think, just be,* I pep-talked myself.

*Okay, this is the deal. Lock your belongings in the bloody wire cage under the bed, have a nice, hopefully hot shower—everything will seem better after a shower. Then head downstairs and get your bearings with the group, and grab something to eat. Some drink and food will set you right.*

It all sounded so convincing in my head but the cold, hard reality was hard to handle. There was little toilet paper, the showers were blocked so the water didn't drain properly, and they didn't have a door so water sprayed all over the floor. The bathroom was tiny, so I constantly smacked my limbs against the wall and shower and bathroom door while drying off. It was soooo annoying. I wiped a clean spot on the mirror, reflecting a weary yet determined reflection.

'Just you wait, Jan and John Buzzo, until I get home,' I said, promising to serve them a piece of my mind when I returned, before scoffing at how cocky I sounded. Home seemed like an eternity away, and at this rate I'd be lucky if I survived the night.

# Chapter Five

I was greeted by a sign in joyous cursive, saying, 'Welcome Bellisimo Tour', accompanied by a picture of a sun and a flower. I wanted to knock the sign off the easel with my fist. The sign should have read 'Welcome to Hell', illustrated with a cockroach and a pubic hair on a piece of soap. I guess I wasn't in the party mood, but as I walked into the back courtyard area it seemed that I was the only one who wasn't. A series of heads turned, revealing smiling, flushed faces. As they registered my entry, they paused their conversations to burst into cheers. I stilled in my tracks, caught between confusion and surprise.

A tall, blond male yelled out, cupping his hands at either side of his mouth, 'Last one at the meet-and-greet has to do a nudey run around the courtyard,' eliciting uproarious laughter and hoots from his audience.

This couldn't be the group; surely this wasn't my destiny.

With little time to react, the sound of Maria's heels closed in, followed by a quick whack to my upper chest that had me reeling back on my heels.

'Ow!' I clutched my chest, stunned at her random violence, and rather surprised at the petite woman's strength. I felt a strip of paper under my hand—a rectangular sticker bearing my name and a smiley face adhered crookedly to my top.

'Come, meet everybody, Sammi.' Maria dragged me towards the long table. 'Everyone, this is Sammi from Australia; Sammi completes the puzzle of our little family, please make her feel welcome.'

'You're late, Sammi,' said a raven-haired girl, her teeth gnashing on the straw of her drink, looking me over. Even though she smiled, her eyes said something else altogether. My attention dipped to her name badge. I had known girls like 'Jodie' before; she was the residential mean girl. I hoped I was wrong.

She, like the tall, blond boy, had an Australian accent, and it seemed that it would have been just like any given night at the local pub back home, until the boy Jodie was partially draped over—'Johnny', according to his badge— leant forward and offered me his hand.

'Better late than never,' he said with an unmistakable American drawl and kind blue eyes. I smiled, comforted by them, until I saw Jodie's 'Back off, bitch' look.

'Okaaaaaay.' I turned promptly toward Big Mouth Blondy, who shook my hand with a wink. '*Ciao, bella.*'

'Speak much Italian, do you . . .' My eyes searched for a badge.

'Nate, and I speak enough to get by.'

Nate was tall, athletic with short-cropped hair and a devilish twinkle in his eyes. He was cute, but definitely the kind your mother warned you about. No doubt I would find out his story, and everyone else's for that matter.

Aside from two other Aussies—best friends from the Gold Coast, Harper and Kylie—there was Gary from the UK, who seemed reluctant to pull his attention out of his book for long enough to shake my hand.

'We call him Bookworm Gary,' Nate murmured out the side of his mouth in an effort to be discreet, but failing. Despite the less-than-warm welcome, I felt for the Brit; he was probably like me, wishing to be anywhere but here. Nate was firing through the group quickly, going onto the table behind.

'Gwendal and Marina from France, Em from Ireland . . .'

I began to zone out, until Nate pointed a finger down to the very end of the table.

'And this bloke who, like me, is far too cool to wear a name, is actually a local; isn't that right, mate?'

My eyes followed the direction of his finger and stilled. The local may not have had a name but he had a very familiar face. I would have recognised him anywhere; the mysterious Gino Bond who had seen me at my sweaty, messy worst was here, except this time there was no humour in his visage. Instead, as his attention flicked from me to Nate, I saw an ill-disguised look of contempt that said, 'I'm not your mate.'

Nate didn't need a translator to get the drift, and he slowly sat back down.

'Aaand I think that's everyone,' he said, clearing his throat.

I stood still at the head of the table, once again finding myself staring at the man from across the way, feeling that same strange sense that neither of us wanted to break away, like some kind of telepathic competition. Just as my brows pinched and his mouth creased just like before, I remembered the reason he had found me so damn amusing last time, feeling slightly annoyed and totally embarrassed.

Next to me, Maria laughed. 'Do you two know each other?' she asked in a lighthearted manner, like it couldn't possibly be true.

'N—'

'Yes.'

*Wait, what?*

The man lazily took a sip from his wine glass before clarifying. 'Me and Miss Shorten go way back.'

*He knew my name?*

No doubt I looked just as surprised as Maria, and had I been sitting, I would have been on the edge of my seat, eager for the next detail, because I had no idea what he was talking about.

'We go all the way back to the hotel reception,' he said, a new lightness sparkling in his eyes.

Maria seemed even more confused, but I wasn't. Instead I smiled. 'That's right, we go waaaay back.'

The only real movement among the group was Nate chewing loudly on a piece of bread, and Jodie's head snapping between the two of us as if she couldn't believe we could possibly know each other.

'Oh, Marcello, I can never tell if you are serious or not,' scoffed Maria.

*Marcello.*

I looked at him again; for some strange reason, knowing his name completely transformed him. He wasn't the dark, mysterious stranger from across the room, he was now very much a somebody. And that somebody was actually a part of this tour group? Now I was confused; why would a local need or want to do a Bellissimo trip? Maybe he had led a sheltered life, although this didn't seem to be the case. He looked worldly, street smart, and held himself with confidence—basically the total opposite to me. If he wanted to see the sights, why on earth would he want to hang out with a motley crew like us, in a dive like this? It made no sense.

Jodie laughed. 'Why don't you take a picture? It will last longer.'

I snapped out of my trance. Oh, God, had I been staring? I had totally been staring. I blanched, quickly motioning for Nate to shift aside so I could move into the seat next to him and hopefully disappear.

*Don't look at him, Sammi, just focus on Maria.*

Maria, who still stood at the end of the table holding court. 'Now that you are all here, let's raise a toast.' She beamed, lifting her wine glass into the air; it took only a second for a glass of red wine to be passed to me, thanks to Johnny. He gave me a wink, as if to say 'I have your back'.

'Here's to new friends!' Maria toasted.

Holding up our glasses, we toasted with a multitude of clinks.

'To new friends!' And I don't know why, but my eyes moved exactly to the direction I promised they wouldn't: straight to Marcello. Again his dark brown eyes caught mine and held me in place, but this time Marcello broke the trance simply by smiling and lifting his drink at the same time as I did, a mischievous curve to his brow. I laughed, actually laughed, then tilted my head in acknowledgement and lifted my glass in his direction.

*To new friends.*

# Chapter Six

Local red wine, empty stomach, jet lag and eight flights of stairs all made for a deadly combination.

I was confident that the wine hadn't gone straight to my head, but to my legs. I had excused myself from the meet-and-greet, muttering about going to find *il bagno*, while in reality I had every intention of sneaking up to my room, or dorm rather, and crashing into my questionably clean sheets and passing out. There certainly was an upside to drinking away your worries; with my fuzzy vision and the lights off, I could be sleeping at the Ritz for all I knew. According to Maria, who had outlined every minute detail of our Roman itinerary, the first day was a free day, meaning we could settle into our little rats' nest, get acquainted with one another, recover from our travels/hangovers and prepare ourselves for the following day of adventure. Cheers to that! Although now I was seriously regretting all those cheers.

*Cheers to new friends!*

*Cheers to new adventures!*

*Cheers to Rome!*

*Cheers to a free day!*

Holding on to the banister, I slid around rather ungraciously and plonked myself onto the bottom step of the staircase. I wasn't going anywhere just yet.

'That's okay, Sammi, we'll just rest up here for a tick until the room stops spinning and then we'll be up those steps in a blaze of glory,' I said, hoping that the lies I was telling myself would give me enough encouragement to make it so. But despite the broken terracotta tile poking me in the butt, I felt strangely comfortable resting my temple against the cool iron of the banister.

'Just a little bit longer,' I muttered, my eyes feeling slightly heavy as I blinked slowly. Zoning out into a glorious haze until I heard footsteps.

'Oh, shit, Maria.' I sat up straight, but then it occurred to me that they didn't sound like Maria's steps—they weren't short and sharp and clicky like hers were. These were slower, heavier and more determined. I peered through the gap in the banister, squinting through one eye in an attempt to focus, but there was no need to—I would have recognised him anywhere.

Marcello walked like a jungle cat, stalking through reception, sliding on his coat, adjusting his collar and glancing back as if ensuring no one was seeing him go.

*He was sneaking off too. Ha!*

It was then that I recognised the white paper strip with black scrawl was stuck onto the breast pocket of his jacket.

'Don't forget your name badge,' I called out, before cursing myself and clamping my hand over my big bloody mouth.

Marcello came to a halt so abruptly that his shoes screeched on the floor, his head snapping in my direction as he squinted into the darkness, confused.

I tried in vain to slide further into the shadows, but it was no use. I saw it the moment his brows lifted in recognition; he had spotted me. He slowly turned and started making his way over.

*Oh, shit-shit-shit.*

He came to stand before me, lifting his elbow to rest casually on the banister as he looked down with amused interest.

I didn't know what to say now he was here, and I was in no fit state to hold a conversation. I should have let him go on his merry little way right out the front door. Then my foggy brain slowly made a connection between Marcello and his planned exit.

'You're not staying here?' I asked, mainly to myself, but he had a wry smile lining his face.

'At Luce del Sole?' he said, looking around facetiously, like it was some glorious kingdom.

'*Si*,' I said.

He breathed out a laugh, crossing his arms over his chest and leaning against the banister. 'No,' he said.

I nodded. Smart man.

My next question was where he was staying, but I stopped myself quickly. I didn't need or want to know. All I needed to worry about was where *I* was staying and how the hell I was going to get there.

I willed myself to stand, pulling myself up in the most inelegant fashion. I probably wouldn't have made it if it weren't for the firm grip of a warm hand on my upper arm.

'I'm good,' I lied, pulling away from his grasp and clutching to the banister with white-knuckled intensity. If I could anchor myself long enough for the room to stop spinning I could at least pretend I was okay; well, until Marcello walked off into the night. But, of course, he didn't; he simply stood there on the lower step and slid his hands into his pockets, his dark, serious eyes ever watchful.

'You don't look so good,' he said.

I instinctively ran my hand over the top of my head. Oh, God, did I look like a cockatoo again?

'This bloody Italian summer air will be the death of me.' Oh, yes, curse my life. Standing before a gorgeous Italian man in Rome with a belly full of wine: how torturous.

*Sure, this isn't the Taj Mahal, but get a grip, Sammi—you're in Rome! Rome!*

I smiled, allowing myself to sway and get a little giddy with the sudden realisation. Maybe it was the wine kicking in, but all of a sudden I felt very free. I swung on the banister, a little too far, it seemed, as I lost my footing and crashed into Marcello so hard that I swear I knocked all the air out of his lungs.

'Shit, sorry,' I stammered, trying to grab onto the railing again out of fear of falling once Marcello let me go. But he continued to hold on to my shoulders, glowering down on me with what I would have liked to think was concern, but looked more like anger. Sheesh, such a grumpy bum.

'I'm. Fine,' I said, trying to break free from his grasp, but this time he was more insistent.

'I don't think you are,' he said.

'I'm just tired—jet lag.'

'And wine,' he corrected.

'A little.' I measured an inch with my fingers.

Marcello rolled his eyes, his patience wearing thinner by the second. 'Where is your room?'

'I'm not telling you that!'

'Well, I hope your travel insurance covers a broken neck,' he snapped.

My mouth gaped. 'Well, of course it . . .' I stilled, a memory of John Buzzo giving me pause. He was wiping a jam stain from his tie and weighing up whether or not to put his doughnut aside to do it; multi-tasking was not his forte. I felt even less confident about what exactly I had signed up to.

I bit my lip, my hateful mood back in full swing. 'Well, maybe just a little help.'

Marcello stifled his smile, measuring an inch with his fingers. 'Maybe just a little.'

# Chapter Seven

If only my parents knew. I was drunk in a dodgy hotel being escorted to my bedroom by a complete stranger. Maybe I had binge-watched far too many true-crime documentaries but by the sixth floor I decided to try to bring some safety into my plan.

'Here I am!' I lied, moving away from his protective hover to stand by a door. 'Thanks for helping.' I beamed, waiting for Marcello to descend the stairs.

'Well, goodnight,' I said, grabbing the door handle and waiting, but he was unmoving.

'You best get inside, lock the door behind you. I'll wait until you're in and safe.' There was some kind of glimmer in his eyes, something that said he saw right through me, and he was loving every minute of catching me out in my lie. I stared him down.

'Don't be ridiculous, I am quite safe.' And with that the door whipped open, and I was suddenly face-to-hairy-chest with a furious-looking man, a towel wrapped under his big belly.

I wasn't sure what he was shouting, but it surely wasn't friendly as the force of his rage had me stepping back until I hit a wall—the living, breathing wall of Marcello. I heard him chuckle against my back. Was he seriously laughing?

'A friend of yours?' he murmured into my ear. I spun around, cutting him down with a hard look.

'Some help you are,' I snapped, before quickly side-stepping away from the still-shouting man. The adrenaline from the incident sobered me, and with a new determination of getting distance between myself, the sixth floor and Marcello, I bolted up the last two flights, breathless, but almost home-free. The end was in sight and I could see my door—right before I tripped, stubbing my toe and faceplanting hard. A flash of pain struck me with such intensity that I swear the Pope heard my scream from the Vatican.

While earlier I had been preoccupied with the filth of the place, I sure as hell didn't care about it now as I rolled around on the grimy floor, clutching my toe and crying.

'I hate it here,' I sobbed, feeling utterly defeated. The stubbed toe was the final straw in what had been an horrific journey thus far. The gravity of my misery was magnified the moment Marcello trotted up the last of the steps, his easygoing nature and humour falling away when he looked down at me in agony.

'You clearly cannot be left alone.'

'Oh, shut up,' I groaned. The last thing I needed was his smartarse comments, no matter how cool everything sounded in his creamy, rich accent. Or the fact that when he smiled it transformed his entire face. But lucky for him he wasn't smiling now; he simply sighed, moving to sit on the top step near me.

'Let me see,' he said, motioning for me to show him my toe.

'I think I broke it clean off—can you see a pinky lying around somewhere?' I gritted.

'I hope I didn't step on it on the way up,' he joked, looking down the stairs, then around him.

'It hurts so bad,' I said between sobs. I didn't have the energy to resist as Marcello gently lifted my foot onto his lap, watching my face for signs of additional pain. I breathed out, trying to control myself as Marcello brought his attention to my foot.

'Please don't touch it.'

'It's okay, I'm just looking,' he said, softly touching the ankle and turning it to the side.

'How on earth am I going to stump my way around the cobblestone streets of Rome with a bung toe?'

'Well, tomorrow is a free day, so you can rest up,' Marcello said, while I tried to ignore the fact that him massaging my inner sole felt so incredibly good.

I thought about being stuck in the hotel, lying on a bunk bed with the mould and bed bugs, and I swear the pain faded instantly. 'I can think of nothing worse than being bedridden in here.'

The throbbing wasn't so bad right now, but I wasn't ready to tell Marcello that; maybe just a little more foot caressing.

He twisted his face, deep in thought. 'More wine?'

'Ugh, no more wine,' I pleaded. The combination of the fall and the flee from the psycho on the sixth floor had me fatigued, and the lazy circles Marcello's clever fingers drew on my foot were working wonders. Despite the misadventures of the day, sitting next to Marcello, my eyes bloodshot from tears and too much wine, I felt oddly safe. His skin was touching my skin, warm with the friction of his caress, and as I looked up and caught his eyes they sparkled with an old familiarity, which was absurd considering he was a complete stranger to me. But when we looked at each other in a silence stretching beyond any normal measure, there wasn't anything strange or awkward about it. From the very first time we made eye contact at reception, there was no urgency—we were just two people existing in the moment; whatever that moment was, I couldn't say. My eyes broke from his and I glanced up the hall, mentally calculating the steps, or hops, I would need to get to my door. I breathed out a laugh, rubbing my eyes and wishing so badly this day would come to an end.

Marcello squeezed my foot gently with a little smile that pulled at the corner of his mouth. 'What?' he asked.

My shoulders slumped in defeat. 'I'm going to need your help.'

And boy, didn't he love me saying that.

At least twenty-three hops would do it, but I needn't have worried. After helping me to stand, Marcello swiftly lifted me over his shoulder as if I weighed no more than a feather. I squealed at the unexpectedness of it, but the sound quickly died as all the air was pushed out of my lungs, his long strides moving down the hall. Soon Marcello had managed to open the door and dump me on the springy mattress, eliciting a belly laugh from me that seemed to be catching. I heard his laugh for the first time, not his low chuckle from the sixth floor, but a real hearty laugh, the warmth of it hitting my cheeks as his hands grasped my shoulders while he looked down at me, gaining his balance. I couldn't see his face in the dark room, only the fuzzy silhouette of his thick, curly hair from the hall light that glowed behind him, but I could totally imagine what his eyes might have looked like, and I wasn't laughing anymore. The smile slowly slid from my face and I was holding onto his forearms like some kind of anchor. I felt dizzy in a way that I knew had nothing to do with the wine, and breathless from something other than pain. My cheeks were burning, and I didn't realise I had voiced the feeling until Marcello reached out and cupped my cheek.

'You're a little warm, but it is summertime.'

'True,' I said, feeling my bones melt into the mattress. I couldn't quite believe I could feel so at ease with a man lingering over me, his arms caging me in, no less, but I didn't feel threatened; in fact, I didn't want him to go, which meant he absolutely must.

'Goodnight!' I squeaked abruptly, and perhaps a little too loudly. It was not a subtle hint, and Marcello didn't have to be told twice. He edged away and I peeled back the blankets and hopped underneath, lifting the sheet up to my chin as a protective barrier.

'Have a good night,' I said, cringing as the words tumbled out of my mouth.

*Have a good night? Seriously, Sammi?*

Marcello laughed. 'Are you sure you're feeling alright?' He leant down, pressing his hand to my forehead.

'Absolutely, I'll be pounding the pavement by morning,' I said.

*Ugh, seriously, Sammi, stop talking!*

Marcello stepped away. 'Very good,' he said. I may not have been able to see his face, but I could tell from his voice he was smiling. *'Buona notte, Samantha.'*

He was saying goodnight, and nothing sounded sweeter, but there was one small thing I had to say before he left.

'Marcello?'

He paused at the door and turned to me, half his face illuminated by the light from the hall.

I smiled, even though I knew he couldn't see it, but maybe he too would hear it in my voice when I told him, 'Call me Sammi.'

And with the twist of his mouth I was so glad I could see, and a quick nod of understanding, he slowly stepped into the hall and closed the door behind him.

# Chapter Eight

The depths of the night were sliced with light and laughter, stumbling, cursing and the springs of my bed groaning as a figure fell onto the mattress at the foot of my bed.

'Oops,' the voice said, followed by a telltale hiccup.

I groaned, turning away from the sounds and the assault of fluorescent, flickering globes, pulling the sheet with me in an effort to shield myself from them. My room-mates were talking to me but I didn't care. I just had to not think, not move until my head stopped pounding and my gut stopped churning. I wanted no part of this reality: drunk, screeching girls and jostling jocks who said 'Dude' a lot. I hoped Maria would appear to chastise them like a boarding school marm, but this wasn't school. No, this was the epitome of freedom, and although I had thought it was what I wanted, at 3 a.m. I wanted no part of it. I cocooned my ears with my arms and focused desperately on drifting back to sleep, and it almost worked, until another form of light streamed across my face. Warm and intense, it stirred me from my dream of wandering the cobbled streets of Rome in a flowing skirt, large sunhat and glasses, eating gelato without a care in the world. It had seemed so real. The warmth of the sun on my face as I lifted it to the sky, the hot, thick air that smelt like . . . cheese?

*Cheese?*

My eyes slowly peeled open, blinking, confused, until I spied my less-than-thrilling reality in the form of a big hairy toe. My eyes widened, refocusing on the toe that was attached to a huge foot suffering from a severe case of sock tan, leading up to a kneecap, a thigh and a . . . *oh, Jesus!*

I catapulted out of bed. I would have hit the floor harder but the sheet I was twisted in acted like a B-grade bungee cord, slowing my momentum towards the cold, tiled floor. Waking up to a naked man in my bed was not something that happened to me, well, ever.

'Nate! Get out of my bed,' I shouted, struggling to stand and save some dignity while fighting with the off-white sheet. Realising I was as fully clothed as I had been in the courtyard, and that I really didn't want to find out why the sheet was now *off*-white, I refrained from tugging it further. Which was lucky, as it was still connected to Nate and was the only thing providing him with a modicum of modesty. Nate stretched, screeching and moaning, rubbing his hands over his eyes and up through his buzz cut. He rolled onto his side like a lazy tomcat languishing in the sun, then peered up at me with a slow-forming smile. 'Your bed?' he asked.

'Well . . .' I paused, glancing around the room that looked like a clothing bomb had exploded. Aside from the chaos and early-hour drunken antics, everyone had somehow managed to stumble into their own beds; well, Jodie had fallen into Johnny's, her head snugly tucked on top of his shoulder, in a twisted mess of sheets and a whole lot of skin. I wondered if I had managed to sleep through an orgy. I quickly averted my eyes from the sated couple, casting over the mess to Bookworm Gary, who sat on the windowsill, sewing a hole in his sock with intense concentration, to the sleeping body of Harper passed out on the bed in the corner. I focused back on Nate, who now seemed wide awake and looked up at me with interest.

'Um, so my bed is . . . ?'

Nate pointed upwards, to the bunk overhead.

My shoulders slumped, not because I was wrong, but because the top bunk was the bain of my childhood. Being the youngest meant I always drew the short straw, and now, even on my independent, finally-becoming-an-adult holiday, here I was on the top bloody bunk again.

As Nate flung himself back on his squeaky mattress, folding his hands behind his head, my despair didn't go unnoticed. 'What? Don't you want to be on top?' he said, wiggling his brows.

I rolled my eyes, and without a word unravelled my toga-like attire and flung the sheets back over him, trying to step over the wayward shoes and boxer shorts, fighting my way towards the door.

*Pfft, top bunk.*

I held my head high, ignoring the laughter behind me, making my way to the door, where Kylie appeared, toiletries in hand, hair twisted up in a towel; her eyes seemed alight with the same taunting amusement as Nate when she spotted me, stepping to the side to let me through.

*Ugh, juveniles.*

'There she is! Have a good night, then?' she asked, her smile impossibly white against her tan skin.

Yes, ha-bloody-ha, I ended up in Nate's bed; oh, how they must have laughed about that last night. Well, it wouldn't be happening again, and I wanted to say as much, seeing her knowing eyes tick toward Nate, who shared the same smug look.

'Not really,' I said indignantly.

'You sure about that?' she mused.

'Yes, why?'

'Because you look like the cat that got the cream,' yawned Jodie, making everyone laugh.

I turned towards her—she was sitting upright in Johnny's Led Zeppelin T-shirt, combing her hands through her bed-hair and looking at me like she knew a secret.

*Whatever.*

I'd never been in any kind of clique; why begin now?

'If anyone's purring, it's you,' I said, curving my own brow in challenge and swinging away from Jodie's death stare. I sauntered my way past Kylie and through the door. And though I could still hear their sniggers, I did feel kind of badass, having the final word then walking out. If you were going to survive in the pack you couldn't show weakness, you had to hold your ground. And I had done that, yes, sir. I strode with a new kind of confidence into the communal bathroom down the hall, shutting the door and locking it behind me. I was soaring with self-importance, but all that came crashing down the moment I turned around and spied myself in the murky reflection of the mirror.

'Oh, good God, no.'

There, stuck partially to my forehead was a big white label with black scrawl.

*Marcello.*

I groaned, peeling it off and thinking back to last night. Marcello carrying me up the stairs, Marcello pressing his hand against my face to check my temperature.

'Ha-fucking-ha!'

Not so badass anymore.

# Chapter Nine

They say Rome wasn't built in a day—well, clearly it couldn't be seen in one either. Part of me wanted to plunge myself into the essence of Rome, but another part really wanted to escape all these people surrounding me. I figured I would have more than enough time to bond with them, and it wasn't just because they had taunted me about my 'Italian lover' over breakfast, who they were convinced I had slipped away with for a secret rendezvous last night. I couldn't blame them. I mean, I had been bloody stamped with pretty damning evidence. Oh, how wrong they were.

I didn't immediately contemplate a lone adventure. I thought it would probably help my reputation to hang out with them a bit, but overhearing Nate and Kylie's conversation was the clincher.

'Yeah, Colosseum, baby!' Nate pointed to the coloured brochure from our welcome pack.

'Oh my God, isn't that where Russell Crowe was killed?' gasped Kylie, looking over his shoulder.

'Yeah, I think so,' Nate nodded.

I closed my eyes, praying for strength, while Johnny chuckled next to me. 'Here endeth the history lesson,' he said lowly, leaning into me.

I breathed out a laugh—because if you couldn't laugh what could you do?—only to meet the steely gaze of Jodie, the narrowness of her eyebrows warning 'I will cut you'. I straightened, clearing my throat and reaching for my bag. Hopefully I could slip away without any fuss, but Nate noticed my retreat.

'Meeting up with your lover?'

I rolled my eyes. 'Please, ain't nobody got time for that.'

'It's rather funny really,' said Jodie, leisurely examining her nails.

I hooked the strap of my bag over my head and looked at her pointedly.

'You just don't seem like the kind that would snare someone like Marcello.'

The hairs on the back of my neck rose. 'Oh?' I pressed, even though I knew better than to engage in such games.

'Like, no offence, but Marcello could have anyone.'

Something primal twisted inside my gut; it was a not-so-subtle way of saying he was out of my league. It was all I could do not to take the bait. Instead, I casually cleaned my sunglasses on my T-shirt. 'And yet he chooses to have coffee with me,' I lied, sliding on my shades and offering a sweet smile.

'Aha! I knew it,' said Nate, pointing at me. 'Sammi and Marcello sitting in a tree, f-u-c-k-i-n-g.' He sung like he was in a school playground.

It was so far from the truth it was ridiculous, but I kind of enjoyed their ulterior version of me: the lone-wolf Aussie that rocks up late to gatherings and woos sexy local men in the dead of night, instead of the girl who couldn't handle her *vino* and needed the gallant Marcello to put her to bed.

'*Ciao*,' I said with affected confidence, praying that no one would follow, because I wasn't meeting up with Marcello, and I had no idea where I was going.

~

According to Claudio, a jolly, helpful man sitting outside of Hotel Luce del Sole, Rome is a city best savoured like a glass of red wine. I liked that, I liked that very much. And rather than being unnerved by the big unknown, I reminded myself to enjoy it. I had felt positively giddy about venturing out and leaving my group behind and, although it was never really possible to be alone in a city where people flocked for the history, culture and romance, there was something rather spectacular about plunging into the essence of Rome with only myself for company.

*I can do this!*

I just had to keep fed and hydrated, something I quickly learned would never be an issue in Rome. The city was overrun with places to eat, crammed in the mazes of intercepting side streets tucked between Via del Corso and Piazza Novella.

Every corner I took there was another charming building and, despite my bruised toe, I navigated the cobblestone streets like a true local, every step taking me further away from my hotel, utterly gripped and completely overwhelmed by the city. My wandering was interrupted by a familiar figure before me: a pair of brown eyes that sparkled in amusement. I wondered how long he had been watching this unworldly Aussie girl walk up the street like Bambi on ice, eyes wide and mouth agape.

Wearing a blue linen shirt that was pressed to perfection, Marcello certainly didn't have that living-out-of-a-crate-under-the-bed look about him; he looked as though he had enjoyed a luxurious eight-hour sleep and a long, cool shower that he didn't have to share with anyone else. Just standing next to him made me feel sweaty and feral. Out of my depth and as clueless as any tourist.

Looking at Marcello now, for the first time in natural light, I couldn't help but think Jodie was right: someone like this would never entertain someone like me. I was gangly, with brown curly hair that deserved its own postcode. I was more athletic than graceful, more at ease with basketball than dancing. I tanned nicely, sure, but with my brown hair and brown eyes, I was really just brown. No alluring features, no stand-out, head-turning attributes; I was just me. I was fine with being just me, until I shifted under Marcello's silent scrutiny.

'How's the toe?'

I blinked. 'Oh, um, fine. Well, clearly, as I'm wearing heels.' I'd chosen wedges in an attempt to feel feminine and sexy, but had sadly fallen short.

Marcello raised his brows as he examined my footwear; clearly he had as much confidence in me as I had.

'So, you headed somewhere?' I asked, quickly diverting the attention from my feet.

'*Si*, to the Hotel Luce del Sole, to see if they need any assistance.' Marcello stopped, watching me curiously, as the gravity of my predicament sunk in.

Not only had I alluded to sharing a smoking-hot night with Marcello, I had out-and-out lied to my tour group about going on a date with the very man in front of me. If he dropped in on them, it would make me look like an idiot, and a bunny-boiling psycho—not exactly the image to ingratiate me with my fellow travellers.

'What is it?' Marcello asked, no doubt wondering at my impression of a deer in headlights.

'No, no, nothing.' I laughed it off. 'I really was just thinking about changing my footwear. Hey, listen,' I said, moving to guide Marcello in the opposite direction from the hotel, 'everyone is out. I think they've all booked a tour to the Colosseum or something.'

Marcello seemed confused. 'Isn't that a part of your itinerary?'

'I know, right, they're seriously keen, but, yeah, I just didn't want you to trek all the way up there and find that no one was about.' I cringed, hoping my performance had been believable. Marcello's dark eyes dropped to his arm, where I had a hold of him to guide him away. I quickly let go, innocently tucking a stray hair behind my ear with a sweet smile.

I kept the smile plastered to my face, even under the deep-set scrutiny of Marcello's dark stare, the one that said he didn't believe a word I was saying, even as his own sickly sweet smile spread across his face. To anyone looking on, we must have looked like the village idiots, or a pair of serial killers.

I laughed, he laughed—it was all so utterly fake.

Marcello folded his arms, taking a step closer to me. He tapped thoughtfully on his chin as if pondering something.

'Why did you not go with them?'

'Oh, you know, I just needed some downtime. I thought I would just wander the streets and see what I could see.' I shrugged; I was not going to win an acting award anytime soon. There was something so unnerving about the way Marcello looked at me. He wasn't looking down at me; my height was somewhat of a curse when it came to dating— being 5'11' and all legs could really limit the playing field. But Marcello and I were eye to eye, and it felt incredibly intimate, as if we were enclosed in our own private space and not a bustling backstreet in Rome. A tiny part of me wanted to step back, but only a very tiny part.

Marcello rubbed the light dusting of stubble on his jaw as if tortured by an inner decision.

'Still, I'd better call into Hotel Luce de Sole. I'll leave a note for anyone who might need help later on tonight,' he said, stepping away.

'No, wait, stop!' I shouted, reaching out to him once more, grabbing onto his arm. 'I need you!' I said, far too panicked and way too crazy.

Marcello slowly turned to me, smug, his eyes dropping to my hand. I did let go, but a little more slowly this time, afraid he might turn and leg it down the street, and I really didn't want to run after him in wedges.

He curved his dark brow; I swore he was loving every minute of this. 'You need me, do you?'

I balled my hands at my side so tightly my knuckles turned white, fighting not to cringe at my own stupidity and my big mouth.

I smiled sweetly once more, tilting my head. 'Desperately,' I said, my voice dripping with so much sarcasm that I hoped he wouldn't turn and walk away, but my pride had to have some kind of victory.

Marcello shrugged one shoulder lazily. 'You are only human—how can I help?' he asked, turning his full attention back to me.

It was then I knew I had won . . . for now.

'I'll help you—on one very important condition.'

*Oh no.*

'What's that?'

Marcello took his sunglasses from his top pocket, flicking them open and placing them on with a wry smile. 'You are going to have to change your shoes.'

# Chapter Ten

After I quickly donned more comfortable footwear, Marcello, my rather silent and useless guide, walked by my side, dodging and weaving through the hordes of tourists and locals zigzagging across our paths. If I had wanted to wander aimlessly around Rome I could have done so myself; beyond pointing towards a corner to take, or curve to veer down, Marcello said nothing, and I wasn't entirely sure he knew where we were going. It seemed like we walked for an eternity, strolling past charming tan-coloured buildings with intimate balconies brightened with vibrant petunias. As I strained my neck to see the ornate facade of an apartment building framed with shuttered windows and covered with ivy, it occurred to me that it didn't really matter where we were going; each twist and turn brought new variants of colour and scale in this incredibly ancient yet dynamic place.

*This was exactly how any free day should be spent.*

So enraptured was I that the smell of pizza drifting past me almost had me blindly following, until a firm grip on my arm pulled me in the opposite direction, yanking me reluctantly from my stupor. I was kind of annoyed until we exited the narrow little street to find a promenade where the large crowds milled about in interest.

'Scallina Spagna, also known as—'

'The Spanish Steps.' I cut Marcello off, much to his surprise. I may not have been able to speak the language but I knew exactly where we were. It was where Audrey Hepburn bumped into Gregory Peck in *Roman Holiday*, though Marcello didn't need to know my knowledge was thanks to a midday movie binge, especially since he looked a little impressed.

We made our way up the wide, irregular steps, which were a mix of curves, straight flights, vistas and terraces. Without a word to each other, we found a tiny break in the groups of like-minded travellers to rest for a moment and soak up the atmosphere and city views. Marcello leant towards me, almost yelling to be heard over the chattering of the crowd; it was almost as if his inner travel guide kicked in as he educated me on how the steps connected to the lower Piazza di Spagna and the upper Piazza Trinita dei Monti behind us, with its beautiful twin tower church dominating the skyline.

'Aside from all the tourists, beyond all this craziness, the design of these steps has made it popular for artists, painters and poets. The presence of artists attracted many beautiful women to the area, hoping to be taken as models. This then attracted rich Romans and tourists, and over time the steps have attracted all kinds of people from all walks of life; the tradition of the Spanish Steps has lived on ever since.'

'It kind of feels like a massive lounge room.'

Something sparked in Marcello's eyes. 'Piazzas have been serving the community since ancient times, with their broad inviting steps; the fountain is like a neighbourhood sofa.' He pointed below.

I shielded my eyes from the sun, squinting towards the fountain at the base of the stairs. Before I could even ask the significance, Marcello continued; long gone was the silent bystander pointing and pulling me in different directions. As we sat on the Spanish Steps in the sun a new person emerged, a smile adorning his face so warm and bright I could see the two pockets of his dimples on either side of his cheeks; they almost made me forget entirely about the fountain.

'It's called Fontana della Barcaccia, or Fountain of the Old Boat. See how the fountain has the form of a sinking ship? It is said to be based upon a folk legend.'

'Oh?' I said with interest, trying not to look at his distracting dimples.

'The legend tells that a fishing boat was carried all the way to this exact spot during a massive flood of the Tiber River in the sixteenth century.'

'Wow,' I said, trying not to openly stare at his profile. I seemed unable to take in these truly fascinating history lessons due to my awareness of Marcello's jean-clad leg pressed up against mine. I wasn't entirely sure it was the Italian sunshine that had me suddenly feeling all hot and bothered.

'Should we go up?' I said.

'*Si*,' he said, standing up, momentarily blocking the sun and offering to help me stand. I took his hand, which seemed strangely intimate, but I knew he was just being nice.

'*Grazie*,' I said in my painfully Aussie accent; my attempt at the local lingo wasn't lost on Marcello, who laughed and swept his arm in front of him.

'After you.'

By the top of the however-many steps, I was breathless; I wish I could have given credit to the view but the cause was my fitness, or lack thereof. Hours spent eating supermarket-bought pizza and watching *Buffy* had in no way prepared me for this very real adventure. One that had me standing by a very handsome Italian man overlooking the magnificent panorama of St Peter's Basilica and Vatican City.

Still catching my breath, I pointed down the street beyond the old boat fountain. 'What's down there?'

'Ah, Via dei Condotti, one of the most luxurious shopping streets in all of Rome; lots of high-end fashion labels. But you probably don't want to go down there.' Marcello shrugged, crossing his arms and leaning against the terrace. 'I mean, you're probably tired.'

I suddenly straightened, a newfound invigoration setting in. 'What kind of shops?'

'Oh, Dior, Gucci, Louis Vuitton.'

'Let's go.' I set off, ready to descend the steps.

'I just thought—'

I stopped, turning. 'Marcello, I'm a girl, and we have needs, even if we can't afford them,' I said, annoyed that we were wasting time.

Marcello, surprised by my second wind, followed behind as I dodged and weaved through the tourists and vendors. My formerly quiet tour guide proved to be incredibly helpful in turning away unwanted sellers of roses or selfie sticks, answering with a firm 'No' on my behalf. But when I had reached the piazza, the promise of retail bliss powering my steps, Marcello had lagged behind, and my soft, touristy heart was snared by a man from Tunisia and his trinkets. By the time Marcello reached me it was too late; a cheap little bracelet was already half woven in yarn, in the colours of Italy.

'Sammi,' Marcello said in a chastising tone.

'Oh, relax; besides, this is more in my budget than Dior.'

'Do you still want to look?'

'Absolutely, it never hurts to look,' I said, glancing quickly at his matching dimples.

The man braided the bracelet with expert speed. 'Once it breaks, you will have fortune in luck, love and work.'

'Really?' I beamed, examining the thread more intently.

'How convenient,' Marcello scoffed. My eyes flashed up to his, annoyed he had tainted my hope that something, even something as silly as a piece of thread, could bring me good fortune in areas that had not had the greatest of beginnings.

Marcello must have heeded my warning as he rolled his eyes and reached into his pocket, giving the man two euros for his efforts. The man seemed just as surprised as I was.

'*Grazie,*' he beamed, nodding his head several times.

I turned toward Marcello, peering at him. 'Thanks. My shout for gelato, then.'

Marcello's sternness melted away as we moved in step towards Via dei Condotti.

# Chapter Eleven

I felt completely out of place among the wealthy fashion-able locals with their blazer jackets, designer glasses and cravats; I didn't dare step my Converse sneaker inside any fashion label. I, on the other hand, in my tan shorts and army-green singlet top, was a bumbag away from 'tourist chic'. Luckily, there were plenty of other questionable fashions darting about to make me feel more at home. Standing next to Marcello was enough to make anyone feel self-conscious, however; he could easily be used as a muse to be carved out of marble and sat in the middle of a piazza to be admired by the masses. I was admiring him way too much—I'd be caught in the act if I didn't cut it out. I averted my gaze to the impossibly priced handbag on display, which worked in distracting me until I glimpsed Marcello's reflection in the glass.

*And moving on . . .*

Looking around, this city was a lesson in contrasts: the stark yellow exterior of Louis Vuitton nestled opposite a corner flower vendor, the high-pitched buzz of passing Vespas echoing off centuries-old arched doorways, quaint narrow streets flowing with conversations in a dozen different languages. And I was free to lose myself in it all, knowing Marcello would lead me back to my hotel. There was no way I could have navigated my way around without wrestling with a map and anxiously trying to ask other clueless tourists where I was. Marcello had proven his worth.

Last night's wine and lack of sleep, combined with the remnants of jet lag, were beginning to take their toll, and I felt the sudden need to replenish myself with some serious carbs.

'Marcello, is there some place we can eat?'

'*Si*.' He laughed, pointing to a gelato stand.

'No, not gelato, I mean something with substance.'

'You have not tried this gelato.'

'Noooo.' I whined like a petulant child. 'I mean I need to put on twenty kilos and feel the burn of a really good wine down my throat.'

'I promise you will have your fill, but first we walk.'

'Ugh.'

My steps were heavy and I was on the verge of chucking an almighty tantrum. Going hungry in Rome was not something I thought I would have to worry about. The busy area just south of the Spanish Steps had been full of culinary choices, not to mention the mazes of side streets where people sat feasting on simple, fresh food, discussing their plans for the evening. I was envious of them all as I dragged my feet along. But my hunger soon abated when I noticed the thickening of the crowd. I glanced at Marcello, giddy with excitement; he simply raised his brows as he jostled forward. At first I heard the gushing water, growing more constant and intense until reaching the square, then I was met with a truly breathtaking sight. The famous Trevi Fountain, a jewel of water and stone, nestled in the historic centre of the city. And it finally hit me: this was Rome, and I was here—like, really, really here. Nothing could ruin this moment, not even the hordes of jostling tourists vying for optimum selfie positions or desperately shuffling to get nearer to the star attraction. Marcello, so close that I could feel the vibration of his voice on my earlobe, spoke of the significance of the intense and spectacular scene before us. I had known it already, but I was happy enough for Marcello to explain it to me now.

'It is the largest Baroque fountain in the city, and one of the most beautiful in the world. Behind is the Palazzo Poli, a palace that held many lavish parties in the 1830s.'

'Quite the party venue. What about those?' I pointed at the imposing fountain sculptures.

'The Tritons are guiding Oceanus' shell chariot, and attempting to tame the winged hippocamps.'

'Hippocamps?'

Marcello smiled. 'Seahorses.'

'Oh, yeah, right, hippocamps—horses with wings, got it.'

'It is said that if you throw a coin over your shoulder into the water, you will be sure to return to Rome.'

I sighed, not for the whimsical, romantic notion, but for the reality in front of me; getting close enough to the fountain to toss a coin would be nigh on impossible.

'Somehow I don't think we are going to get anywhere near there.'

Marcello seemed disappointed. Yep, I was officially a shit tourist.

'It's just that . . .'

'Let's go,' he said, canting his head to the side and urging me to follow.

'I'm pretty sure that the tour has us coming back here— I'll throw a coin in then,' I said, struggling to weave and keep up.

'If you're sure. Okay, then, come on. So many gods, so little time,' he said with a wink, leading me in yet another direction, littered with more men selling roses and trinkets. This time I was a hardened tourist, turning down each and every one myself.

Marcello flashed a smile at me as if impressed, then continued on.

It was becoming clearer and clearer to me that Rome was like no other place, with its ancient cobblestone streets worn down by centuries of celebration and sorrow. Fountains filled with cool water sat against the backdrops of the white and pink buildings, some glowing in the summer sun, others shaded, affording us refuge from the heat of the day. Souvenir shops with postcards and T-shirts were as common as flower vendors and magazine stands; a car alarm sounding in a distant street seemed to fit in with the chaos that surrounded us for street after street. We wandered into a side alley, where for a fleeting moment it felt like we were the only ones around, until the sound of a motorbike flying up behind us broke the peace. As we moved over to the side and then walked out into another piazza, my stomach reminded me lunch was well overdue.

'Are you deliberately trying to torture me?'

'Just a little further,' he said, leading me into yet another narrow street filled with ravenous tourists in little cafes, taunting me with their delicious bowls of pasta and seafood.

We entered a stretch of stalls featuring jewellers and handmade objects and paintings, artists drawing caricatures of giggling travellers, and row upon row of fake designer handbags. A culmination of hunger and intrigue caught me as I sipped on my lukewarm water bottle and blindly followed Marcello, only to stop so suddenly I banged straight into the back of him. Hot, sweaty and hungry, I scowled at the spilt water on my shoe. When I finally looked up, my annoyance was forgotten as my eyes widened in awe at the sight in front of me.

'Pantheon.' Marcello's dimples were in full force now as he turned around to look at me. 'This is one of my favourite places in Rome,' he said, nodding his head. 'It's so incredibly well preserved, one of the best in all of ancient

Rome, largely due to its continuous use throughout history. Since the seventh century it has been used as a church, dedicated to St Mary and the Martyrs.'

'It's beautiful,' I breathed out.

Marcello seemed like a small boy, gushing with pride. 'Wait until you see inside.'

Behind a steady queue of people, we made our way through the imposing columns and in through the large bronzed doors, our eyes trailing up to the dome-shaped ceiling with mouths agape—well, mine was, anyway. Even in the great vastness of this room, Marcello stayed close to me. It seemed the best way to speak; even in the fray he wanted to tell me things about this city, his city, as if it was meant only for me to know.

'See above us: there is a perfectly circular opening,' he said softly. Marcello pointed upwards, just in case I might have missed what he was talking about, though it was the first thing I had seen when we walked in. 'Rainwater comes down through the opening onto the marble floors.' My eyes trailed down with interest as we walked around the perimeter. 'And around the edges, you can see an actual drainage system that helps get rid of the water.' I shook my head, realising that I hadn't said one word since stepping inside. Being inside the Pantheon seemed to rob me of speech; I felt so small, insignificant,

We made our way to stand before Raphael's tomb, reading the tiny plaque about the great Renaissance artist, and silently paid our respects before leaving through the giant metal doors. I felt completely reenergised, ready to keep exploring this magnificent city, but Marcello had other ideas, stopping right before the Fontana del Pantheon. I stared at the fountain, wondering the particular significance.

Marcello chuckled, seemingly delighted in my confusion as he spun me around and pointed.

'Lunch!'

# Chapter Twelve

It all made sense now. Lunch was easy enough to find, but it all depended on what view you wanted. Seated outside the Hostaria Pantheon with its white-and-red checked tablecloths, freshly poured white wine with a front-row seat to the Pantheon, my guide had chosen well. Marcello raised his glass to me.

'*Salute.*'

I brought mine up to clink against his and we drank in unison. I placed my glass back on the table, melting back into my chair and taking it all in. While there was always a consistent hum around us, a new silence fell between us, and then it occurred to me how strange this all was. I had jokingly alluded to a hot date in front of the others, and now this felt strangely like one.

I shook the thought from my mind.

*Don't be ridiculous, Sammi, let's just refuel the tank and . . .*

'Oh, wow.'

Marcello topped my glass, his brows raised in question.

'*Spaghetti alle vongole veraci*, the *risotto alla crema di scampi*, the *fettuccine mari e monti*,' I read aloud in what was no doubt the worst Italian accent ever, but the choices were just too much. I had died and gone to food heaven.

Marcello read his own selection of the menu.

'*Rigatoni alla carbonara, abbacchio alla scottadito, coratella con ai carciofi*.'

I had absolutely no idea what any of it meant, but I really wanted him to say it again; the way he rolled his tongue around the words was more soothing than the sound of water over marble in *la Fontana di Trevi*. I shifted in my seat and took a deep swig of my wine.

I cleared my throat and placed my napkin in my lap.

'So are you coming out with us tomorrow? Day one of official Bellissimo tour shenanigans.'

Marcello reclined in his chair, sliding his sunglasses off his face and into the thick fold of his dark hair.

'No,' he said simply, and I felt a surge of disappointment inside me. Then I wondered what exactly Marcello had to do with the tour group. Apart from attending the meet-and-greet, and his apparent interest to help show the group around in our downtime, he seemed to have no official role within Bellissimo Tours. Was he Maria's wingman, her business partner, her lover? I didn't sense a romantic vibe between them.

I straightened in my chair, looking at Marcello with a long, assessing stare. He didn't flinch.

'How exactly are you affiliated with the tour?'

Marcello shrugged. 'I'm not.'

My brows rose, pausing for my next hard-hitting question.

*Wait a minute.*

Troubling thoughts ran through my mind: if he wasn't affiliated, what the hell was I doing with him? Walking the streets, seeing the sights, wining and dining with him. He could be a con man, racking up a huge bill for having taken me around the city for the day; he could be spiking my drink and placing me in the boot of a car after lunch, never to be seen again.

'Are you affiliated with the hotel?' I asked as calmly as I could.

Marcello leant his elbows casually on the tabletop, looking directly at me in that way he had. 'No.'

I wanted to press further but our waiter was at our table now, smiling and charming. I pointed at a random item on the menu and fixed my eyes back on Marcello, who ordered with far more thought.

'More wine?' the waiter posed.

My eyes darted to the near-on empty bottle. Christ, I had to slow down; legless in Rome for a second night was not going to happen.

I smiled and covered my glass and the waiter looked at me as if I was a lunatic, like he had never seen such an action before. From an outsider's perspective, Marcello and I must have looked a sight: the paranoid and slightly clammy girl interrogating an Italian runway model. No wonder he looked bemused.

'Sooo, what is it that you do exactly, Marcello?'

*Scam vulnerable tourists.*

Marcello topped up his own glass. 'Oh, a bit of this and a bit of that. What is it that brings you to Rome?'

'Oh no-no-no, I asked first. I have spent far more time with you than anyone else in my entire group, and I already know way too much about them and absolutely nothing about you.'

'Well, I know nothing about you either.' He smiled, satisfied, like we had reached a stalemate, but unlike him I had nothing to hide.

'Okay, well, I am a twenty-two-year-old Gemini who took a gap year three years ago from a Bachelor of Arts course at uni, thinking I would use that one year to work and "find myself", before inevitably re-enrolling, though this time to major in history with the plan to become a high-school teacher because, let's face it, apart from that very splendid path my parents had picked out for me, I really didn't have a bloody clue what I wanted to do with my life or where I was going, and still don't, so in order to pretend like I am living some kind of life I booked a rather haphazard trip with a dodgy-ass travel agent and now I am stuck with a group of people that I really don't like, and all that keeps me from booking an early ticket back home is my pride and the fettucine carbonara that I may have just ordered.'

I sat there for a long, drawn-out moment as Marcello simply looked at me, a little alarmed, perhaps wondering if I planned to drug him and put him in the boot of a car. I rested my hands on the table. Wow, I had never said any of those things out loud, and saying them only made me feel more shit. If I couldn't make something of this holiday then what was going to become of me? I would be back home, broke, living at Mum and Dad's house and even more clueless than before.

If blurting out my rather uninspiring story was meant to encourage Marcello to open up, it was a failure. Instead, he silently topped up my glass and this time I didn't object, quickly taking a deep swig in the hope it would cool my pink cheeks, which were currently burning with mortification.

'I've been working on something new.' Marcello's words stopped me from taking another sip. I slowly placed the glass down, afraid that if I moved he might stop.

'I work with Maria on occasion, but I don't think it's going to work, not this time. The group is too . . . *young*.'

I nodded my head. 'I'm pretty sure they're drunk most of the time, too.'

Marcello laughed, a welcome reprieve from the gloomy turn our afternoon had taken, though I cursed myself for interrupting his story.

Marcello shrugged. 'You win some, you lose some. Tell me, Sammi, what are you doing on this tour? It seems so . . .'

'Not my scene?' I laughed.

Marcello smiled, turning the base of the wine glass from side to side, his eyes moving from the glass to me.

'You seem different,' he said, seriously.

I smiled. 'Well, Marcello,' I said, lifting my glass up for another sip, 'I will take that as an absolute compliment.'

# Chapter Thirteen

When you're headed into the unknown it always takes forever; with the promise of an exciting adventure you can never quite get there fast enough. Heading back is always a much quicker journey. I didn't want to get back to the hotel just yet; sure, my pinky toe throbbed, and I had a matching blister forming on my other foot, but I didn't want the day to end. I stalled as much as I could and, as far as distractions go, a stopover to Giolotti—Rome's most famous gelateria—was a pretty damn good one. As promised at the Spanish Steps, I paid for our iced treats, though Marcello had insisted he pay for lunch; it definitely felt like some bizarre date. In retrospect, I hadn't exactly lied to the others about my plans for the day. The fact that it also included Marcello's raspberry and chocolate gelato, and my pistachio one, well, that was just an added bonus.

We veered down the narrow, familiar street towards the hotel. Our gelatos were long gone and the air hung heavier in the onset of afternoon; it seemed like a lifetime ago that we bumped into one another on this very street, when I had in some way swayed him into showing me around. I thought about how the day might have turned out. Me, hobbling aimlessly in inappropriate footwear, lost, feasting on overpriced tourist food and seeing a fraction of the sites. I thought about how Marcello could easily have ended up showing Jodie and the others all the places he had shown me and something twisted my insides; I didn't like the feeling and I sure as hell didn't understand why. I mean, Marcello didn't belong to me; he wasn't my private tour guide, although in some strange way he kind of felt like it. We stopped outside the hotel, awkwardly standing at the front entrance, facing one another, again just like a first date.

'Umm, thank you, Marcello, today was really great,' I said, fidgeting from side to side. I brushed my hair out of my face, looked down and then up, then placed my hand on my hip, trying for that casual, cool persona, like *hey, whatever*. Ugh, I was the worst.

Marcello, on the other hand, was the epitome of cool and casual; he was so confident and sure of himself he didn't even need to hide behind his shades, and when he looked at me, giving me his sole attention, he did so without apology. If Marcello wanted to look, he looked, and one thing I learnt rather quickly is that I would never win the staring competition, not with him. I don't know if it was the deep, dark brown colour of his eyes that was his advantage, but they sure were mesmerising. Screw it, he had dreamy bloody eyes. No woman stood a chance looking into those.

I stood there, not really knowing what was customary: do I shake hands, curtsy, offer a tip? *Oh, Jesus, should I tip him?* Would that be embarrassing? What was more embarrassing was the way Marcello was looking at me now, his eyes narrowed, fixed to the side a little. Oh, God, did I have gelato on my face?

But before I could wipe at my cheek, Marcello stepped forward and lightly touched my face.

'You got a bit of sun today.'

If my face wasn't already burning from the Italian sunshine, the feel of Marcello's skin against mine seared like a brand.

I swallowed. 'Did I?'

He smiled, nodding and letting his hand fall to the side. He was very close to me and I suddenly felt really hot, or maybe it was the sunburn? I looked down, then back at Marcello, who definitely had the darkest eyes I had ever seen, so dark they were almost as black as his lashes ... aaaand now I was staring and he was staring right back at me. I stopped my awkward fidgeting and just stood there, aware of my uneven breathing and his proximity. Could he hear the crazy beating of my heart? I swear it was threatening to leap out of my chest; that couldn't be good.

'Well, thanks for not drugging me and selling me off as a sex slave,' I half laughed.

Marcello's beautiful dark eyes double-blinked and I saw a flash of horror mixed with confusion. I instantly cursed my big mouth.

*For fuck's sake—internal thoughts, Sammi, remember?*

I laughed nervously, stepping back to put space between us, no doubt much to Marcello's relief.

'See, told you I was different.'

And before I waited for him to answer, I turned on my heel and headed into the hotel.

'*Ciao*, Gabriello!' I saluted to the man behind the desk, who, like most of his guests, probably assumed I was drunk. *No, just mortified*, I thought, taking to the stairs, only wincing slightly at the building pain of my bruised, blistered feet.

Who would have ever believed I'd be so relieved to see the inside of Hotel Luce del Sole? Certainly not me, not in a million years. And I wouldn't call it a sense of nostalgia, but as I made my way up each aged, grimy step to the eighth floor I found myself smiling, wondering if any of my tour buddies had as good a day as me. Had they seen the things I had, learnt as much, tasted in the delights of delicious Italian food, and been immersed in the history with skin heated by the Mediterranean sun? Whatever they had done, I couldn't imagine them enjoying their day as much as me, I thought smugly, twisting the handle of my room with a contented sigh, pushing it open to—

'Oh, Jesus Christ!' I shielded my eyes, turning so quickly I walked straight into the door, flinging it closed and trapping me inside the room with an alarmed scream and rustling sheets for company.

'Get out, GET OUT!' Jodie screamed.

'I'm so sorry, I didn't see, I'm gone, I am so gone,' I babbled, scrabbling for the door, opening it and flinging myself into the hall, shutting it firmly behind me. I leant against the wall, my heart racing as I squeezed my eyes shut, trying so desperately to unsee the tableau from a moment ago. But try as I might, there was no amount of squeezing my eyes or wishing away that would work; the images danced a sick and twisted loop around my brain, images of Jodie's ankles around ... Bookworm Gary's ears.

*Jodie and Bookworm Gary?*

'Holy shit.'

~

I had so many plans: shower; get changed; have a little snooze on my top bunk bed. Scribble down all the sights I had seen—well, not all of them—and message my parents about how amazing my day had been, minus Marcello and the live sex show. But right now I was far too terrified to venture through that door. Instead, I decided the safest bet was to sit at the Hotel Luce del Sole bar, if you could call it that: it was really just a tiny bench wedged in the corner of the hotel restaurant. It wasn't even busy enough to have a full-time bartender; the deeply sighing hotel desk manager, Gabriello, had to split his time between front reception and coming to top up my drink. After the first time, I sipped very slowly, comforted by the solitude and enjoying the dark corner, until an unmistakable sound sliced through my quiet contentment. It was like an insane tourist running with the bulls, except replace 'run for your lives' with an obnoxiously loud rendition of 'That's Amore'. I shrunk away from Nate and Johnny, who were wearing matching, skin-tight 'I Love Roma' T-shirts. I could only imagine how well they would have fit in holidaying and bar-hopping in Bali, but, lucky me, of all the tours in the world, they had to book mine.

'Hey, S-S-S-S-Samantha,' Nate called out, spotting me and diverting his path from the stairs towards me, Johnny in tow.

'Oh, kill me now,' I muttered under my breath, spinning on my stool and pretending I was shocked to see them.

'Looks like someone's had a good day,' I said.

*Not as good as mine, and definitely not as good as Jodie's.*

I forced my fake smile wider, hoping it didn't seem creepy, or as if I was hiding anything.

'Well, looks like you can't wipe the smile off your face so I'm guessing you and Marcello had a pretty good time,' Johnny said with a wiggle of his brows.

I couldn't quite bring myself to look at him; were Johnny and Jodie a thing? They seemed like a couple last night, and this morning for that matter; was she cheating on him? I shook the millions of questions from my mind.

Not my business. My smile morphed into something else, something real as I thought back to my day.

'Yeah, we really did,' I said, enjoying the fact that, unlike this morning, I wasn't actually lying.

Nate pulled up the stool next to me, his huge frame engulfing what was left of the tiny corner bar. I edged back a little but our knees still touched. Nate slid my drink over and without apology took a big sip, before grimacing and reeling back in disgust.

'Ugh, that's just nasty.' He shuddered.

Johnny curiously picked up the drink and sniffed it, his questioning eyes lifting to me.

I sighed, rolling my eyes and taking my drink from him. 'Yes, heaven forbid that a drink doesn't have alcohol in it.'

'No alcohol?' Johnny repeated, as if certainly such a concept weren't possible. 'You mean, like one of those mocktails?' he asked in apparent distaste.

I shrugged, taking a deep draw on my straw, trying not to think about where Nate's mouth might have been in the past twenty-four hours.

'Oh, hell, no!' Nate exclaimed, taking the drink from me and chucking the straw into the air.

'Hey!' I protested.

'You are coming out with us,' he said, as if it wasn't up for negotiation.

'What, where?' My heart started to race, in a way that was less 'oh goody' and more 'oh God'. Obviously I had trust issues.

'Honestly, Sammi, you need to remove that stick from up your butt and come out with us tonight.' Johnny whacked me on the arm like one of the lads.

Rubbing at the pain and scowling, I said, 'I don't have a stick up my butt.'

'Good, then get ready.' Nate leapt off the stool, victorious, and pushed Johnny into motion.

My shoulders slumped. I really didn't want to go out, the thought of consuming alcohol while suffering a mild case of sunstroke did nothing for me. Nor did I like the idea of being trapped in a confined space with the likes of Jodie. Then, as if conjured from my imagination, she appeared, blocking the boys' path on the stairs.

'What are you two so pleased about?' she asked.

'Sammi's coming out with us!' exclaimed Johnny, with way too much excitement. I wanted to hide. If there was one thing I had learnt it was to keep my distance from Johnny: he belonged to Jodie. Apparently she had quite the collection; would Nate be safe? Should Marcello be warned? I felt a pang of something inside me, deep in my gut, at the thought of Jodie's tentacle-like arms flailing over Marcello. I didn't like this primal feeling, which disturbed me more than I could say. In fact, it disturbed me almost as much as the way Jodie was looking at me now, her catlike eyes boring into me from above.

'Oh, goody!' she said with no enthusiasm whatsoever.

'Hey, Sammi, Jodie will help you get ready,' Nate called out before turning back to Jodie. 'Something really short, okay?'

'You're such a pig,' Jodie sneered, moving to let them barrel up the stairs.

'Oh, come on, you love it.' He laughed, flexing his muscles. It could have been a shared moment between girls, for Jodie and I to look at one another conspiratorially and say, 'Men!' with a massive eye roll, but there was no bonding, no camaraderie. All I got from Jodie was a filthy 'I loathe everything about you' death stare before she continued down the steps and through reception.

I sighed; if this was a preview of things to come, I seriously had to clear the air.

'Hey, Jodie, wait,' I called out, abandoning my mocktail and limping after her.

Jodie swung around, stepping up into my face. 'If you tell Johnny, I swear to God I will destroy you.'

I stepped back, stunned. Jodie's wild eyes stared into mine, her finger pushing into my shoulder. With her being a whole foot shorter than me, the situation had the potential to be comical if I wasn't so intimidated by her.

'It's none of my business,' I said, holding up my hands in surrender; if there was a white flag I would have flown it.

'Damn straight it's not, so keep your mouth shut.'

I nodded. 'Or you will destroy me, got it.' It sounded like a threat made from a Marvel comic-book villain, but I did not mistake the meaning in Jodie's manic eyes, and I had no doubt she would happily serve time if it meant making me pay. I would have to have had a death wish to mess with Jodie, all five foot of her.

She flicked her hair in a departing 'Fuck you' motion before walking out the front door; somehow I think it was safe to say we would not be braiding each other's hair tonight and giggling about boys as we got ready to paint the streets of Rome red. I just hoped that we didn't paint them blood red.

# Chapter Fourteen

There was one saving grace; well, two, actually. And they were in the form of two besties—and part-time bikini-clad Meter Maids—Harper and Kylie. Lovely girls, in large part because they didn't want to harm me in any way. They were the kind of girls you could giggle with about boys and share hairspray and fashion advice. I could probably learn a thing or two from these effervescent eighteen-year-olds, who were not related and yet looked almost identical with their straightened bleach-blonde hair, a shade-too-dark spray tans, and manufactured, impossibly white teeth. They were the epitome of youth, and enjoying their own gap year, after which, bless their hearts, they actually believed they would go back to uni. That's what we all say; it was the very thing I had proclaimed three years ago and counting. Looking in the mirror, I felt like a librarian next to them; as I stood between them, applying foundation to take the red tinge out of my skin, they looked like matching Barbie bookends. Coming up to my shoulders, we were going to look ridiculous out on the dance floor together; I only hoped they would be wearing perilously high heels, otherwise I would have to seek refuge in the shadow of Nate the Giant. I really didn't want to be hanging out and drinking shots with him, though Harper was only too happy to do that for me.

'Nate is so fucking hot,' she said, pumping the crusty remnants of her mascara tube.

'Noooo, I'm more of a Team Johnny kind of girl. I can't believe he hooked up with Jodie last night,' pouted Kylie.

I tried not to falter with my foundation at the mentioning of her name. 'They aren't really a thing, are they, though? I mean, they're not exclusive or anything, right?'

I could only hope that was the case, otherwise I had witnessed certain infidelity; no wonder Jodie wanted me dead.

'Well, I think Johnny is pretty cruisy, but seriously, don't even look at Johnny sideways, Jodie is very territorial.' Harper looked at me in the reflection of the mirror; her belated words of wisdom bonding me to her. At least someone was on my side.

'It's just so bloody unfair. How am I ever going to make my moves on Johnny if she's there giving me daggers?' complained Kylie. The scene was reminiscent of getting ready for a school social. We were all talking about who we wanted to 'get with', and the residential mean girl who ruined our lives. Except we were wedged in a dank, grimy bathroom with cracked, mouldy tiles and no natural light, which made make-up application rather difficult.

'So, is Marcello coming out tonight?' Harper bumped me playfully with her hip, causing me to draw a clumsy, jagged kink in my winged eyeliner. My almost-lie about Marcello and I had really landed me in it; clearly everyone wanted to know about Marcello.

'Umm, I don't think so, he isn't really linked to the tour in any way,' I said, still troubled by not knowing exactly how he fitted in. It was my goal to find out exactly who Marcello was; maybe tonight I would become Maria's wingwoman. I rubbed away the streak of black, not keen for the Cleopatra look. Reapplying my eye make-up more carefully, I began to get excited about our night on the town. According to the mad ramblings of the boys, complimentary T-shirts were provided because they booked online, as well as a complimentary welcoming shot and something called the 'Power Hour' with as many wines, beers and mixed drinks as you wanted, followed by drinking games and traditional pizza. It sounded messy. It sounded, dare I say it, amazing.

I tried to think back to the last time I had been out pub-crawling. It was a mortifyingly long time. Embarking on a break from my studies, I hadn't really expected to be lonely. I mean, it's not like I'd moved to the other side of the world. My friends moved away to go to uni; they came back most weekends in the beginning, but soon it became less, and then they got new friends, new social agendas and stopped coming home at all. I had tried to head to the city on weekends, to meet my old mates on their new turf, but it had always felt awkward, like I didn't belong in their world anymore. As time went on, it kind of felt like I didn't really belong anywhere. I had, in a way, become institutionalised by my own making.

Standing in front of the murky mirror in a Roman hostel, I had an epiphany. It was time to break out of my self-made shell. What was the saying? When in Rome, do as the Romans do. I wasn't entirely sure what that meant for me tonight, but it felt really freeing. For all the pitfalls and less-than-ideal living arrangements, in the space of twenty-four hours I had never felt so liberated, which I knew had at least a little to do with a particular someone I'd spent my day with. I tried not to think too much about that as I flicked my thick curly hair over my shoulders and examined myself one last time before declaring, 'Alright, let's do this!'

~

Maria was wedged in a corner booth, being peer-group pressured into taking a shot, which she did like a trooper. I stood awkwardly to the side with a foul-tasting alcoholic beverage that I had been nursing for longer than I cared to admit. I wanted to stay semi-coherent; I had planned to corner Maria and subtly question her about Marcello, but I really struggled to get near her, which was probably just as well because I was also struggling with how to broach the subject without seeming like a stalker. There was also another barrier: the music in the bar was so painfully loud—clearly not the ideal place to have a conversation, as I came to learn first-hand when a voice screamed in my ear: 'Here, you'll like this one.'

I turned to see Johnny next to me, passing me a fresh drink that looked clean, cold and crisp next to my horrendous, now-warm drink that looked like a watered-down sunrise.

'Oh, thanks. What is it?' I asked, taking a tentative sip and liking what I sampled.

'Well, let's just say it ain't no mocktail,' he said, smiling broadly. I laughed, allowing myself to get lost in that smile until a memory of fierce eyes slapped me into reality. I glanced around, swearing that Jodie was lurking in the shadows, watching on.

Before I could distance myself, Johnny took the drink from my hand and placed it on our table, then slid his hand into mine. I froze. 'Come on—I love this song,' he said, canting his head and pulling me towards the dance floor.

'Oh no, Johnny, I really don't want to . . .'

But there was no escaping his pull—he was far stronger than me. Fight as I might, with an awkward twirl onto the dance floor we were soon lost in the crush of flailing bodies, battering around like a ball in a pinball machine while Phoenix's 'Rome' belted out. I could only hope that we were hidden from prying eyes as Johnny was dancing up close next to me, holding my hand. And maybe it was the new taste of my drink, or the hidden crush of the dancing crowd and the beat of the music, but I finally lost myself. I forgot about prying eyes and consequences; I was having the best time, until I made the mistake of looking at the heated stare of Johnny. His arms had somehow encircled my waist, and I felt a new panic as a small, sexy smile tugged at the side of his mouth, like a question being posed, his face so close to mine. I suddenly felt hot, like I couldn't breathe. Jodie's eyes, Kylie's pout, Nate's high five and Maria's curved brow flashed in my mind. I looked up into Johnny's blue eyes—and don't get me wrong, they were a really beautiful blue—attached to an equally nice face, a hard, built body that I could feel under my hands that rested on his biceps and—holy shit, what was that pressed against my hip?

Ordinarily this all wouldn't have been so shocking; I mean, I wasn't a prude and Johnny was gorgeous, but what unsettled me more than his unexpected erection was the fact that his eyes weren't the ones I wanted to look into. They weren't the very vivid brown eyes I wanted to get lost in; his smile wasn't home to two dimples that made me want to stare at any given chance in case they emerged. And regardless of how fast my heart was beating and how I bit my lip at the tempting notion of giving in to Johnny, I took the only exit I could think of, sliding my hands up to his shoulders and yelling into his ear, 'I think I am going to be sick.'

Here's a tip for travellers worthy of any *Lonely Planet* guide: if you need to quickly exit a situation or avoid a certain event real fast, just utter those magical words. Aside from the rather comical wide-eyed look of horror you will receive, you will have your way out. Johnny led out of the crowd, ducking and weaving, pushing and shouting, carving a fast retreat to the exit and blasting into the cool, Italian night air. Though I didn't really feel sick, the blissful fresh air was a welcome reprieve from the stuffy, loud interior of the bar. Actually, I felt fine, elated even, thinking that, hey, I hadn't lost my charm, I still had it. I smiled and breathed in the night air deeply.

'Johnny, you are my knight in shining armour,' I called out, spinning, until an image caused me to skid to a halt. Johnny walked into the back of me and would have knocked me over if he hadn't grabbed my hips and drawn me back against him.

'Whoa, watch ya lookin' at . . .' Johnny paused as my widened eyes locked onto a pair of very familiar brown eyes. My heart stopped, but not for the unexpected joy of bumping into Marcello out the back of a club in the heart of Rome; no, not at all. My heart stopped because my eyes broke from Marcello to the figure standing next to him, the vision of my nightmares.

Jodie.

# Chapter Fifteen

'Samantha?'

It was like being struck by a bolt of lightning; I only got called by my full name when I was in deep trouble, which it seemed I now was. I followed Jodie's eyes and realised that Johnny still had his hands at my hips, and Johnny and I had been seen giggling and swaying in a darkened Roman street like a pair of young lovers. I quickly pulled his hands away, putting distance between us, trying to choose between explaining that it wasn't what it looked like or laughing it all off. Johnny turned to look at me, offended by my sudden repulsion; I was now caught by three sets of confused eyes.

'What the hell are you doing?' Jodie spoke as if her blood was boiling under her skin, her poor attempt at concealing her rage perhaps more frightening than the rage itself. But I really wasn't concerned with answering as my gaze set on the cool, calm exterior of Marcello, who looked from me to Johnny and back again, as if he was silently putting two and two together. My heart dropped. There was no two and two, there was nothing going on. But then my eyes flicked from him to Jodie and my own sudden realisation settled.

'I thought you weren't coming out tonight?' *And what the hell was he doing with her?*

Marcello's brows furrowed as he glanced at Jodie and back at me, as if he was just as troubled by the assumption. Jodie, on the other hand, seemed oh so smug.

'Marcello was just showing me the sights,' she said, glancing at Johnny and then back at me, as if to say a silent 'Fuck you'.

I didn't know what was happening to me, maybe rage was a contagious thing, but seeing Jodie loop her arm through Marcello's made me feel ill. To think of him walking and telling her stories of times gone by made me feel like a complete fool. Had I honestly thought that he had told me things, shown me things today that were special? I was so naive.

*So. Stupid.*

I smiled. 'Yeah, he is really good at that,' I said, before turning and heading into what I thought would be the last place I wanted to go, until I realised that place was out in the street with Marcello and Jodie. *If I never see those brown eyes again it will be fine with me*, I thought. I just wished that I really believed it. I wove my way back into the dark, narrow halls crammed with people laughing, drinking, fist-pumping, dry-humping: all the good stuff.

*Lucky them*, I thought bitterly, turning a corner, relieved to see the friendly faces of Harper and Kylie in a spot where the music, while still loud, was a little duller and you didn't have to yell for conversation. Unless, of course, you were just getting yelled at, like I was now. Harper placed herself protectively in front of Kylie, who looked upset.

'What's wrong? Kylie, are you okay?'

'You have some nerve.' Harper glared at me; it was a look I was getting accustomed to.

'Sorry?'

'You knew she liked Johnny, and yet there you were dry-humping him on the dance floor in front of everyone.'

'I was not!' I said, way too high-pitched. Was she for real?

'Everyone is laughing at you, Sammi.'

Her words landed like a physical blow, a quick uppercut that robbed me of my breath. I didn't know what to say; the thought of them all making fun of me made me feel like I was in high school all over again.

'It's funny, I really didn't think you were the kind,' said Harper, shaking her head and looking almost like she was sorry for me.

'Oh, and what kind is that exactly?'

It was a question I wished I hadn't asked, but the words had fallen out of my mouth anyway. Before Harper could answer, Kylie pushed herself up from the wall and looked at me dead on with bloodshot eyes.

'A total snake in the grass,' she bit out, before tugging Harper away and leaving me on my own, my mouth agape.

*What the hell?*

The only bridge I'd managed to build in this insane group had been set on fire. Now I was stuck in no-man's-land; I didn't want to go back to the street, where Marcello was probably pointing to the night sky and telling Jodie about old Roman legends—that, or he was wrestling with Johnny on the cobblestones to win the girl. Or I could go back to the table where apparently I was a laughing stock. Was it because of my dance moves, or was it because me landing someone like Johnny was so unlikely? They must have really split a stitch over the possibility of me and Marcello.

Ugh. I pushed myself forward, if not towards the group then towards the bar; there was still time left in the 'Power Hour' to down a good number of drinks. I slammed a shot down my gullet, eliciting a cheer from a group of locals, encouraging me to reach for another, slamming one drink down after another while Icona Pop's 'I Love It' blasted in the background so hard I could feel the floor vibrate.

I toasted my newfound friends. *'Salute!'*

I came to Rome on my own, and I was going to leave here on my own.

Before too long my self-pity had morphed into something else entirely.

I LOVED Rome! And this snake was going to slide onto the dance floor and rip it up. What's the saying—dance as if no one was watching? Well, that was me. A lone wolf, having the time of my life. I didn't need anyone, not even to show me the sights. I had a map, a brain. *Screw you, Marcello, whoever you are.* And maybe I was seeing things, and Lord knew after several shots I was seeing double, but I felt a hand grab my arm, turning me around, and there he was.

'Speak of the devil!' I shouted.

'What?' he yelled over the music, confused.

Oh yeah, another internal thought again.

'Having a lovely evening?' I asked, still dancing from side to side, my words dripping with sarcasm.

'Not as much as you, it would seem,' he said, his eyes following me, watching my awesome dance moves as he stood stoically still.

'Me? Oh, I am having a great time!' I raised my hands to the sky as if summoning the dance gods.

Marcello was laughing at me, actually fucking laughing at me. Like all the rest of them, no doubt; well, screw them, screw him and this place, wherever the hell this place was. We had arrived by taxi and been unceremoniously dumped out the front, our wrists tagged and pushed inside like cattle. Now if I wanted to exit dramatically, marching off mid-conversation into the night, I really didn't have a clue where to go. Ugh. Instead, I opted to skulk back to the bar until Marcello grabbed my hand.

'I think that's a bad idea.'

'Well, not as bad an idea as getting snared in Jodie's spider web.'

I nodded at the thought. If I was a snake and she was a spider, I could totally beat her in a fight.

'Jodie came to me—she didn't know where the night-club was.'

'Oh, howww convenient.'

Marcello ran his hands through his hair, almost as if he was praying for strength; it was the first time I had really seen him exasperated.

'This is exactly why I don't want to work with you,' he said.

'With me?'

'Not you—them, this, the whole thing,' he shouted.

I frowned; how much had I had to drink? Marcello wasn't making any sense, and it had nothing to do with a language barrier.

'I think you need a drink,' I said.

He simply shook his head, looking at me like he didn't know whether to strangle me or follow me to the bar.

'Come on, it's my shout,' I said, pulling him towards the bar.

He scoffed. 'It's for free.'

I smiled. 'Oh, and so it is.'

~

It didn't take me long to figure out exactly what Marcello's official role was in the group. He was the fun police, outlawing my happiness by ordering me water instead of booze and wedging himself firmly between me and the barman.

'Really? I'm on holidays and you are cutting off the tap.'

'You will thank me in the morning.'

I paused, thinking about what the morning meant exactly; ugh, a fully planned day of sightseeing. I could feel my skin screaming in protest at a day in the sun. I should have opted for an ice bath and slathering myself in after-sun gel. I took the water from Marcello without a word.

'Well, I will just pace myself tomorrow,' I said, taking a sip from my glass.

Marcello laughed. 'Don't bet on it. Maria runs a tight ship; if you're late she will leave you behind, make no mistake. She acts like one of the gang but she will never mess with site operators; you are replaceable. Relationships formed in business will win every time.'

I glanced at the fun-loving Maria flirting with Nate and couldn't imagine her leaving a man behind. She was like the mother of the group, and hopefully not one who would be in the bed under mine later on. I wouldn't put it past any of them, bunch of deviants. My eyes locked on to a very solemn-looking Bookworm Gary on the edge of the dance floor, nursing a beer and looking utterly miserable. I followed his forlorn look across to the opposite side of the room, where Jodie and Johnny stood, clearly in a heated argument. It was like a love triangle from a seriously fucked-up YA novel.

'Should I ask? No, actually, don't worry—I've had my fill of teen angst for one night. Goodnight, Sammi.'

Marcello nodded before moving to step around me.

'Oh, what, not going to escort me to bed tonight?' The words came out before I could realise how incredibly suggestive they sounded. Marcello stopped and looked at me, a little smirk tugging at the corner of his mouth.

'I think Johnny can help you out.' Marcello looked over my shoulder, causing me to turn and be met with Johnny, leaning against the bar next to me. I cringed, not wanting anything to do with Johnny and his psycho woman, who was thankfully nowhere to be seen.

I turned back to Marcello, tilting my head in mockery, but he simply flashed those dimples and leant into me, speaking into my ear. 'Behave.'

And just like that he was gone.

# Chapter Sixteen

'Marcello, wait. Don't make me run—I have a sore pinky!'

It wasn't the kind of impassioned cry you'd see in a movie script, not something you'd hear Deborah Kerr yell as she ran after Cary Grant. But this was the world according to Sammi Shorten and, as much as running after a gorgeous Italian man in a darkened street in Rome wasn't exactly a usual Friday night, here I was.

Marcello stopped, turning to take in the sight of a lone woman running down the street, shoes in hand, hair wild, sunburned skin on show, pulling up in front of him with hands on knees, breathless. How he didn't turn and run I will never know. Instead, he simply stood there and looked at me like he didn't know exactly what to do with me; I probably looked like an item that belonged in a lost property pile. And with me standing next to the unwrinkled, well-cut, tall, dark and handsome figure of Marcello, no wonder people were laughing at me—it was a bloody joke.

In the light of an illuminated bar sign, it was painfully
clear. He was not for me; he was not in my league and
despite the courage of a few drinks, chasing after him
with some romantic, whimsical notion was utterly insane.
It was a sobering moment, one that had me stepping back
and shaking my head.

'Sammi?' Marcello edged forward.

'No, never mind. I'm good,' I said, holding up my
shoes and spinning so quickly in the opposite direction
that I didn't see the blinding light of the buzzing Vespa
in my path. It happened all too fast: lights, screaming,
horn blasting, tyre skidding, the vice-like grip swooping
around my body and dragging me backwards and slamming me against something hard and cold. All the
breath was knocked from my lungs, and loud, angry
Italian shouts echoed in the streets between the rider and
Marcello, insults exchanged in a wall of infinite noise as
the world spun and shock settled in. I felt painfully aware
of everything. The noises, the lights, the rough edge of the
doorway I was pressed against, the warmth and protection
of Marcello holding firmly onto me, keeping me up, my
shaking body held by his firm grip as he slid his hand up
to cup my cheeks, tilting my ashen face to meet his.

'Are you okay?'

Was I? I wasn't so sure, so I answered in the only way
I could communicate. My chin trembled and I shook my
head. Marcello breathed out, like ten years of his own life
had been robbed from him, smiling and caressing the side

of my neck; nestled under the thick mane of my hair, he simply mirrored my head shaking, drawing me into him and wrapping me into a tight, warm embrace.

'You are a disaster.' The vibration of his words were warm against my temple.

'I know,' I agreed, anchoring myself to him. I couldn't stop shaking. I didn't want to lose my shit but I lifted my head anyway, tears welling in my eyes; no use trying to hide how truly pathetic I was.

'Are you hurt?'

'No, I was just thinking that . . .' My voice broke; I wiped at my cheek and looked away.

Marcello lifted my chin. 'Thinking what?' he asked gently.

'I have no faith that my shitty travel agent's insurance covers serious maiming by a Vespa.'

Marcello's mouth twisted. 'You mean, you didn't tick the "maiming by Vespa" box?'

'I can pretty much guarantee it.'

'That's a raw deal,' he agreed.

'I didn't sign up for this,' I sniffed.

'What? You didn't sign up for being wedged up against a doorway by a handsome stranger?'

My eyes flicked up to Marcello's face, smiling beyond my misty vision. I saw a lightness in him; the dimples were there and they were the best kind of distraction.

'Well, no, I did actually sign up for that,' I joked. 'That was extra.'

Marcello's thumb made slow, lazy circles against the nape of my neck. 'Extra?'

I nodded, pressing my lips together, I was shaking for a whole other reason now, my chest rising and falling in laboured breaths that were out of rhythm against Marcello's. If this was what the aftermath of being saved from certain death was all about, I would have thrown myself into the path of a Vespa a long time ago.

And as if his eyes, and his hands, his heat—and, God, did he smell amazing—weren't all too much, he bloody smiled as he moved in closer, lowering his head and whispering against my mouth.

'Well, I hope it was worth it,' he said, lips lowered onto mine, kissing me so softly, so sweetly, stopping me from breathing. In that moment I knew, feeling his arms circle around my waist, that it was worth it. It had all been worth it. Letting go, being free, throwing caution to the wind, running down a street shoeless and almost getting run over, it had all been worth it. I felt it in the warmth of his body against me, in his deepening kiss as my hands scooped into his hair, encouraging him with the small sounds of approval as his hands fisted at my dress, pulling me closer to him. Softness, careening into a heated hunger. My shoulder rubbed against the coarse stone doorway, verging on pain, until I felt the press of Marcello's thigh between my legs, and his tongue delve into my mouth. I had all but forgotten my name as he kissed a trail down along my neck, a scorching path that had me catching my breath and blinking the stars from my vision, feeling the delicious friction between us. I didn't know the laws here; was it sociably acceptable to have sex on a darkened doorstep? I knew you weren't allowed to eat food on the Spanish Steps; surely this was far more depraved.

I blocked out those voices inside my head—*No time for negativity*—as I shifted, moving to push Marcello against the door, so hard his back hit. I took great delight in the way his brows rose in surprise. I giggled against his mouth, taking control and being far less gentle than he had been with me. Maybe it was the alcohol that gave me the courage, or the brink of something ready to explode inside me that had me so ready for this, whatever this was.

Rome had never looked so good: Marcello's hands sliding up across my dress towards my breast, kissing me back harder, faster and more eagerly. The moment was broken by the echoing, drunken singing that would haunt me long after this trip was over.

'When the moon hits your eye like a big pizza pie, that's amore!'

I rolled my eyes. 'Nate.' I breathed out a laugh, glancing back at Marcello who had frozen, listening to the approach of the nearing chorus. I expected to see those dimples, for him to laugh and shake his head. But instead something flashed across his face when I looked at him, and the act of him breaking away from me so fast was like a slap. He moved to lean against the alcove of the door, his hands in his pockets. I stood there, chilled by the sudden exposure I felt now that he had put space between us; was he that embarrassed to be seen with me? I frowned at him, offended and ready to ask what the hell he was doing when Nate appeared, his arm slung around Kylie's shoulder, who seemed to have miraculously recovered from her heartbreak over Johnny.

'Marcelloooooo, *come stai*,' Nate sung into the air.

Marcello smiled at me, trying to include me into the moment, but I wasn't exactly feeling the funny vibe, too pissed to be lighthearted right now.

'Oops, we weren't interrupting, were we?' Nate whispered, or at least attempted to.

'Of course not,' I said, wrapping my arms around myself and pushing away from the door. 'Are you guys heading back?' I asked, moving to stand with them in the street.

'*Si*,' Nate said, followed by a hiccup.

'Good, I'm coming too.'

'Sweeeet, party at Hotel Luce del Sole,' Nate yelled.

Kylie looked between me and Marcello, her bloody woman's intuition not missing a beat, the air so thick with tension I could see her brain ticking over in thought.

'You're not coming, Marcello?'

I hated her in that moment, but not more than I hated him when he answered, 'No, I think I'm going to call it a night.' His eyes flicked to me, but I wasn't interested in the staring game right now. I simply walked away, not even giving him the courtesy of saying goodnight.

I marched with my arms braced around myself, warding off an invisible chill, so angry I had to make sure I didn't let my rage step me too far away from Nate and Kylie, who followed behind. They were there, I could hear them, but I wouldn't look back to check where or how far. I was done looking back.

I might be many things—a joke, a snake—but I would never be someone's dirty little secret in the dark.

*Ever.*

# Chapter Seventeen

*C*oncentrate on the cracks, Sammi, keep focusing on
the cracks.

It was the only way I could stop the world from spinning, staring down and hiding in the shadow of Nate's
six-foot-three shadow as the blistering Italian sun beat
down on us.

'What's the matter, Sammi? You don't look so good.'

I swallowed deeply, shaking my head and placing my
finger to my lips to urge silence. I could feel the chunks
rising, and staring at the cracks in the pavement helped
keep me from filling them with the remnants of last night.
Ugh, now I didn't want to look at them. I tilted my head
up to the sunshine, thinking some vitamin D might help.
Wrong! I wanted to hiss at the sun that threatened to pierce
through my Ray-Bans; the throbbing of my brain and the
burn of my skin was enough to make me feel nauseous.
Worse still, we were standing in the longest line I had ever
seen in my life.

'How much longer?' I groaned, shielding my face from the sun and pressing my rapidly warming water bottle to my neck. I looked on at the group, amazed at their ability to recover from last night's binge drinking. But worse than the effects of the alcohol were the vague memories of pissed-off meter maids, shots at the bar borne of desperation and the very real and very vivid memory of kissing Marcello. The way he pressed me against the rough edges of the building, the feel of his tongue in my mouth, his hand sliding up my thigh.

'I think I need to sit down,' I announced, feeling the world fall away before I made the move to sit, my vision going dark as someone's arms broke my fall, muffled voices and shadows dancing around me.

Air whipped at my face, followed by a drenching of water that felt icy against my burning skin. I flinched, coughing and spluttering.

'I think she has alcohol poisoning.' Harper's voice seemed so far away that I felt like I was hallucinating, but when I opened my eyes to see her big brown ones filled with concern I realised I was back in the land of the living.

'And here I was thinking I was going to have to offer mouth-to-mouth,' Nate said, suggestively.

Now I knew this wasn't a hallucination.

My eyes shifted to Nate's upside down smile; my head was resting on his thigh.

'Why am I always waking up with your penis near my face?'

Nate shrugged. 'Just lucky, I guess.'

Ordinarily I would have been mortified at having released my internal thoughts without edit, but for now I was far too sick and sorry to care about it, lying on my back like a starfish on a rocky street in Rome, which was, incidentally, really uncomfortable.

'Man, you better get up before Maria gets back. I haven't been standing here for the past hour only to miss out because you can't handle your grog.'

'Oh, Jodie, always so selfless.' Nate laughed, helping me to sit up, which was a monumental effort. I rubbed at the back of my head, which hammered with pain, double-checking there was no blood. I examined my clean hand, before mustering enough energy to glower up at Jodie, standing there with her arms crossed.

'Don't look at me like that,' she said.

'Like what?' Maria's heels appeared out of nowhere, her dazzling smile accented by hot cherry lipstick that matched her dress. Following Jodie's eyeline, she saw me on the ground, white and beaded with sweat.

'What's going on?'

Before I could answer, Nate moved to sit cross-legged beside me. 'Oh, we're just taking ten, Maria. We like to switch things up.'

I didn't have it in me to fake it, nor to continue in line. 'I think I got too much sun yesterday,' I confessed. It wasn't *exactly* a lie. Then I remembered Maria was at the bar with us last night, batting her eyes at Nate. *Oh, God, had Maria seen me knocking back drinks at the bar like a sailor?*

Jodie snorted. If I had the strength I would have kicked her feet out from underneath her.

'Well, you certainly don't look very well. Let's get you out of the heat,' Maria said, her voice laced with concern. She was probably worried about how my potential hospitalisation would affect her Trip Advisor rating.

'Would you mind if I head back to the hotel? I think I just need to take a nap.' Having the room to myself would be amazing. I would sleep off my hangover, drink plenty of water and have a decent, sensible meal and an early night. The thought of eating made my stomach roil distressingly, but I knew I needed to get some food into me . . . and keep it down. We were leaving Rome tomorrow so I really had to sort myself out; being trapped on a bus feeling like this was not an option.

'But you're going to miss the Colosseum tour.' Bookworm Gary seemed deeply concerned, unable to understand my decision to opt out of the longest queue on earth. As I stared up at the imposing, arched grandeur of *Il Colosseo* I felt only a dizzying nausea, proof that I was in no fit state to appreciate the historic wonder. Nate helped me to stand as I swayed and tried not to fall in front of Maria, who was, thankfully, distracted with her cell phone.

'Sorry, guys,' I said, and meant it too. While we weren't exactly the tightest crew, I didn't want to spoil anyone's day—well, except perhaps Jodie's.

Harper rubbed my arm. 'You do look really bad,' she said with a pout. I knew she didn't mean anything by it, our drunken tiff forgotten in the bright light of day, but it didn't make me feel any better. Maybe I was being precious, I thought, examining the group before me, a picture of health. Johnny had matched me drink for drink and he seemed fine. Kylie and Harper had sipped ridiculously large, seriously strong cocktails and they were positively chipper; was I really such a lightweight? Maybe I should put on my big-girl pants and just tough it out. But as we shuffled forward, I realised that they were the first actual steps we had taken in the line. Could I handle walking around a space that was over twenty-four thousand square metres when I had just fainted after standing still?

I was so done.

Just as I was about to admit my defeat to them all, Maria ended her phone call.

'Come, Sammi—I have organised for you to get back to the hotel.'

I wasn't going to lie—I was flooded with so much relief that my shoulders visibly sagged. Though the bus that had dropped us off what seemed like hours before lacked air-conditioning and apparently any form of suspension, I awaited its return as if it were a solid gold chariot turning up to my rescue.

'Thanks, Maria,' I said quietly, zapped of energy but also sorry that I was being so difficult, walking away from the group and leaving them to themselves and their high-functioning livers. Seriously, how did they do it? Freaks.

Maria walked me to the edge of the promenade, where I could lean against a blissfully cool stone wall in the shade of the buildings and take small, quenching sips of water from a Roman drinking fountain, thoughtfully installed to keep tourists hydrated on hot summer days. I fantasised that the water might have magical healing powers, or provide eternal youth, or something. Or at least provide the drinker with the power to get through one day without embarrassing themselves, which would be mighty useful right now. Alas, it was not so, but I did feel slightly better.

'Sorry to be such a nuisance, Maria.'

'Oh, don't worry.' She waved away my words. 'It happens all the time.'

I straightened a little, energised by the thought that I was not alone in my idiocy. 'Really?' I asked.

Maria cocked her head to the side, her brow crinkling as she searched her memory for the last time such an event had occurred. With a quick intake of breath, she went to speak but then stopped, shaking her head and mumbling under her breath. She pursed her lips and tapped her chin.

Yep, there was no one else like me. I had been told as much yesterday. I was different. I was the only twenty-something who could not manage to drink, dance and enjoy the sheer abandonment of my youth. Instead, I felt like a ninety-year-old woman who needed sensible shoes and an afternoon nap. I should never have come here. I should have just saved my money and watched *Roman Holiday* again from the safety of my own recliner, where the Pepsi Max flowed and the bowls of Samboy salt-and-vinegar chips were eternal.

'Anyway, not to worry, you'll be resting soon.' Maria rubbed my shoulder, sympathetically.

I inhaled deeply, longing for the churning, long-since serviced sound of the little white bus pulling up, its doors screeching only partly open until the driver pulled them all the way apart. Right now it was my only fantasy, however sad that was.

Eager for a distraction, I surveyed the surrounding crowds, all kitted out with comfortable shoes, water bottles, backpacks and simmering excitement. A man pushed a sleeping child in a pram. A group of laughing girls tried to navigate the challenge of their selfie stick. A couple had a barely contained argument in front of their children, all of them hot and exhausted before their day had even begun. It was the credo of tourists: see as much as you can, snap as many pictures as you can, look happy—even if that means faking it—and keep going, no matter the cost. Later they'd all be swearing over their hotel internet access while adding filters and then uploading dream holiday snaps to their social media pages in a desperate bid to make everyone back home envious; I mean, they were only human. I, on the other hand, was a terrible poster girl for my generation. I hadn't uploaded anything; my phone had a few snaps of some of yesterday's sights, but mostly I'd been too lost, too in awe, too invested in what I was seeing. Not counting on wiping myself out in the first few days, I had assumed that I would get to see it all again—that I would have the chance to play catch-up and be a better ultimate tourist; to show my parents a slideshow of photos that they could brag to their friends about in supermarket aisles.

'Yes, Claire is still in Paris—oh, and did I mention Sammi is in Rome now?'

I felt a pang of homesickness, but more than that I felt a sudden urge to call my sister, to beg her to come to Rome and hold a cold compress to my forehead and tuck me into some clean sheets. But as much as I wanted that, there was a part of me that never wanted to tell anyone, ever, how much of a lame human being I was. I couldn't blame it on heatstroke. I blamed it on my ill-fated attempt at letting go of my inhibitions and living life with abandon. For me, that apparently translated to poor decision-making, like deciding to kiss Marcello. This way of living clearly led to trouble. As much as I would be sad to leave Rome tomorrow, my departure couldn't come soon enough. One more night of laying low and this city, and the beautiful brown-eyed man, would be left behind.

He would be the one good thing I could relay to my grandchildren in many years to come. I could build it up as an enchanting, epic story of love in Rome; Marcello, the man I never saw again, who simply slid into the night, never to be heard from again. It certainly sounded a lot more magical than my current sequence of events: a drunken pash followed by the mother of all hangovers, which saw me trying to keep the chunks down out the front of the Colosseum. Nope, the other version was so much sweeter.

I smiled to myself, remembering the pulse of the music, the flash of the lights and Marcello's hot mouth on my neck as I laughed and pressed into him, his skin burning and sliding against mine as if no one was watching. I felt my cheeks heat at the memory of the man who made me feel unexpected things, who made the blood pump in my veins and my heart beat erratically. In one day he had given me more of Rome than I had ever expected—a unique view of the city that doesn't feature in the glossy tour guides. As I smiled to myself, sifting through the small pros of my short stay here, I tried not to let my heart feel too heavy about the mysterious Roman. He was just a memory now, a hot, sordid memory overruled by how quickly he had moved away, not wanting to be seen with me.

I slid down the wall, taking a moment to rest my forehead on my knees and indulge in replays of last night, so vivid it was like I was back there again. The burn of the shots of off-brand liquor at the bar, the look of dark, deep-set eyes watching me with amusement. With the cool stone at my back, a moment to rest in the shade and the memories of a not altogether bad evening, I felt much better; the nausea had eased and the world had stopped spinning. I had worked through the worst and, although I wasn't going to head back into the line, I would be climbing aboard the bus feeling much better.

I breathed a sigh of relief. *You're going to be okay, Sammi.*

And then I heard his name.

'About time, Marcello!' Maria's voice rang out.

I lifted my head and saw that unmistakable figure in the distance, making his way towards us, and I felt my stomach twist again. I didn't feel so good anymore.

# Chapter Eighteen

There was no bus, no golden chariot; instead, there was Marcello and a helmet held out to me.

I recoiled. 'What is that?'

His eyes dipped to his hand, confused. But I wasn't referring to what he was holding; my attention was fiercely locked on what was behind him. Marcello's eyes eventually followed.

'I am not getting on that,' I said, crossing my arms and taking a step back.

Maria touched the side of my arm tentatively. 'It really is the fastest way to get back, and far more comfortable than you would expect.'

'Where's the bus?'

Maria sighed, looking at her phone. 'Pietro is not answering his phone. He won't be back here for another three hours for pick-up.'

I paused. Was three hours really so long in the scheme of things? I looked at Marcello, my knight in shining armour, though there was nothing shiny about him. He was dressed in all black: black jeans, black tee, black boots, black mood. The cheery, smouldering Marcello I kissed last night had been replaced by a cold, distant stranger. Maria looked between the two of us, our body language speaking volumes, my arms crossed, his insouciant lean. It was like she was working with two defiant children. The fact he seemed so unimpressed about having to help me made me all the madder; had he regretted last night so much? While I was seated on the cobblestones lost in dreamy reminiscing about what could have been the one highlight of my Roman adventure, he was dragged here to help Maria clean up my mess.

*A story to tell my grandchildren? Jesus, Sammi, wake up.*

'Sammi, I'm sorry, but I have to get back to the group and I can't leave without knowing what you want to do.' Maria's voice snapped me out of my death stare and I blanched.

*Shit, it's not always about you, Sammi.*

'Sorry, Maria, of course. Look, I think I will wait for the bus. I have water and shade and I'll be—'

'Get on!' The helmet was thrust into my chest and I juggled the black, shiny dome, watching on with an open mouth as Marcello made his way back to his Vespa. I swallowed, seeing the determination in his stride as he slid onto his bike, placing on his own helmet.

Maria giggled. 'I don't think waiting for the bus is going to be necessary.'

I gripped the helmet. 'Is he always like this?'

Maria shrugged. 'That's Marcello.'

I turned away from his angry eyes, lowering my voice. 'Maria, how is Marcello associated with the group?'

Maria sighed. 'It's complicated.'

Her answer gave me absolutely no confidence; I was about to climb onto the back of a tiny death trap with this man. Maria led me over to the Vespa; it felt like a funeral procession, or a walk to the gallows. I would have sooner taken my chances with possible heatstroke and dehydration than be forced to wrap my arms around Marcello.

'I can't believe you haven't told Sammi what a terrible person I am,' Maria quipped as Marcello fastened the strap at his chin.

'I am not convinced you are,' he said, gripping the handles and looking at her with interest.

'Well, we'll see,' she said.

Marcello shook his head. 'So you still haven't made up your mind.'

'I told you I would think about it.'

'And?'

'I'm still thinking,' she snapped.

'And then what? Tomorrow you are gone and again . . . nothing.'

Their words were heated and my attention snapped between them like a tennis match. Was this a lovers' quarrel? What was she equivocating about? Whatever it was, it clearly burned Marcello's blood. If he looked unhappy before, he looked near on homicidal now.

'Just give me time, and when we come back, who knows?'

Marcello scoffed. 'That's what you said last time, and the time before that.'

Marcello started the Vespa. Though I didn't know much about them, I could tell that he had started it rather violently, and not how you were supposed to do it. I didn't know if it was my eagerness to leave this awkward conversation behind, but I clipped on my helmet and jumped on the back of Marcello's Vespa so quickly that I barely had enough time to secure my arms around his ribs before he peeled away from Maria and sped into the fray of death-defying traffic.

Oh, God, what had I done? I had climbed on the back of a Vespa with a madman, quite literally.

I had heard that the best way to see Rome, in fact the only way to see Rome, was on a Vespa, but with my eyes firmly closed and my koala-like grip around Marcello I wasn't going to see anything. All I could do was feel and hear the sensations that would only amplify my terror if I opened my eyes.

'Can't breathe!' Marcello laughed, yelling above the soaring sounds of traffic and chaos. Only then did I open my eyes a little.

'Oh, sorry,' I shouted, loosening the tiniest amount but still clinging firmly.

Marcello peered back at me, and maybe it was the distance he had put between him and Maria or the wind in his face and the sunshine on our shoulders, or maybe it was just this particular angle, but his dimples were back, and his bright white smile flashed as he glanced at me.

'Keep your eyes open,' he said, and I could feel the vibration of his laughter in my chest.

'Just watch what you're doing,' I yelled, gripping tighter once more as he expertly veered around a honking car.

'Well, stop distracting me,' he said, veering down a side street. The buzzing of the motor echoing off the curved buildings and my head turned upwards as the coloured flags of strung-up washing whizzed by. We sped along places and paths that no bus could possibly go, and I don't know if it was exactly the shortest route back to Hotel Luce del Sole, but it certainly was the most distracting. In a good way. I felt the cool wind at my cheeks, and any sickness I had felt was replaced by a new energy, a thrill in the pit of my stomach and the safety I felt whenever I was with Marcello. It was something I pushed to the back of my mind, even as I found myself resting my chin on his shoulder, my body melting into his. I didn't know if he could tell from the change in my posture, but Marcello glanced back at me again, fleetingly. There was no missing the lightness in his eyes, the flash of something shared; he looked, dare I say it, happy, and it was the kind of look that could fill you with warmth better than any sunshine could. I didn't want it to be over, I wanted him to keep driving long past Hotel Luce del Sole; I didn't care if we never made it. With the promise in Marcello's face in stark contrast to the reality of what awaited me at my hotel, I hoped that my telepathic pleas to Marcello would work.

*Please, keep going, just a little longer.*

# Chapter Nineteen

had helmet hair, my cheeks were flushed, and I clung on to Marcello far too long; he literally had to peel my hands off his waist. As he helped me from the back of the Vespa my legs felt like jelly, the vibrations still running through my body. The last thing I felt I needed now was to lie down and sleep; I felt alive and Marcello knew it, smirking as he took my helmet from me.

'What?' I tried to look serious but was never any good at having a poker face.

'See? That wasn't so bad.'

I shrugged. 'I could just as easily have waited for the bus.'

And there it was, Marcello's broad, brilliant smile as he locked the helmet into the back storage compartment, an action that made me kind of sad because it meant that our joyride was over.

Like everything with us, the moment of lightheartedness was fleeting and an awkward silence fell when he turned to me, looking at me as if waiting for direction. The idea that I was the one who should know what to say or do was utterly ridiculous; I struggled to 'adult' at the best of times, let alone in matters of the heart. There were a thousand questions brewing inside my head, most of which began with 'So, about last night . . .'

Did he regret it? Was it just one of those things fuelled by music, alcohol, hormones and a near-death experience? Or should we blame it on Rome? I imagined his potential responses: he was bored, he always hooked up with Maria's tour groups, he was trying to make Maria jealous . . .

Maria. My mind wandered into the myriad of questions about what exactly was going on between the two of them.

'I told you I would think about it,' she had said, and he'd been angry about it. Maria had said it was complicated, but what kind of complicated, and why did the very thought of it make my insides twist? Was this why he didn't want anyone to see us together last night? I wanted to ask all these questions, even though I was afraid of the answers. I needed to know if Marcello was the bad guy— or, even worse, was I? Was I unwittingly involved in some kind of Roman love triangle? Oh, wouldn't Jodie just love that, the dull, mousey girl of the group who can't hold her liquor embroiled in some tawdry love affair.

I looked at him closely; while obviously telepathy wasn't our thing, there was something in his expression that said, 'Ask me, go on.' But then I caught myself. It wasn't the first time I had imagined something; why should this be any different? I wondered if he could read the multitude of conflicting emotions in my face. Would he see, 'Who are you, and what's your story?', 'How dare you pash and dash last night!' or 'I really want to kiss you again—want to come up?' I cleared my throat and looked away, hoping he wasn't that perceptive.

'Anyway, thanks for the ride,' I said, stepping away from the Vespa and dodging the pedestrians in our narrow street.

'How are you feeling now?' he asked, genuinely concerned.

*Confused.*

'Yeah, much better. I think if I have a lie-down I'll be right.'

A flash of Marcello on top of me, naked and between my thighs, smiling down at me in a twist of sheets and a creaking bunk bed, caused me to blink rapidly in an effort to clear the image away.

'Are you sure you're okay?' he asked, not entirely convinced.

*Please, God, don't let him be able to read minds.*

I swallowed. 'Of course.'

We stood there a moment longer. Was this it? Was this to be how my last day in Rome ended? Would this be the last time I saw Marcello? Why, WHY didn't I throw that bloody coin into the fountain? I had a vision of Jodie doing that very thing, and if that idiot secured herself a ticket back here then the world really was an unjust place.

I breathed out a laugh.

'What?'

I shook my head. 'I am officially the worst tourist.'

'Oh, I don't know. You have seen some things . . . *done* some things,' he said, a little curve to his mouth.

*Was he flirting with me?*

'I have,' I admitted.

Marcello's lip tucked in under his teeth; he chewed thoughtfully as he seemed to weigh up the next question. He looked down, then asked, 'Any regrets?'

Whoa, there was a loaded question.

I stared at him for a long time, so long that he eventually lifted his eyes to meet mine. Of course I had regrets: the coin tossing, the binge drinking, the stopping at a kiss and not giving myself something more to remember from that heated night. But I couldn't voice any of that, and a simple 'yes' would leave him guessing in far too cruel a way, though a part of me wished I could. I imagined walking away with a hair flick, without a backwards glance. That's what Jodie would have done, but I wasn't that cool— or that mean—and I was okay with that.

'Well, in the immortal words of my travel agent . . .' I held out my hand to shake, unsure what else to do. *Ugh, what are you doing?*

Marcello's brow curved slowly, taking my hand into his with interest. 'Yes?'

I shook his hand as if finalising a business deal, and it felt all kinds of wrong. 'No regrets,' I said, then dropped his hand, deciding this would be my grand exit. It wasn't exactly the microphone drop I had wanted; it wasn't a departure any red-blooded male would remember a woman for. If anything, turning away and heading through the doorway of the hotel, I could just imagine the look of utter confusion spread across Marcello's face. With every step up to my thankfully vacant dorm room, I cursed Jan Buzzo for sending me on this trip, and myself for being so goddamn awkward.

# Chapter Twenty

*shook his hand? I shook his fucking hand!*

Marcello's last memory of me could so easily have been of me pressing him up against the wall, my tongue in his mouth. But no, instead it would be a handshake. I pulled the pillow over my face to muffle the groans of despair, until I remembered I didn't know where that pillow had been. I cringed and threw it away.

I sighed, fidgeting on my top bunk and linking my hands behind my head for support. *Come on, Sammi, go to sleep. That's why you left the tour, to rest and replenish. Make it count.* If I wasn't going to be getting my money's worth exploring the Vatican's treasures, I could at least prep myself for what was to come. Pompeii, the Amalfi Coast, Florence, Venice! There was so much to discover in this stunning country. Besides, technically today wasn't the last I would see of this place, as the tour would bring us back here to fly home. As I opened my eyes to stare at the now-familiar brown water stain on the ceiling above me, it occurred to me that I really shouldn't be in any hurry to come back here. What did I expect, that Marcello would be waiting at the bar downstairs, champagne and roses in hand, ready to ride off into the sunset with me on his Vespa? That kind of thing only happened to my sister. My eyes flashed open again, this time with purpose.

Claire!

If anyone made me feel less chaotic about my own existence it was my sister. She was often stressed and unpredictable but it was more to do with décor colours and reservations for dinner. It was the kind of chaotic life she now thrived in since being with her Parisian celebrity chef boyfriend Louis, by far the most exciting and exotic thing to happen to the Shorten family. Maybe a chat with my sister would help calm my addled brain, and I could finally get some shut-eye.

I got out of bed and walked down to the hotel kiosk to send Claire an email. The kiosk, or 'business centre', was littered with scrunched-up pieces of paper, an over-flowing wastepaper basket and the remnants of coffee cup rings around the grimy keyboard. The large, box-shaped computer screen that sat on a flaky, rickety old desk looked like it was a thousand years old, perhaps one of Rome's most ancient relics even. I took the liberty of dragging over a chair that was missing from the desk, making myself comfortable and waiting for the painfully slow dial-up to connect me to civilisation.

I had emailed Claire about my travel plans when I'd first booked my trip, giddy and terrified about what lay ahead, but I'd not yet had a response. Logging into my Gmail, I wished for a message from her about a surprise meet-up in Venice, or a girls' weekend in Tuscany. But she and Louis were always busy—always doing something fabulous—so it came as little surprise that my inbox was empty, aside from the usual spammy twenty-percent-off sales from Dotti and Jeans West. There was, however, a response from my dad, who was far more computer-savvy than Mum. I had told them of my free day spent sitting on the Spanish Steps, seeing the Trevi Fountain and lunching outside the Pantheon—had even included a couple of snapshots—careful to paint the perfect picture of the globetrotting daughter. I left out the small detail of dry-humping my gorgeous Roman tour guide; there were some things better left unsaid.

Dad's message read.

*Looks great! Miss you heaps, the cupboard has never been so full. Have fun, be safe, love you. Mum and Dad X*

I could totally see Dad typing a reply with one finger at a time, squinting up at the screen, while in the background Mum yelled out instructions that Dad would choose to ignore. It may not have been a full-page spread like Claire would have written me, but it was typically Dad, giving all the important directives, as well as a Dad joke, which is always a bonus.

*Dearest Parentals,*

*Can't wait to smash that cupboard if I ever come back home. Loving Rome! Made lots of nice friends, who are all God-worshipping, law-abiding citizens of the world. Having an early night for Pompeii and the Amalfi Coast tomorrow! Will send some more snaps!*

*Love you, miss you.*
*Ciao Sammi xx*

I read over my lies and hit send, then clicked on 'compose new email'. I started hitting the keyboard furiously.

*Claire-Bear,*
*I HATE ROME!*
   *Okay, so that sounds a little harsh, but seriously. I am staying at an utter dive!!!*

I stopped typing and glanced around; what if the hotel monitored emails? Could they have some kind of keyword alert? I took a moment's pause, then shrugged and kept typing—maybe they would learn a thing or two.

*Hotel Luce del Sole apparently translates to Hotel Sunshine! But trust me, there is no sunshine here; instead, I am being housed in cattle-class accommodation with a group of binge-drinking lunatics, led by Jodie bitch-face, whose personality resembles that blonde child from* Lord of the Flies *but with less charm.*

*Everyone is out enjoying the Vatican and I am here in
the hotel kiosk, sunburnt, hungover and all alone.*

I read over my email. I've got to say, I found myself kind
of annoying. Although it was factually true, I was nevertheless, what was the word . . .

'You total BITCH!'

*Holy shit.*

I spun around in my chair so fast that I knocked my
knee on the desk. 'Jodie!'

What the hell was this all about?

'Yeah, old bitch-face was forced by Maria to come check
on you.'

Oh, my God, had she read everything?

I was tempted to point out that it wasn't polite to read
over some one's shoulder, but the way she was looking
at me right now—as if she wanted to rip me in half—
made me think better of it.

'You didn't have to do that.'

She scoffed. 'So I see—looks like there is nothing wrong
with you.'

I swallowed; if only she knew how ill I felt right now.
'Where are . . .'

'Oh, the binge-drinking lunatics? They'll be back
later,' she said, moving to exit the small alcove of the
kiosk.

'Jodie, wait!' I leapt after her, pulling at her arm, but
she violently pulled herself away from my grasp.

'I'm sorry, I was just sending a frustrated email to my sister. I was just blowing off some steam.'

'How about you do everyone a favour and just go home? We're obviously not good enough for you, so why would you want to lower your standards?'

'I never said I was too good.'

'You don't have to; when you don't hang out with anyone aside from the Italian Stallion, it's bleedingly obvious that you would rather be anywhere else.'

My mind shifted back to my email. *Italian Stallion*— had I typed that in my email too? No, no, I would never have said that, though that probably wasn't the most important issue at hand.

'Jodie, please don't say anything to the others. I've just had a bad few days. I've never been overseas before and I'm trying to fit in; it's not something that comes easily to me.'

I hoped my earnest words would make her feel at least a little empathetic, but any time I thought back to 'bitch-face' I wanted the ground to open up and swallow me. Jodie stared me down, her fisted hands at her side. I almost would have preferred she hit me, get it over with and done with, rather than the threats and mind games she no doubt had in store for the rest of the tour.

I then said what I thought might help my case—so she would know that I had no intentions of getting involved, that it really wasn't any of my business. 'Jodie, I never said anything to Johnny about you and Gary.'

I knew it was a catastrophic mistake the moment the words left my mouth. Fire flashed in her eyes and she stepped forward, into my face. 'Don't you dare threaten me!'

'What? I wasn't . . .'

'You think you can blackmail me?'

The back of my legs hit the desk; I was caged in like an animal.

'I am not blackmailing, I'm just saying it's none of my business.'

'Yeah, well, by writing shit about me, you're now my business, and if you think I am going to turn a blind eye while you try and be everyone's BFF, then you have another thing coming.'

As far as threats went, that was right up there. And, much like with a drunk person or a two-year-old, I knew better than to try to reason with her.

I straightened, stepping up into her face and looking into her eyes. 'Do what you need to do,' I said, pushing past her, pretending to be badass when all I wanted to do was run and hide. I felt exposed, like someone had read my high-school diary and was about to announce my secrets at assembly. I just knew it wouldn't be the last I would hear of it. I walked to reception, waiting patiently for Gabriello to come serve me. Guilt clawing at my insides, my head spinning over the things that I had written.

*Just breathe, Sammi, in-out-in. Don't cry. Do. Not. Cry.*

'*Ciao*, Sammi. *Come stai*?'

'*Ciao*, Gabriello, um, listen, I'm not feeling so good, is there a chance I might be able to book a room just for tonight? I just need a quiet space to get some rest.'

*And prevent my head from getting mounted on a stick.*

'*Si*, I am sure we can help you out.' He typed on the keyboard, while I gripped the edge of the reception desk, wondering where Jodie was now. Was she waiting to get me alone? Had she slipped out the back to run to the group to tell them what I really thought of them? Or had she slid upstairs to pee in my shampoo bottle or, God, on my toothbrush?

'Ah, you are in luck. It's not the most spacious suite, but if you want some peace and quiet for the night it will do.'

Did he actually refer to rooms here as suites? Jeez, he was optimistic.

'I'll take it, *grazie*.'

Gabriello printed out the new booking and slid it across for me to sign.

Level two, room ten. I felt a surge of relief knowing that I was floors away from them.

'*Ciao-ciao*, Gabriello, bitch-face is off to catch up with her friends.'

Jodie walked through reception, putting on her sunnies and flashing me a bright smile as she headed for the door.

Gabriello's face twisted in distaste. 'She is a strange one,' he said, shaking his head.

I watched her disappear out into the street.

'Yeah, you have no idea.'

# Chapter Twenty-One

My 'suite' was a small, dark, windowless room with a bed shoved in the corner. Waiting was the worst, but doing so in what could only be described as a cell really did make me feel like a dead woman walking. I might as well have been placed under the staircase.

I sat on the edge of the mattress, tears welling in my eyes, thinking how I didn't even get to press send on my email to Claire. Mum and Dad would be telling her right now what an amazing time I was having with all my newfound friends, when in truth I was hiding, too ashamed to face the others knowing Jodie would have told all. Once again I didn't recall social isolation being featured in the glossy tourist booklet; come to Italy and be an outcast! If I had wanted to feel that way, I could have easily stayed home.

I had come all this way and spent a chunk of my savings only to be here, hiding, feeling sorry for myself? I stood up and began pacing my block-shaped room, angered by

Jodie's snooping, but also embarrassed at being caught out. Maybe Jodie did have the right to hate me from the start—maybe she was a good judge after all. Had I acted aloof, as if I thought I was better than them? No, I was just different, that's all; if I wasn't on this trip I certainly wouldn't be friends with them. We were only going to be together for a short time; when I first stepped into the meet-and-greet, I'd doubted I'd be forming any lifelong friendships.

I stopped my self-righteous thoughts.

*Oh, wow, Sammi! Will you listen to yourself?*

Within two seconds of meeting the members of the group I had made a judgement that they weren't my type, which, in no uncertain terms, made me Miss Judgey McJudgeface of Judgement Town. I had even gone as far as to book another room to escape the backlash; how was that going to look? I had visions of them laughing from their bunk beds.

'*See, too good to even share a room.*'

I buried my head in my hands.

'Oh, God, I am a snobby bitch,' I groaned, lifting my head and running my hands back through my hair. I hadn't given anyone a chance.

*Except for one.*

One very different person, one who from the very first moment had stood out, one who I'd been trying to work out ever since. Never once had I thought myself too good for him; if anything, the general consensus was he was far too good for me. I wished he was here with me now, telling me local myths, flashing me those adorable dimples, looking confused when he didn't quite understand my meaning, touching me, kissing me . . .

I snapped out of my daydream.

'No, no, I wasn't a bitch,' I mumbled to myself, throwing myself back onto my bed. I swallowed some painkillers to alleviate my pounding head, and soon my eyes became heavy and my body sank into the mattress. Drifting off in my tiny little box room, I repeated sleepily to myself, 'I am not a bitch.'

~

Thunder, there was thunder jolting me awake.

*No, wait a minute.*

Thump-thump-thump. 'Sammi, open up!'

*Oh, shit, they've found me. At my door with flaming torches and pitchforks, no doubt.*

I scrambled out of my bed, ripping the sheets from me, struggling to navigate the unfamiliar surroundings in my darkened room. What time was it? How long had I been asleep? Had I even locked the door?

The handle twisted, the door creaked and light leaked into the room, threatening to expose me. Holding up my hand to shield my eyes, I squinted at the darkened figure in my doorway. The light was impossibly bright; spots danced in my vision until the fluorescent beam flickered above me.

'Hot damn, look at you.' Johnny's Californian drawl was deep and filled the entire space. He didn't seem angry; his words were an observation, and sounded shocked if anything. I knew I wasn't exactly the most attractive person upon waking, but I really didn't need to be reminded about my frizz-ball hair and squinty eyes at a time like this.

'Just getting some rest,' I croaked, smoothing down my hair, wondering if the red tinge of my skin was worse now. I had slathered on the sunscreen, I had moisturised, kept hydrated. I felt good, the painkillers had worked a treat, so why was Johnny looking at me like that? Did I have drool on my chin?

'What's that on your face?'

I touched my chin, wiping at the skin.

*Nope, no drool.*

'What?'

Johnny grimaced, walking closer to me, reaching up to capture my chin and turn my face to the light. 'You have giant welts on your cheek.'

'What?' My hand flew up, searching, until I felt an unmistakable lump on my face, then another.

'What the . . .'

Johnny broke into a smile. 'Haven't you heard the old saying: "Don't let the bed bugs bite"?'

'Oh, shut up!' I said, pushing past him, skimming along the halls in search of a bathroom on the unfamiliar second floor. Instead, I found a murky hall mirror above a table featuring a dusty faux floral arrangement. I pressed my face up close to the mirror, whimpering at the sight.

'I look like the Elephant Woman!'

'Oh, I think that's a bit harsh,' Johnny said.

I cupped my cheeks, staring at my reflection, which had instantly become itchy from the heat of my palms. All I could do was shake my head as the tears welled in my eyes. I turned to Johnny. 'I have bloody bed bugs!' I shouted.

'It would appear so,' Johnny said; at least he was trying his best not to laugh. But I knew no matter how much time would pass I would never find it funny. Instead, I simply burst into tears, the salty streaks probably fuelling the swelling of my bites.

'Oh, hey, hey, come on, you don't look that bad.' Johnny reached out, rubbing my shoulder. 'Why are you in that room anyway—are you in quarantine or something?'

I sniffed, shaking my head. 'You mean you don't know?'

'Know what?'

'What, Jodie hasn't come running to you reciting my email word for word?'

Johnny's brows pinched. 'What email?'

I wiped my eyes, my sobs stilled by his apparent and genuine confusion.

'Did Jodie come back to the group?'

'Yeah, she said you were asleep, that she didn't want to wake you.'

Now I was the one who was confused, my hand slowly falling from my face. Had I dreamt it? Had there even been an email? No, it was definitely real; what was Jodie playing at?

'W-what are you doing here?'

Johnny sighed. 'So many questions! Maria is organising a dinner tonight, a kind of farewell to Rome, I guess. It's all provided in our package so you better get ready,' he said, backing away down the hall.

'What? Dinner tonight? I can't go out like this.'

'Come on, Sammi, anyone would think you're trying to avoid us.' He laughed, but his words hit a nerve inside me.

*Too good for us.*

I didn't think that, and even if, for reasons unknown to me, she hadn't told them about the email, the last thing I needed was for them to jump to that conclusion on their own. The first three days had been a disaster, the fault all my own, but I still had seven days with these people. If I was going to get the most out of this trip then I had better slap myself and get my shit together.

'Where's dinner?' I asked unenthusiastically.

Johnny grinned. 'Atta girl! It's at a restaurant called That's Amore. We meet down at reception at six,' he said, setting off down the hall. As he walked away, he said over his shoulder, 'Oh and, ah, just in case you're thinking about changing your mind, Marcello will be there.'

I slowly turned back to the mirror, a look of complete and utter dread spread across my lumpy face.

'Oh, fuck!'

# Chapter Twenty-Two

had spent the afternoon in my stripped-down, barren room, standing with a cold can of Coke pressed to my cheek and the assurance that new bedding would be in place by the time I returned from dinner; apparently there were no other dungeons available, and I was still too chicken to return to my dorm room.

As much as I tried to rearrange my hair, nothing disguised my disfiguration; short of stepping out in a Phantom of the Opera mask, there was nothing I could do to reduce the hideous-looking bite marks. Apparently I was allergic to bed bugs. Awesome.

I had nothing in my possession that would work—I needed heavy-duty concealer. I took it upon myself to risk detection, scooting up to the girls' bathroom and hitting the jackpot. Primers, hair products, brushes, blushes, contouring powder, eyeliners and bronzers were strewn all over the vanity. I sifted through foundation sponges, lipstick-stained tissues and eye-shadow pallets as quickly as I could.

*Come on, Sammi, in and out, the perfect crime.*

Just a smidge, I thought, a teeny-tiny dollop of foundation, dabbed lightly onto my skin to disguise the redness. And what do you know? It did exactly that. There was no redness in sight because now, in my reflection, the red had been replaced with a large orange blob on my face, the kind no amount of blending could save. To avoid being labelled a make-up thief, or mistaken as an Oompa Loompa, I rubbed the foundation off, making my face even redder than before. But it was necessary: the girls already thought I was moving in on Kylie's man, they might not appreciate me moving in on their make-up—some things were simply sacred.

~

I had wanted to really make Marcello's head turn tonight, but now I would be making everyone's head turn for all the wrong reasons. I descended the stairs in my navy maxi dress, long and flowing, skin aglow now that the burn had mellowed to a tan, and I was well rested. But, thanks to the bed bugs, none of that mattered. At least I was having a good hair day; my hair was out and swept to the side, my attempt at some kind of hair veil. As I entered the lounge near reception, without looking I could sense he was there, a dark spot in my peripheral vision. I concentrated on every single step I took, praying I wouldn't trip on the length of my skirt and flail down the last of the stairs. Upon reaching the bottom, I breathed a sigh of relief and tried, as best I could, to walk towards the group in a carefree, elegant way. I strategically placed myself, turning my offending cheek to the wall while I attempted for lighthearted banter with an extremely confused-looking Bookworm Gary.

I smiled, sipping on my pop-top water bottle, before slipping it into my bag.

*Just shut up, Bookworm, and play along.*

Everyone I had wanted to avoid had come to dinner. Jodie sat with Harper and Kylie in one big, happy sisterhood. As usual I could hear Nate, though he didn't necessarily have to be in the same room for that. I glanced around the small space, trying not to let my eyes fall on that particular black figure across the room. I was just going to ignore him. With Maria being such a stickler for punctuality, I assumed that Marina and Gwendal from France and Em from Ireland, who were all bunking in together on the sixth floor, had not received the dinner memo.

'Where is everyone?' I asked Gary.

'Marina and Gwendal are having some kind of an anniversary dinner somewhere, and the Irish girl . . .'

'Em.'

'Yeah, she went home.'

My head snapped around. 'She went home?'

Gary did a double-take, his expression deepening. 'Ah, yeah, she said she wouldn't stay another minute in this hole of a hotel, so she cancelled the rest of her tour . . . what happened to your face?' Gary's nose was screwed up.

I turned away from him, my mind reeling.

*Em cancelled her trip? Bloody good on her.*

And then I thought it was quite the shame; Em sounded like my kind of girl. Who knows, maybe if we'd been assigned the same room we might have become best friends.

Johnny had never said so explicitly, but the last dinner in Rome with the group had that kind of 'this is compulsory' feeling about it, and sure, there was a part of me that had wanted to see Marcello again.

I mentally slapped myself.

*Don't you even go there, Sammi.*

So he was here—so what? If anything, it was going to make for a hell of an awkward night. Yep, I was definitely going to keep my distance, from everyone. In fact, I was probably doing them a favour: by shielding my unsightly face they wouldn't be turned off their food. You might even say I was being considerate . . . and, okay, a little egotistical.

Maybe it wasn't that bad? I did have a tendency to be melodramatic. Gary was easily distressed. Just as I was beginning to convince myself that I was overreacting, Johnny walked past me, tilting his head and wincing.

'Are you okay? That looks, really, really bad,' he whispered, like he was in on the hideous secret.

*Kill me now.*

'Thanks,' I deadpanned. It was official, I looked monstrous. I would have to choose my place at the table very carefully. Johnny shucked my jaw sympathetically, as if to say, 'Chin up, tiger,' then went to get a drink.

'Alright, people, *avanti, avanti*! Let's go,' Maria sing-songed, floating through the reception in a beautiful floral-patterned dress that only she could get away with, her petite frame and ample bosom on display.

I took a moment to glance in the mirror: Marcello was in the lounge. He was sitting there in a beautiful black suit, white collared shirt casually open, and dampened hair. Even from far away he looked gorgeous, wearing an impressive scowl as if he wished not to be here. And why was he here? Was he getting a cut of Maria's commission somehow? Helping her out by taking clueless members of the group under his wing? Well, if that was the case, he deserved a decent cut based on his lip service alone. As much as I hadn't wanted our awkward handshake to be his last memory of me, I really didn't want it to be like this; me dancing around all night, trying to avoid him catching a glimpse of my face. Though, truth be known, I couldn't only blame the bite marks. Screw it, tonight I would just try to enjoy my dinner. As far as I could tell, Jodie hadn't said anything to the others about my email; she hadn't even cast me daggers, choosing to ignore me, which was fine by me.

We converged out on the street, our smart-casual dress a stark contrast to the grimy hotel façade, making us look lost and slightly out of place. The evening was warm and clear and the streets were filled with the chaos I was becoming accustomed to, the happy mess of holiday-makers wandering in our paths. The dodging and weaving didn't unsettle me so much as the unknown ambush I was likely to suffer at the hands of my own group if Jodie ever decided to drop the bombshell.

We walked along the streets in cliques: Jodie, Nate and Johnny walked out in front, followed by the besties, then me and my new BFF, the solemn, serious Bookworm Gary, who shuffled along with his hands in his pockets. I didn't care to think about Maria and Marcello, who led the pack, and tried to resist looking forward in case I caught a glimpse of them and their seemingly civil conversation. I was happy to linger further back with Gary, who seemed to share my 'out of sight, out of mind' philosophy. Maybe Gary and I could be mates: we weren't party animals or attention seekers, we didn't need loud, boisterous conversations, we were merely soaking up everything around us—even if I could tell that, much like me, he was trying to avoid his lingering fascination with a certain person. I would never in a million years understand how Jodie and Gary came about, but I really didn't want to think about it either.

I chose instead to focus on dinner. According to Maria, That's Amore was located only a few steps away from the Trevi Fountain. I had a chance to turf my coin in after all, though choosing to do so would depend on how the evening played out; if it was a disaster, I may never want to return to Rome.

It turned out That's Amore was not just a song that Nate had been singing since our arrival in Rome (and had since been threatened by Maria to not sing again), it was a bright, warm and cosy restaurant abuzz with good cheer and intoxicating smells. Even though the restaurant was busy the staff were friendly and willing to help with recommendations. The owner made his way around the tables, showing a genuine interest in his customers and conversing with each one. One of the things I had come to love about Rome was the people, and I had noticed that if you made an effort to speak the language, no matter how terribly, it was like opening a door to the friendly and passionate locals.

*Don't look at Marcello, Sammi. Be strong.*

Walking through the restaurant, my eyes drifted along the framed black-and-white photos of old movie stars hung on the floral-imprinted walls, aglow with golden lighting. I looked with particular interest, staring at a candid snap of James Dean and Sammy Davis Jnr wearing an eyepatch. Approaching our table, I saw that I was in luck: the seat nearest the wall, on the left, was empty. My lumpy face might yet avoid detection!

*Oh, shit.*

My seat was opposite Marcello.

He slowly unbuttoned his jacket before pulling out the chair opposite and sliding into position, making himself quite comfortable. Ignoring him would be near on impossible, and I could only find the wall art interesting for so long. I would just have to become fascinated by whoever was going to sit next to me, ask lots of questions and keep the small talk flowing. I shifted my chair aside to make room, only to watch in horror as Jodie sat next to me, looking red carpet ready in a halter-neck dress, heavy eye make-up and straightened, sleek hair falling down her back. Did she not realise what she was doing, the situation she was putting me in?

She scooted in her chair and turned to me with a beaming smile. 'Oh, hey, Sammi—you look lovely tonight.'

Oh, she knew exactly what she was doing alright. She was here to torture me.

# Chapter Twenty-Three

I wasn't sure which was worse—that Marcello was seemingly ignoring me or that Jodie very much wasn't. If anything, having her hair straightened seemed to have the effect of a personality transplant. She clearly picked up the awkward vibe Marcello and I were giving off and made a particular effort to include us both in the conversation. It was enough to make my welts itch.

Jodie lifted her wine, clinking on the side of her stem, summoning the table's attention. 'Time for a toast!' she declared, and everyone seemed just as unsettled by Jodie Version 2.0 as I was. 'I just want to thank Maria and Marcello, and, well, all of you really, for such a great start to our Italian adventure.'

By this point I had given up trying to hide my blemishes; my thick hair had become a torturous form of insulation and, with the intimate placing of our table and the warm summer's night, I was fanning myself with my menu, pushing my hair back and looking eagerly for our main meals. Gnocchi would make everything alright; I believed fully in the curative power of potato pasta. I wished the waiter would come and deliver it right now and interrupt Jodie's long-winded speech.

'All my life I have dreamed of Italy. Since I was a little girl I wanted to explore this magical city . . .'

I sipped my drink, thinking if I waited for the actual toast I might die of thirst. Everyone seemed transfixed by Jodie, who now stood up at the table, hand on her heart. Good God, was she getting misty-eyed? I kept my barely contained smile hidden behind my wine glass and stared down at the tablecloth.

*Don't laugh, don't laugh.*

'And then my mum said to me, Jodie, you need to follow your dreams . . . you need to follow your heart.'

*Don't snort, don't even breathe.*

I closed my eyes, finding the inner will to control myself; had Jodie been drugged? Who was this affable imposter and what had she done with the real Jodie?

When my imagination brought up the image of Jodie climbing onto her chair and breaking out into the chorus of 'Climb Every Mountain' I nearly lost it, dribbling a small mouthful of wine onto the tabletop. I felt something press against my foot and looked up to see Marcello, who was also struggling to keep a straight face, although he managed to appear fully focused on Jodie, nodding as if entranced by her words. He kept his foot pressed firmly on top of mine as I watched him, smiling and waiting for him to crack, almost hoping that he would. I cocked my brow and placed my hand on my chin, staring at him, pretending to care. He blinked rapidly, breathing in and refocusing as he pressed down on my foot harder.

But it only made me want to do it all the more.

'Anyway, here's to you all. New friends!' Jodie lifted her glass up and, much to my absolute shock, turned to me first, looking me in the eye and clinking against my glass.

I sat stunned, incoherently repeating 'To new friends' and clinking my glass against hers. I half expected to see her true self in the reflection of her eyes, but there was nothing, just sparkling warmth I had never seen before; well, not when she looked at me. Maybe I had been too judgemental, too quick to assess Jodie's character, and got her all wrong. Maybe we had just got off on the wrong foot—she judged me, I judged her—and seeing the email had caused her to reflect on her behaviour and turn over a new leaf.

With Marcello's foot still touching mine, and the toast of solidarity between me and Jodie, I was suddenly grateful that I had come out for our last Roman supper. There was something about the energy in the restaurant, a buzz of activity that amounted to more than the flow of the wine and the delicious plates piling onto our table. We had turned a corner, we all had; even Bookworm Gary seemed to be merry with his red wine-stained lips and flushed cheeks. Harper and Kylie's cackles rang out over the chatter in the restaurant, so raucous that I couldn't help but laugh with them. By the time my tiramisu was delivered I had lifted my hair up into a messy, casual bun on top of my head, caring little about the twins on my cheek. If Marcello noticed them, he didn't say. As I went to take my first mouthful of the indulgent sweet he slid his fork into my dessert, carving off a cheeky slice and licking off the cream with a little wink that made my tummy flutter. I pressed my other foot on top of his and he smiled, running his tongue along his lips and savouring the flavour.

'Okay, everyone, I hate to be the bearer of bad news, but we have a big day tomorrow and I want everyone there on time—I mean it.' Maria pointed to Nate.

A collective groan sounded from the table, a group of kids begging their camp leaders to let them stay up just a little longer. And despite our actions last night, tonight we acted like the mature adults we were supposed to be. Johnny slung his arm around Jodie and Nate opened the door for Kylie, followed by a cheerful Gary talking Harper's ear off about the history of Pompeii. With wine consumed at a more moderate, civilised level, I hooked my bag over my head, sliding it to the front and making a straight line for the door, skimming past Maria, who chatted to the owner in words my Italian high-school lessons wouldn't help me with.

With a full belly and an unexpected evening of, dare I say, good vibes, I didn't mind walking on my own. Wandering had a new meaning here; as evening fell and the harsh summer sun inched its way out of the piazzas, a local evening ritual had already begun—the Italian tradition of *passeggiata*, a gentle, slow stroll through the main streets, where new romances begin and new life is on display. Italians tended to dress up for *passeggiata*, while tourists were much easier to spot in their shorts and daypacks. Maybe tonight, in my dinner attire, I might even be mistaken for a local? Now, that I wouldn't mind at all.

I felt many things: overfull, a warm buzz from good wine, excitement for what tomorrow held and a certain sadness at leaving a city I hadn't even begun to scratch the surface of. I wandered down Via della Stamperia, watching as the others zigzagged their way into the distance, about to call out for them to hold up when I was slowed by a hand gripping my arm. I turned to see Marcello next to me, his questioning eyes ticking over my face and the same boyish, dimpled grin appearing. It was the Marcello who was infectious in his warmth, the one who was easy to get lost with, the kind you wanted to kiss in doorways. It would be so easy to smile back, to walk on together as if nothing was amiss; instead, despite the butterflies in my tummy, I lifted my chin.

'Are you lost?' I asked, an air of innocence in my question.

'No, but you might be.'

I scoffed. 'I know exactly where I am,' I lied with confidence, knowing I was following the others, but as I turned my smiled faded. They were gone—they hadn't bothered to wait for me.

*Unbelievable.*

Marcello laughed, sliding his hand into mine and pulling me into step. 'Come on.'

'Is this the way?' I asked, three of my steps equal to one of his. I bunched my skirt in my hand and lengthened my stride in a bid to keep up. 'Where are we going?'

'To finish what we started.'

My eyes were wide, my mouth agape; was he going to drag me back to the nightclub and ravish me against a doorway? As unlikely as that sounded, I nevertheless quickened my pace.

'What are you talking about . . .'

But as we increased our pace up the street, I didn't need Marcello to answer. It all became clear as I turned to Marcello, who reached into his pocket and turned to me, pulling up my hand and placing something into my palm.

'Last night in Rome—make it count.'

My eyes dipped to a silver coin in my palm. I smiled, looking from my hand to the Trevi Fountain.

I breathed out a laugh. 'I knew it was close to the restaurant but I didn't realise it was this close.'

It was surreal knowing all the things this fountain had seen. Movie sets, centuries of lovers' quarrels, the wishes of a billion travellers. It was like I could feel my soul being refuelled by the fountain and the energy flowing all around us. I could think of no better way to end the night than being here; ending my stay in Rome the way it started, with Marcello.

He took my hand again and pulled me through the crowds; this time I didn't hesitate as he slid and darted through the crowd with expert ease until finally we stopped right in front of the fountain. I breathed in the magic and smiled at Marcello, who motioned with his finger to turn around. I giggled, doing exactly as he instructed, biting my lip and closing my eyes. I took a moment, not knowing if I had to wish for my return or to simply throw the coin and let the myth do its thing. Not wanting to risk it, I did both.

# Chapter Twenty-Four

I wasn't ready for goodbye. This time was different, I felt it, and I know he did too. It resonated in the silence that fell between us, after I thanked him for walking me home and wished him good luck with everything, thinking that 'everything' was general enough to cover any area of his life, which I still knew nothing about. No doubt Maria would finish this tour and then go through all the same motions again with a new bunch of horny tourists vying to find love or a fling in the Eternal City.

With my belated bonding with my group and a new city to conquer, I could make one of two decisions: I could walk inside and bid Marcello goodbye, or I could voice the less reasonable, more terrifying notion that was screaming in my head, one that would usually require a lot more alcohol for me to even contemplate.

'Umm, so did you want to come in . . .'

*Don't say nightcap, Sammi, don't say nightcap—that's so lame.*

I had a brain freeze; oh, God, what was I asking? To come in and have a mocktail? For all he knew, I was still bunk buddies with six other people; yeah, that sounded like an attractive proposition.

Marcello's mouth curved as he watched me squirm. He crossed his arms and waited for me to fumble my way into a deeper hole. Finally, he saved me, clearing his throat and asking, 'Don't you have to get up early tomorrow?'

*Great, now he was looking for a way out. He's not interested, Sammi, take a hint!*

I shrugged. 'I had a lot of rest today.'

Something changed in his expression, as if those simple words held a deeper meaning; maybe they did. Now the ball was in his court, but I wasn't going to beg.

I decided to give him one last chance. In a tone that sounded far more flippant than I felt, I said, 'I just thought I would give you the grand tour of my new room.'

That got his attention. 'New room?'

I laughed. 'I am not sure if I've been upgraded or downgraded, but it's all mine.' I held out my arms like it was a blessing from the gods.

Marcello broke into a broad smile, stepping forward. 'It's not a linen cupboard, is it?'

'I'll let you be the judge of that,' I said, walking through reception, ever aware of him following. Gabriello looked up from his paper at the front desk, adjusting his spectacles and nodding to us.

'*Buona notte*, Gabriello,' I sing-songed.

He shook his head. *Oh, the things he must have seen*, I thought.

'*Buona notte*, Sammi,' he sighed.

We had only made our way up the first lot of steps before Gabriello called out once more. 'Oh, Sammi, before you go.'

We stopped midway, turning to see Gabriello at the base of the stairs.

'We have washed all the linen in your room and replaced the mattress as you requested.'

My smile fell away, watching Gabriello wink and double back to the front desk. I wanted to die.

Marcello slowly made his way up the steps until he stood beside me, smirking. 'Expecting company, were you?' His brows rose in question.

I pointed to my face. 'Bugs! I had bed bugs,' I said, a bit too loudly, for once grateful there was evidence of the foul creatures on my face.

Marcello laughed, moving past me on the stairs. 'A likely story,' he said.

I glared at his back, shaking my head and following in his footsteps.

'This one.' I pointed.

Marcello moved to stand to the side of the door while I rummaged through my bag for the key, a key that appeared to have been swallowed up in the abyss. Biting the side of my mouth, the more I searched, the more flustered I got— and the more aware I became of Marcello, standing there watching, and waiting for me to open the door. Mercifully I found it in a side pocket; blowing out a breath and offering a small smile, I slid in the key and unlocked my cell door. Pushing it open and turning on the light, I saw the bed— my new bed—had been freshly made, and there was a lingering smell of bug spray in the air.

'Ah, home, crap home,' I sighed, pulling off my bag and throwing it on top of the chair next to the door. Marcello stepped in, his serious gaze taking in the small, windowless room, and closed the door behind him.

'Wow, this is . . .'

'Charming, quaint, cosy?'

'Awful, this is really awful.'

I laughed, because I had learned the first time I had stepped into this room that if you didn't laugh you cried; seeing as I hadn't been able to find the funny side to it, I had done exactly that for most of the afternoon. I sat down on my bed-bug mattress and cried. Now, thanks to the clean sheets, the fact that I didn't have to worry about other people waking me up with their body gases, snoring and squeaky bed springs, and the happy knowledge that I only had to endure one more night in this rat-hole, made it easier for me to snigger at the depressingly low quality of my accommodation. I also felt strangely alive, thanks to my jaw-droppingly gorgeous companion, despite the fact that he made the room feel even smaller than it already was. I couldn't exactly offer him a drink, or even turn on a TV or radio for background noise. I was now painfully aware that there wasn't actually anything to do in here . . . aside from the obvious. We both stared at the freshly made bed.

'Well, we could always break it in,' I joked, but the speed with which Marcello's head spun around caused the laughter to die in my throat. *Bad joke, BAD joke.*

I detected the hint of a smile as he slowly peeled off his dinner jacket, throwing it over the chair on top of my bag.

'Anything to get me into your bed, huh?'

Okay, that was it. I was no longer speaking about anything other than the weather—my mouth was obviously too big and too unfiltered for decent conversation. As charming and gorgeous and attentive as he had been, I still knew nothing about this man—who was, oh, God, sitting on the edge of my bed, unbuttoning and rolling up his cuffs. I mean, I knew what bloody Jodie's childhood dreams were, for God's sake; how did I know nothing, not one single thing, about the man who was on my bed?

In an effort to restore some of my dignity, I moved his jacket and my bag aside to sit opposite him in the chair.

Marcello curved his brow. 'So far away?'

I tilted my head. 'I tell you what, I'll scoot my chair closer with every question you answer.'

Marcello's face turned dark. Clearly he didn't like the sound of those rules, which made me all the more eager to ask. What was he hiding?

'Deal?'

He gave me a slow nod.

Bingo!

'What's your name, your full name?'

'Marcello Lorenzo Bambozzi.'

*Excellent.*

I slid my chair forward an inch; Marcello folded his arms as if he found my tiny little movement annoying.

'How old are you?'

'*Ventisei.*'

I knew enough to know that was twenty-six in English.

I slid my chair closer. 'All answers in English, please.'

He held up his hands. '*Scusa.*'

As small as the room was, I was still out of arm's reach and now the questions really mattered: what did I want to know?

'How do you know Maria?'

'We grew up together.'

I nodded. 'Childhood sweethearts?'

Marcello laughed, shaking his head and crooking his finger. 'That's two moves.'

A girl could try.

I was getting closer now; if he reached out he could touch my knees. I thought carefully about my last few questions.

'Today, when you were talking with Maria, what did she have to think about?'

It was a stupid question, a question that pushed him too far and was none of my business. I wouldn't have blamed him if he got up and grabbed his coat. But instead he sighed contemplatively and looked at the distance between us, weighing up the pros and cons of answering.

'We are going into business together—well, trying to.'

Damn. He had answered the question but it left more unanswered questions rolling around inside my head. I begrudgingly scooted forward, knowing that I had one more question to ask, at best.

*Make it count, Sammi.*

I looked at Marcello, straight in his eyes, because I wanted to see how they would change when I asked him my next question.

'Last night, when you kissed me and then walked away, was it because you regretted it?'

Something flashed in Marcello's eyes alright: sheer disbelief. His eyes searched my face as if he expected me to tell him I was joking, but I was deadly serious. He didn't answer; instead, he stared at me for a long moment and, before I could warn him that I wasn't moving an inch until he answered, he grabbed the arms of my chair and dragged me towards him. The jolt was so unexpected that I yelped. My breathing rapidly increased at finding my mouth so near his as his intense, dark eyes bored into mine.

He shook his head. '*No, mi dispiace niente,*' he whispered against my mouth.

I glowered at him, close to losing it as I warred between wanting to taste his lips and needing to remain in control.

'I said, in English.'

A wolfish smile spread across Marcello's face. 'No, I regret nothing,' he said, leaning in and kissing me as if there was no tomorrow. And, for us, there wouldn't be—there was only now.

# Chapter Twenty-Five

This was happening, this was really happening. Marcello helped me pull my dress up over my head as I straddled him on the bed. My hands made quick work of the buttons on his shirt, pulling it apart and revealing his ridiculous landscape of muscle and curves, my hands sliding over to admire its beauty, more intriguing than any map I had ever followed. Marcello was just as interested in my dips and curves. He sat up and kissed my rib cage, while sliding his hand up to unhook my bra. He peeled one strap over my shoulder, exposing the pink bud on my milky, untanned breast, which he took into his mouth, circling his tongue and sucking, before shifting his attention to my other breast.

My head fell back, breath escaping me as I stared, unseeing, at the ceiling, pushing into his mouth. Despite the heady sensations, the slight flicker of the fluorescent light bulb began to frustrate me; in my need for Marcello

I hadn't even worried about the light, but now I wanted to slide away my final barrier.

'Wait a minute, I'm just going to turn off the light,' I breathed against his mouth, edging away. Marcello looked disappointed but he didn't stop me. As I moved to the door I took a moment to look at him, splayed out on my bed, and for a moment I was afraid to turn off the light, that somehow he might disappear. He lay against my pillows, watching me and working on unbuckling and unzipping his pants with a cocky grin. It was all the motivation I needed to flick the switch, blushing so fiercely I had to take a moment before I slowly made my way back to the bed.

My knees hit the edge of the mattress and Marcello's hand snaked out, pulling me towards him, encircling me with his strong arms and coaxing me to open my mouth to him. Like a magician's sleight of hand, I hadn't even noticed he was sliding down my panties until they were pooling at my feet. I breathed hard against his mouth, and smiled.

*I, Sammi Shorten, unworldly, boring, mousey traveller, am about to have a one-night stand in Italy, with a gorgeous man with a—OH, MY GOD—*

I could feel the hard length of him digging into my hip; skimming my hand down over him, I felt my heart stop. He wasn't going to fit—there was just no way. I couldn't even remember the last time I had had sex: eight, nine months ago? This was no way to ease back into the game. I tried to keep my voice from shaking.

'Um, do you have . . . protection?'

Would there be a condom big enough?

Marcello kissed the corner of my mouth. 'Of course.'

Happy to hear we were on the same page, I rewarded him with a kiss, sliding my tongue inside while exploring the long, hard length of him in my hand, pumping and kissing him so hard I heard him groan against my lips, from pleasure or pain I couldn't tell. It only made me move faster, loving the feel of him, almost wishing I had left the light on so I could see his face as I worked him into a frenzy. I revelled in the power of having Marcello, so confident in everything he did, at my mercy, and hearing him swear in his native tongue turned me on all the more. Just when I thought he couldn't take any more, the power was reversed and Marcello moved my hand away, flipping me onto my back and pushing my legs apart; without missing a beat his head dipped between my thighs.

'Holy shit!' I slapped my hand over my mouth, muting the unearthly whimpers and swearing that I had no control over, as Marcello dug his fingers into my thighs and pushed his tongue deep inside me, tasting and teasing. Caught between heaven and hell, I rocked into him, cupping the back of his head and encouraging him, pleading with him not to stop—until it became too much. I couldn't take any more and I was pushing him away, but he clamped my thighs open until I screamed so loud I was certain they would hear me on the eighth floor.

My body limp, beaded with sweat and practically hyperventilating, I could hear the vibration of Marcello's laughter against my thigh. I didn't know if I loved or hated him in that moment, all I knew was that he was a genius. He crawled up my body, rolling to the side; he leant his head on his hand, catching his own breath.

'You sure?' he asked; it was a simple question, one that meant this was over if I wanted it to be. Fooling around with a sexy stranger on holiday was one thing, but letting him inside me, giving a piece of myself away, well, that wasn't me. I don't know if he guessed that, or if he was just doing the right thing, but I was glad he asked; as adamant as I had thought I was about wanting to go further, now I wasn't so certain.

'Don't be mad . . .'

Marcello's hand, which had been sliding over my skin, stopped abruptly at my words. I couldn't see his face and didn't know what his eyes conveyed, but I knew how he felt the moment he moved his hand up to my face, touching me so gently and caressing the horrid bumps on my face. He breathed out a laugh and I could just make out the silhouette of his head shaking.

'You are completely mad, but I could never be mad at you.'

I smiled, melting against his hand and feeling the warmth and sincerity of his words. I cursed Pompeii, and Venice and every destination that had me leaving tomorrow, because I knew that if I had more time there would be no reservations, which was utterly insane. *Oh, sure, Sammi, because a seven-night-stand would make this so much more meaningful. Idiot.*

Regardless, what we had was us, here, tonight. My body was still reeling from the aftermath of my orgasm, but if this night was truly going to be one to remember then it couldn't possibly end like this.

Marcello, being the gentleman, rolled onto his back, probably thinking of any number of turn-offs to get rid of his erection. I smiled and rolled over to kiss his shoulder, sliding my hand over his rib cage, then slowly down his six-pack and lower still. I could hear him swallow hard as I touched him.

'Sammi.' He said my name as a warning, strained.

I moved over him, kissing his jaw, his neck, his chest, his nipple.

Marcello ran his fingers through my hair. 'Sammi, what are you doing?' I didn't answer, I simply trailed a determined line down, down. Marcello fisted his hands into my hair, his hips pushing forward as I took him into my mouth.

'*Cazzo dell'inferno!*' he gritted.

Whatever that meant, I hoped it was a good thing.

# Chapter Twenty-Six

I lay in the shadows, the sheets tucked under my arms, listening to the deep, rhythmic breaths of Marcello next to me. He had shown me many things these past few days, but tonight was something else entirely and, while I couldn't wipe the goofy grin from my face, I kind of wanted to high-five myself. Girls like me didn't do things like this, and they certainly didn't do them with men who looked like that.

I peered to the side, seeing nothing more than a darkened lump in the bed, but I knew he was there, his right leg crossed over mine. I was wide awake, shifting and sighing really loudly, hoping that Marcello might stir, but nothing. I yawned loudly, then turned towards him heavily, making sure to squeak the springs on the bed. Nothing. I stared at where I thought his head might be on the pillow next to mine, considering giving him a little pinch and blaming it on a bed bug, but knowing there was no waking him from his deep sleep.

I rolled back over, thinking it was probably just as well—there was no telling what would happen if he woke up. *Best I just lie here and think pure thoughts.* It lasted all of five seconds. 'Oh, who am I kidding?' I ripped the sheets off me, rummaging around the floor for my dress; it had been flung off so fast I had no clue of its whereabouts. My hands skimmed over a hairbrush, lip gloss, Marcello's jacket, a chair leg and my handbag with its entire contents seemingly spilled everywhere. It was as if the room had been ransacked: the things you do in the heat of the moment.

*Aha!*

I pulled it over my head but it got stuck midway and I panicked, picturing the scene that could soon play out; Marcello waking up in the dim light to see my silhouette, arms trapped and starkers from the waist down, banging into the limited furniture of my room. Yep, real attractive. But even when I finally managed to pull the dress down my body there was still no movement. I crept to the bed, leaning over and placing my hand over his face until I felt the warmth of his breath against my palm. Excellent, my bedroom skills hadn't killed him. Laughing at my overactive imagination, I backed away from the bed. I skimmed my bare feet along to the door, opening it slowly and peering out, wary not to be caught.

*Doing what, going to the bathroom?*

Besides, what was there to worry about? Everyone was safely tucked away on the eighth floor, so there was no one to see me here. I straightened my spine and made my way down the hall to the bathroom, only to twist the handle and find it locked.

'Ugh, seriously?'

'You might want to go to another bathroom, there's no spray in here,' the muffled voice yelled through the door.

'Oh, that's just gross,' I said, recoiling from the doorway and heading for the stairs. I wanted to make myself look semi-respectable; the light of day might not pierce through any part of my windowless room, but Marcello was sure to wake up and turn on the light sooner or later, and when he did I wanted him to see me at my best. I would be lying there, hair soft and flowing on the pillow, with fresh breath and lips shimmering with berry gloss, pretending I always woke up like this.

With my toiletries trapped in the bathroom of eternal stench, I had no choice. As much as I didn't want to, I headed up to the eighth-floor bathroom. I didn't need orange foundation, just a reasonable toilet, a smidge of someone's toothpaste to rinse with, and a light misting of—I picked up the bottle and squinted—Britney Spears perfume? I would be back down and in my room in no time, nothing amiss. I was getting pretty good at sneaking around, I thought to myself, washing my hands and scrunching my hair. Marvelling at my post-orgasmic glow, I wondered if I would look different to the others, more worldly, more womanly. I certainly felt like I had an air of contentment about me, until I opened the bathroom door and was stopped dead in my tracks.

'Oh, hey, Jodie.'

She stood there half asleep, with hair all a mess and raccoon eyes from sleeping in her make-up. Seeing me, she straightened, her brows rising in surprise. Now was the time I would learn if dinner had all been an act or if she really had changed her tune.

'Oh, hey, where have you been?' she asked.

'Oh, I, um, I'm bunking on the second floor for tonight.'

She looked confused. 'Why?'

'Oh, I just felt really crook today and thought I would need a solid night's sleep, plus I didn't want whatever I had to be contagious.'

Jodie laughed. 'You can't catch a hangover.'

*Valid point.*

A silence fell between us; Jodie hadn't sneered or glared at me, which I took as a positive sign that the water was well and truly flowing under the bridge now.

'Did you end up emailing your sister?' she asked casually, as if it was just an ordinary catch-up between siblings rather than a scathing indictment of my tour group.

'Umm, no, not that one. I might send her one tomorrow before we go. My sister lives in Paris so I want her to come and see me in Venice before we head home.'

'Oh, that sounds nice,' she said, yawning, her concentration wavering.

'Yeah,' I said, kind of enjoying just talking with this new Jodie.

'Hey, Jodie, listen. I'm sorry about the email, I really didn't mean the things I wrote, I was just . . .'

'Eh, don't sweat it, I've been called worse,' she said, waving my words away.

'Well, I appreciate you not saying anything to the others.'

She burst out laughing, way too loud; I flinched, glancing down the hall, wondering if her cackle might wake the others.

'Oh, Sammi, you didn't honestly think I would destroy you, did you?'

I laughed haltingly. 'Of course not,' I lied, looking into her intense green eyes.

'Good, now toddle back down to the second floor and get some sleep.'

Ha! If only she knew what awaited me in my bed.

''Night,' I said, stepping around her and heading straight for the stairs.

'Oh, Sammi?'

I paused on the top step.

'Have you set your alarm? Remember, you won't have Nate's farts to rouse you in the morning.'

'Oh, crap, no, I haven't.'

My distraction, in the form of a certain Italian god incarnate, had meant an early morning wake-up call was the last thing on my mind.

'Don't sweat it, I'll wake you—you know what Maria's like. What room are you in?'

'210.'

'Got it—see you in the morning.'

'*Si!*' I said, perhaps a little too enthusiastically. Jodie looked at me as if I were a complete dork, rolling her eyes and stepping into the bathroom.

With that settled, all I had to do was make my way back to my man. I mentally slapped myself: Marcello wasn't my anything. I just had to keep remembering that.

~

I had planned to sneak back into my room and under the covers in my bed, secure in the knowledge that Marcello slept like the dead. So when I opened the door and the bedroom light shone in my eyes, and I was greeted by the sight of Marcello perched on the edge of my bed, dressed and tying his shoes, you can imagine my surprise.

'Oh, hey,' I said, folding and unfolding my arms, shifting to shut the door behind me, before busying myself with picking up the chair I had knocked over. Spotting my knickers on the floor among the debris of my spilled belongings, I scooped them up quick smart; God only knew where my bra was. Marcello rested his elbows on his knees, looking up at me; I was relieved to see he was smirking in that boyish way that he had, entertained by my complete awkwardness.

I really hadn't put too much thought into the aftermath of what we had done, to how different it could be between us; I had a flashback to how he had slid his fingers inside me, and the primal noises I'd been unable to contain as he wickedly took control of my body. Surely the woman who had done those things was another person, not the same creature blushing profusely in front of him. Had he planned to slink away in the night while he thought I was gone? Had I caught him mid-escape? I felt sick. I wasn't under any grand illusion that he would give me a promise ring and swear to wait for me, but I didn't think it would end like this. Perhaps I was a fool to think that there had been another kind of connection between us, that this had been more than just fooling around. I mean, he made me come three times—surely that was a sign of a connection?

I tried to keep it casual, to act like my stomach wasn't in knots, that I wasn't overanalysing everything in that moment. What would Jodie do? How would she behave after a hookup?

I yawned, playing bored. 'What time is it?' I asked.

'It's late—you should get some sleep,' he said, standing up, pushing his hands in his pockets and watching me with guarded interest.

'True that!' I agreed, stretching my arms like I was ready for bed.

Marcello's brows narrowed like he wasn't quite sure what to say, or how to react to my careless attitude. It felt kind of good to protect myself. So he was going to leave without saying goodbye? He may as well leave now and shut the door after him.

I padded past him, leaping onto the bed and sliding under the sheets. 'Hey, can you turn the light out before you go? Thanks,' I said sweetly, like I really wasn't bothered one way or another.

Marcello turned to me. 'Are you feeling okay?'

I shrugged. 'Fine, why?'

'You're being weird.'

'No, I'm not.'

Yeah, I totally was.

Marcello crossed his arms, looking at me pointedly.

'Okay, well, in that case, I'm going to leave the light on, because I'm going to the bathroom and I thought that I probably should not do that naked.'

My fake smile faded. 'You mean you're not leaving?'

'Sorry, did you want me to?' He half laughed the question.

My instinct was to say no, to drag myself desperately up onto my haunches and beg that he stay. Instead my mouth gaped as I struggled to voice a single word, and the smile slipped from Marcello's face.

*Say something, Sammi, anything.*

Marcello looked away and bent to scoop up his crumpled jacket from the floor, shoving it under his arm. This was not how I wanted to remember him; I wanted to see those dimples appear, for him to smile in that sexy, knowing way he did that made my breath catch. Instead I just stared at him, the silence agonising because I didn't know what to say to end it.

I didn't know how to prepare for this. This was goodbye; it was as if we were simply committing each other to memory. Besides, what was the point of having him stay a few hours longer, knowing I was leaving in the morning.

I didn't wanted to give into the aching feeling, the feeling of wanting something I couldn't have, something that lasted longer than a night. It reminded me how out of step I was with the rest of my generation, for whom hooking up was a common occurrence. Going on an overseas tour with a bunch of twenty-somethings? Well, it just came with the territory. Wake-explore-drink-party-sex-sleep-repeat: it was part of the reason I felt so out of place in my group. I didn't want to do that, which made me feel completely prudish; even with the one person I had actually connected with, I still couldn't go all the way. My guarded, sensible self was kind of infuriating. Why couldn't I just let go, binge-drink and bed-hop with abandonment? Somehow the very thought of that seemed to taint the fleeting hours I had spent with Marcello. I couldn't help but be filled with more swirling, confused thoughts that had me feeling lost, unsure where to go from here. I sank down into the mattress, feeling the fatigue and sadness claim me as I smelled him on my pillow.

Staring up at the ceiling, I linked my hands across my belly and swallowed deeply.

'I have a pretty early start so . . .' My words fell away. I didn't dare look at him now. I had to be brutal, act cool, like there were no strings attached; after all, that was how it was. I could only imagine how relieved he would be at being given an out. But still he stood there; I could feel his eyes boring into me, and I thought he might say something, but I heard the door open and my heart stopped.

*Don't go, just . . . stay.*

But my rational mind told me to keep my thoughts to myself, and for once I listened. Just as I thought I would be okay hearing that door close behind him, Marcello's voice sliced through the room.

'Safe travels, Samantha Shorten.'

And before I could throw myself out of bed and blurt out that I really didn't want him to go, the door had closed and Marcello was gone.

# Chapter Twenty-Seven

I dreamt I was falling, jolted awake by that stomach-dropping, heart-stopping feeling.

Thank God it was just a dream. A dream about impending death, but a dream nonetheless. I was in my bed and awake of my own accord. I couldn't have had more than three hours' sleep, but I felt rather rested, considering. I gave it until three o'clock for me to hit the wall, but hopefully by then we would be well on our way to our next adventure. I had to grab my suitcase from upstairs; yesterday I'd only had the energy to bring a spare outfit and some toiletries downstairs with me, energy which had apparently magically restored itself for my evening with Marcello.

Memories from last night had me walking around in a daze as I got out of bed and headed to the mercifully open door to the bathroom. Lost in my troubled thoughts, I almost choked on my toothpaste when I was startled by the loudest knock on the bathroom door.

'Jurst ugh mirnute.' I spat. 'Jodie, is that you?'

Bang-bang-bang.

'Okay, okay, I'm up, I'm out, jeez.'

Rinsing my mouth and securing the towel around my hair, I packed the last of my toiletries up like I always did; I mean, you just couldn't trust who might be lurking around for a squirt of foundation or a spray of perfume. I shoved the bag under my arm and all but ran to the door to put a stop to the insistent knocking.

'Bloody hell, I said that I was re—'

I whipped the door open so fast I almost stepped right into the singlet-covered chest of a man with wild, woolly white hair and a newspaper under his arm. Most definitely not Jodie.

'*Fretta, non ho tutto il giorno!*' the man yelled.

'Ah, sorry, all yours,' I said, stepping aside as he made his way in with a huff, slamming the door and locking it behind me.

Making my way back to my room, I decided to traipse up to the eighth floor to wake up the group. They would thank me from sparing them Maria's wrath; my awakening would be like birdsong compared with that of the passionately punctual Maria. Ascending the stairs, I took comfort in knowing that the circus I was about to join on the road would at least provide a distraction from Marcello.

Making my way up past the sixth floor, I took a moment to glance at the door that I had tried to trick Marcello into believing was mine. That was, until an angry, hairy-chested man came out and abused me. Seriously, what was with me and hairy men?

I sighed. Marcello wasn't hairy. Despite his thick black hair, and brows most women would kill for, he was all silky smooth. And I really had to stop thinking about him.

*It was just a summer fling, Sammi, let it go.*

I put it down to naivety. I had never had a summer romance before, and certainly not one in Italy, so I was bound to go a little gooey. And, really, I had done pretty bloody well for myself; wait until my friends back home asked about my holiday. I would tell them all about the tall, dark stranger I invited into my bed on a hot Roman night. Of course, they probably wouldn't believe me, and I didn't exactly have any photo evidence that included him. As far as anyone would know, Marcello was a figment of my wild imagination, and in some ways I wished he was—then maybe there wouldn't be a dull ache inside me every time I thought about him and how things had ended last night.

I walked up the last few steps to the eighth floor, impressed at my lack of exhaustion. The first night up these very stairs I had thought I might pass out from a lack of oxygen to the brain, but now I could hardly even feel the burn, conditioned by my sightseeing wanderings. I hadn't quite got over the door-opening incident with Jodie and Gary, so was relieved to see that the door had been left ajar; I only hoped that, unlike other mornings, Nate had a sheet wrapped firmly around him. I slid my hand through the door, taking great delight in flicking the light switch off and on like my dad used to do, ensuring I woke up in a foul mood on school days.

'Wakey-wakey, rise and shi—'

I flung open the door, lighting up the room and coming to an abrupt halt.

'What the . . . ?'

The room was in its usual disarray, sheets and pillows flung, beds crooked and shifted, an apple core on the floor and an empty can of Coke on the windowsill. But more disturbing than any of that was the fact that the room was completely empty. No twisted, half-naked, snoring, drooling, farting bumps in the beds.

I stepped over a blanket, bending down to pull out a squeaky crate from under the bed. It was well and truly empty—they all were. I sat back on my haunches, looking around, confused. Even my own things were gone.

*Where was everyone?*

I walked back down the hall, opening up the bathroom door. The vanity was clear of all products, a wastebasket full of make-up-stained tissues and some eyeliner shavings in the sink were all that was left. The room was misty and damp, proof that someone had taken a shower not too long ago.

*Nice one, guys. You could have bloody woken me!*

Heading downstairs, I was pissed off, and felt a little rejected; clearly they didn't want me at the breakfast gathering in the courtyard as was outlined in the itinerary. I felt kind of nervous making my way through reception. I wondered if Marcello would be at the breakfast table, here to see us off—or, more specifically, me. But then I shook that absurdity from my thoughts. I was probably a distant memory to him now, and here I was daydreaming that he would be standing in the courtyard with a single rose.

*Settle down, Sammi.*

I walked through the arched doorway that led into the courtyard overgrown with potato vine and flaky mint-coloured picnic tables . . . empty picnic tables, apart from the elderly couple drinking coffee and playing with their expensive-looking camera.

I made my way over to the breakfast buffet feeling something twist in my stomach, and I knew it wasn't hunger pains. Pouring myself a juice, I hoped that there might be a clue lingering somewhere. Maybe they had left a note somewhere, or a message with reception. A young staff member I had seen around the hotel moved along the table, collecting spoons, lifting and stacking bain-maries and wiping down the grubby surfaces. He looked pointedly at the carafe of juice I had just poured from.

'Oh, *scusi*,' I said, handing him the carafe and stepping away to allow him to continue cleaning.

'I am sorry, *signora*, but breakfast is over.'

I breathed out a laugh. 'That's okay, I'm not really that hung—wait, what?'

The man pressed his lips together and lifted up his hands in a 'what can you do?' gesture. 'I am sorry, breakfast is over.'

'W-what time is it?' I blurted out, trying to remember the serving times. Did it differ depending on the day of the week?

The man looked at me, confused. I was one step away from grabbing him by the arms, shaking the shit out of him and yelling, '*WHAT FUCKING TIME IS IT?!*'

'*Dieci e trenta*—ten-thirty.'

'What? That can't be, there must be some mistake.'

The man looked forlorn. '*Mi dispiace*,' he said, bowing his head and stepping quickly away from the mad woman.

I couldn't blame him—my mouth was hanging open and my eyes were wide and crazed.

'No, no, no, this cannot be,' I mumbled to myself, walking past the grey nomads and back into the hotel. I stood in front of reception in a daze, turning to look at the clock in the lounge area where I could see the breakfast waiter had indeed told the truth. I felt my world drop away. I pushed past the line of people checking in, earning myself some choice Italian abuse and a couple of dirty looks, but I didn't care. I gripped the edge of the desk so hard that my nails bit into the wood.

'Gabriello!' I yelled, despite the fact that he was standing right behind the counter. He ignored me for a long moment, stamping the paperwork and handing a credit card back to a young couple with a smile.

'You need to wait your turn,' he said, without even looking at me.

'Gabriello, please, where is everyone?'

'Everyone?'

'The tour group, my tour group, Maria, Bellissimo Tours, Nate, Jodie, Johnny.' I continued rattling off the names of more group members, but I had his attention the moment I said Maria.

'They are gone,' he said, as if it were bleedingly obvious.

'Gone?'

'*Si*, they checked out a few hours ago.'

'A FEW HOURS AGO?'

It was like there was an echo in the room.

Gabriello shifted awkwardly, offering the people behind me an apologetic 'nothing to see here' smile.

I gripped the bench harder, the crazed Aussie having a meltdown. I shook my head, barely believing this was real. Surely this was some practical joke, the group would come leaping out from behind the pillar and yell, 'Just kidding!' Then, through the fog of my brain, a remembered warning sounded in my mind: 'if you're late she will leave you behind, make no mistake.'

Like a zombie, I lifted my head to see Gabriello watching me, wary that I might lose it completely and start tearing the place apart. I was confident that I wouldn't do that, too numb and weary to muster such a reaction. I know I had longed for a distraction, but this? All I could do was stand and stare and shake my head, over and over, until the words finally formed in my mouth as I looked up at Gabriello once more.

'They left me. They really fucking left me.'

# Chapter Twenty-Eight

I got lost once. In Chadstone Shopping Plaza when I was six years old. Nothing too traumatising, I had spent most of my time in the Barbie doll section, fantasising about the next purchase I would beg my mum for. I had been alright—I'd known where I was, no drama. In fact, at the time, I hadn't known what all the fuss was about. This, on the other hand, was very different. There were no hot-pink glittery distractions and I didn't know what to do or where to go. I was so screwed.

I couldn't believe they left me. And where the hell was my stuff?

I sat slumped in the lounge area, cold to my core, struggling to believe the harsh reality of what had happened.

My mind flashed to Jodie's sparkling smile at dinner as she lifted her glass to me. *'To new friends.'* To our chat in the bathroom, her laughter as she said, *'Oh, Sammi, you didn't really think I would destroy you, did you?'* And her promise to wake me.

I buried my head in my hands. I was such an idiot. How had I not learned that when something seemed too good to be true, it always likely was? Had I been so eager for her to like me that I simply discounted all the dirty looks and threats? Well, she had done a pretty good job. Jodie: one, me: zero. Unless of course I was just being paranoid; surely someone couldn't be that evil . . . could they?

After all I had been through in this hell-hole, I thought that I would welcome the sight of Gabriello wheeling my suitcase towards me but, at this point in time, all I could think about was trying to come up with some kind of plan.

'Here you go; it was in the luggage holding area.'

'How thoughtful,' I said bitterly, imagining Jodie lovingly zipping up my luggage and dragging it to reception.

Gabriello sat at the coffee table opposite me, his eyes full of concern. '*Signora*, I do not understand. Was your sister not meeting you here?'

I blinked, looking at him. 'My sister?'

He shifted in his seat. 'Luciano said he overheard the crazy one telling Maria that you had cancelled the tour because you were catching up with your sister.'

Bingo! The crazy one—Jodie.

Though I had my suspicions, hearing the exact details of how Jodie had plotted my downfall made it all the worse. She had turned my plan to meet up with my sister in Venice into a means to destroy me. Wow, if I hadn't stayed in another room, would she have laced my gnocchi with a sedative? Or clubbed me over the back of the head with her make-up bag? My leg was jigging up and down, I was so mad. In the space of a few hours I had gone from ecstasy to agony, from wanting to track Jodie down and tell her what for to just wanting to grab my bags and leave this place forever.

'I am guessing this is not the case.'

My crazed eyes flicked up to Gabriello. 'No, no, it wasn't.'

I sighed, rubbing my hands on my thighs. Which was worse—the feeling of abandonment or the reality of having to spend another night here?

'What are you going to do?' Gabriello asked tentatively.

I shrugged. 'Drag myself back to my room, take stock, form a plan B.' Though part of me was hell-bent on revenge, most of me was happy to never see them again.

'Ah, yes, about that,' said Gabriello, his face twisting in distress.

'What?'

He looked as though he was struggling to form the words, dreading what he was about to say. The penny finally dropped.

'Oh, of course I will pay for my extra nights here, don't think I'm going to be dodgy about it. I hadn't planned for it but I will fix it up right now.' I went to stand but Gabriello stopped me.

'No, Sammi, it is not the money.'

'Oh.' I slowly sat back down.

'Your room is already booked by someone else.'

'Oh, I see. Well, if I have to move, I have to move.'

'Unfortunately the hotel is fully booked. I am afraid that you will have to find alternative arrangements.'

Well, today was just getting better and better.

'Of course we can help you find another hotel—Luciano can even take you there.'

He was being kind, sympathetic, helpful—all the right things—but I was so overwhelmed in that moment that nothing could have made me feel any better. Until my glorious Plan B hit me like a freight train.

'Thanks, Gabriello, but I think I'm sorted,' I said. 'Would you mind if I stored my luggage until I need it?'

'Of course, for however long you need.'

'*Grazie.*' I beamed, hopping to my feet and making a determined path to the internet kiosk, thinking that perhaps not all hope was lost. There would just be a slight detour in my plans.

~

I had never been to Paris, although I felt like I had from listening to Claire, who spoke, at length, of its beauty. I was suddenly filled with excitement. I was trading in a not-altogether-cheap, bug-infested hotel for free accommodation in the city of lights. Screw you, Jodie! As gutted as I was not to be exploring more of Italy, survival mode kicked in. I was not going to run home with my tail between my legs. But when I did choose to go home, I would storm through the doors of Jan and John Buzzo's travel agency and demand a refund. 'Bellissimo' was a really misleading word. As the brochures didn't showcase a girl crying and disfigured by bug bites, I'd be calling them out on false advertising.

I pulled up a chair, mentally pushing the Buzzos to the back of my mind; besides, it was the weekend, so contacting them about my disastrous abandonment by my tour group was not going to get me anywhere today. But what I could get was a plane ticket to Paris, to be comforted by my big sister. I felt better already, moving to turn on the computer screen, only to still.

'You've got to be kidding me.' I lifted the tiny yellow Post-it note from the computer screen that read:

*GUASTO! (OUT OF ORDER)*

What was going on with my life right now? Was I cursed? What had I done in a past life to deserve this? The beautiful man in my bed last night was just a way for the universe to lull me into a false sense of security, because come the light of day—bam! The universe had whacked me straight between the eyes, repeatedly. Just like it always did.

I sighed, sliding out of the chair and dragging myself to the front desk, where Gabriello seemed to be even less excited to see me. I slapped down the Post-it note on the counter.

'Can I please use the phone?'

# Chapter Twenty-Nine

Finding Claire on any given day was always a process of elimination. Useless at answering her phone, she could be anywhere between her and Louis' apartment, Louis' restaurant, Noire, and Hotel Trocadero, where Claire spent a lot of her time. I opted for the last; with a little help from the operator, I was put through to the Hotel Trocadero, as I had been a million times before.

'*Bonjour,* Hotel Trocadero, how can I help you?'

I smiled, feeling better already at hearing Cecile's friendly voice.

'*Bonjour,* Cecile, it's Sammi.'

'Ah, *oui,* Sammi, but of course, I would know that voice anywhere.'

'What gave it away? The hideous Aussie accent?'

'Oh, Sammi, your voice could never be hideous.'

I breathed out a laugh, loving the way she pronounced hideous with her accent.

*Idious.*

'How can I help you?'

'I am trying to track down my sister. Is she with you guys today?'

There was a pause at the other end of the line, so long that I wondered if I had been cut off.

'Hello?'

'Oh, sorry, Sammi, I am here.' Cecile sounded a little panicked.

'Oh, so is Claire there? It's kind of important I speak with her.'

'Is it an emergency?' Cecile sounded cagey. I half expected her to ask for a secret password next.

'Very much so. I am in Rome at the moment and I just really need to speak to her.'

'Oh, Sammi, don't you know? Well, of course not—she told me not to say anything. It was meant to be a surprise. Oh, I am confused.' Cecile definitely sounded panicked, which only made my heart beat faster.

'Told you what?'

'It was meant to be a surprise.'

'Cecile, please, I'm about two seconds away from booking a plane ticket to come to Paris.'

'No!' Cecile blurted out. 'No, you mustn't do that.'

'Cecile, what is going on?' I gripped the phone so hard that I feared I might snap it in two; I glanced at Gabriello, who was watching me with interest. I pulled at the cord, though it had very little slack from behind the desk, and turned away for some privacy.

'Cecile, please,' I begged.

Again with the silence, followed by a sigh. 'Okay, but you never heard it from me.'

'Heard what?' I snapped, my patience now paper-thin.

'Claire wanted to surprise you when you got home from Italy. She didn't want to interrupt your holiday, seeing as you were having such a good time.'

I scoffed. Trust Mum and Dad to pass that on; oh, how wrong they were.

'So Claire and Louis decided to fly home to Australia and be there when you got back; oh, please don't tell them I told you, please act surprised when you see them. They were even going to pick you up from the airport.'

'Australia? You mean they're home?'

'Well, almost; they left last night.'

I closed my eyes; of all the times for Claire to be spontaneous, I really wished it hadn't been now.

'Sammi, are you there?'

The silence was now my fault. I faked a laugh. 'Yeah, I'm fine, thanks for telling me. I will act surprised, I promise.'

'Of course, if you want to come to Paris we would be more than happy to help you.'

'Thanks, Cecile, but I better wait until Claire is there to show me around. She would never forgive me if she couldn't take me to her favourite patisserie.'

'Oh, but of course.' Cecile laughed, understanding the passion Claire had for baked goods.

Thanking Cecile and bidding her goodbye, I hung up the phone with an even clearer, if somewhat deflated, purpose.

I might as well go home. There was nothing for me here, now; the thought of booking another tour made me shudder, and the idea of exploring in the footsteps of the Bellissimo tour in order to discover Italy left me with a bad taste in my mouth. Nope, Italy was tainted alright, thanks to Jodie. I dialled the operator, motioning for a pen and paper from Gabriello. No, my mind was clear. I let the fact of my sister's sweet act numb the pain of me going home; at least I'd be able to see and hug her, the true comfort I needed after this disastrous holiday. I could feel my nerves stilling, just thinking of it.

*Home.*

I pulled the cap off the pen with my teeth as I spoke to a sales consultant at Alitalia, asking to book the next flight to Melbourne. I felt good about it; with every click on the other end of the line and the helpful woman rattling off times and dates, I felt in control again, a step closer to home and ready to leave this place once and for all.

'Passport number? Hang on a second, I just have to . . .' I clamped the phone between my ear and shoulder, delving into the side pocket of my bag, rummaging and scraping through the interior, much as I had when trying to find the key with Marcello. A memory of his dark eyes moment-arily distracted me from my mission.

*Not now, Sammi, focus!*

Finally my fingers skimmed over the familiar rectangular passport holder.

'Eureka! Okay, sorry about that, my passport number is . . . oh, God.'

'*Signora?*' The voice on the other end of the phone suddenly sounded faint, and very far away.

'I'll have to call you back,' I said, leaving the phone sitting on its side on the counter as I rummaged more violently through my bag. 'No, this can't be happening, this can't be happening.'

Gabriello placed the receiver gently back on the hook. 'What's wrong?'

'My passport, I can't find my passport!' I shouted, upending my bag onto the floor and sifting through the pile.

*Just breathe, Sammi, it has to be here somewhere. It just has to be.*

Gabriello was by my side in a flash, probably more concerned about calming me down and stopping me from frightening the other guests.

'Stay calm, you will find it. Have you checked your suitcase, your room?'

'I keep it in this bag, in this cover. I always keep it here, it couldn't possibly be anywhere else.'

'Is there anything else missing from your bag?'

I ran my fingers through my hair, before searching more violently through my bag's contents, now strewn all over the floor. 'No, no, everything else is here, just not my passport,' I said, flicking up the navy-blue cover, triple-checking in case I had made a mistake.

'I'll check with housekeeping to see if they have come across anything; Luciano!' Gabriello called out to the front door where he stood. 'Come, help Sammi retrace her steps—she can't find her passport.'

But as Luciano came to my side, reeking again of cigarettes but ready to offer a helping hand, I was resigned to the fact, shaking my head and holding up my hands. 'It's no use, it's gone,' I said, my voice trembling. My eyes welled with hot tears; it was all too much.

'Come on, Sammi, you can't give up like that. People lose their things all the time, even passports, and we always end up finding them,' said Luciano.

'That's right, always slipping down the sides of furniture, or falling onto the floor or under a bed. I will get the entire staff to tear this place apart until we find it,' said Gabriello.

It should have given me hope, but it didn't because I knew it was futile. I knew with a deep-seated bitterness that they would never find it, because I knew exactly where it was—or, more importantly, who had it. I could picture her right now, sitting on a bus winding along the Amalfi Coast, smiling like the Cheshire Cat. Jodie had wanted to destroy me, so well done to her.

She had finally succeeded.

# Chapter Thirty

True to their word, Gabriello and the staff of Hotel Luce del Sole tore the place apart. I humoured them, going through my suitcase, retracing my steps, but I knew it was futile. I knew where it was and all I could do was walk around like a zombie, beyond tears, beyond anger; I felt nothing. With no place to go, no passport and no clue, I simply stood back at reception, staring at the phone, ready to make the call that would no doubt crumble my stoic façade. I was about to tell the very people who didn't believe I could do it—travel overseas, be responsible, be an adult—that they were right. As sympathetic as I knew they would be, I also knew that the first thing that would pop into their minds would be 'I told you so'.

Yep, I was going to call my parents.

'They left without me' would be interpreted as 'I missed the bus'. 'My passport got taken' would be construed as 'I lost it'. 'I have no place to stay, the hotel is booked out' would be 'I have no organisational skills, I can't be left alone in the world'. I could already hear my mother's voice in my head. Feeling like I wanted to vomit into the nearest pot plant, I picked up the receiver for a third time and took in a deep breath. I had no idea what I was being charged for these calls; with my luck, the bill would probably leave me penniless.

The phone was ringing, and with each trill my vision became more blurry as I sniffed and wiped away tears.

*Come on, Sammi, keep it together, keep it together.*

I just really needed something to go my way for once. Was it too much to ask that one of the cleaning staff appear around the corner with a winning smile, holding my passport aloft? I could almost forgive Jodie if it turned out she was innocent of that crime.

With no sudden emergence of a cleaning lady, I was now running out of hope. I just needed a sign, a little helping hand; it didn't have to be big, I wasn't greedy, just something, anything. But then I heard my mother's voice and I closed my eyes, wanting nothing more than the ground to open up and swallow me whole. This was it, the point where my parents' illusion of me was shattered by my own admission.

I opened my eyes, streaks of salty tears carving a path down my face, but I wasn't sobbing—I was too exhausted for that—I was merely leaking.

'Hello, is someone there?'

And just as I was about to speak, my focus shifted towards the desk, searching for a tissue, when I paused, frozen in place by the sight of a small item on the counter.

'Listen, you sicko, I don't know what game you're playing at, but go and breathe down someone else's phone,' my mother shouted, hanging up in my ear. The line went dead, which was the most beautiful sound I had ever heard.

I put the phone down, blindly slotting it back on the receiver, and stood there for a long, long moment, blinking, barely believing what I was seeing. There, on the far end of the reception desk, with the brochures and daily news-papers, was a shiny little card, black and glossy. I reached out and picked it up, holding up the card to the light. I had asked for a sign and, as my tear-stained face broke into a slow smile, I felt that I finally had it.

There, in bold, proud letters across the card, read:

**MARCELLO BAMBOZZI – LOCAL ARTIST.**

Not knowing how many Marcello Bambozzis there were in this part of Italy, I flipped over the card, looking for more information. Sure enough, smiling back at me from a black-and-white image were the dimples I'd become addicted to.

Luciano's voice filtered in from behind me, but still I focused on the card.

'I'm sorry, Sammi, but we haven't been able to find your passport anywhere.'

'Very good,' I said staring at the photo of Marcello, leaning against a wall, looking so cool and casual that he could have been modelling for Ralph Lauren.

'S-sorry, *signora*?'

Oh, right; I spun around, facing a very confused Luciano.

'Luciano, what's this?' I said, passing him the card.

'Oh, Marcello's card.'

'*Si*, but what for?'

It said local artist, but that seemed unlikely; surely he was a tour guide of sorts.

'Marcello is an excellent artist. I am surprised none of you took up his lessons.'

'Lessons, what lessons?'

Luciano seemed intrigued by my response. 'I see,' he said. 'So Maria reneged on her promises.'

'I'm sorry, but I don't know what you're talking about.'

Luciano blinked up at me, suddenly concerned he had said too much.

'Luciano, please, I've had a truly shit day, lay some juicy gossip on me.'

He smiled, glancing at the clock in the lounge. 'Well, I am due for a break—do you have a moment?'

I laughed. 'Luciano, I have nothing but time on my hands.'

~

Luciano sat opposite me, placing down the sweetest gift of all: an espresso.

'*Molto bene, grazie*,' I sighed, picking it up and inhaling the glorious aroma.

'*Prego,*' he said, relaxing in his chair and keeping a watch on the time. The poor fella had a ten-minute break and he was spending it with me. I could tell by the way he was jigging his leg up and down that he was dying for a cigarette; still, maybe that meant that he wouldn't beat around the bush and tell me the deal between Maria and Marcello.

'So?' I prompted.

'So.' Luciano edged closer, lowering his voice. 'Marcello agreed to help Maria with her tour business: making connections with restaurants, showing people around, helping with questions.'

*Bedding the women.*

I slapped that thought from my mind, refocusing on what Luciano was saying.

'In doing so, Maria had to help Marcello in return.'

I was now on the edge of my seat, feeling rather nervous; what did she have to do? Bear his children, marry each other by the time they were thirty, what?

'Marcello wanted Maria to bring her tour group to his studio in order to do a session, a lesson on painting, maybe build in a luncheon and some local knowledge; it is a new thing he's trying and he was relying on Maria to help generate interest and word of mouth.'

'And she backed out?'

'Well, I think she is a bit sceptical about how it would fit into her tour, which is already quite full, as you know. I don't know if she thought it through when she agreed to help.'

I tried to imagine Nate or even Johnny sitting in a light-filled room with an easel in front of them, serenely painting a bowl of fruit. I couldn't see it.

'Seems a bit unfair to not hold up her end of the bargain; why does Marcello bother continuing to help her when she refuses to reciprocate?'

'Oh, I think he thinks he can persuade her, that all he needs to do is convince her it's a good idea.'

It all made sense now; that day when he came to pick me up from the Colosseum they argued about whether or not she had made up her mind. And now she was gone with her group, not even having mentioned Marcello's lesson to them. I suddenly felt angry for him.

'Seriously, he should just cut all ties with her.'

Luciano laughed. 'Well, what's the old saying, blood is thicker than water?'

I paused mid-sip. 'Blood?'

'Si, Maria is his sister.'

Missing my mouth and spilling hot coffee on my shirt, I cared little about the mess or the burn, quickly brushing at my top and placing down my cup. Surely I had misheard. 'WHAT?!'

'It's not something they advertise.'

'Clearly not,' I said, thinking back to all the moments I had felt threatened by Maria, worried that maybe there was something more. And then a memory popped into my head. I had asked Marcello last night how he knew Maria and he had referred to growing up with her.

Ugh! I had read this all wrong.

'So basically it's a whole sibling rivalry thing?'

'I suppose, though I doubt Marcello has much faith in her promises after this group. I think that's why he dropped in those cards—he's trying to drum up business on his own. He only just dropped those in a few days ago. He must have seen the writing on the wall.'

A few days ago? My mind flashed back to the first time our eyes had met, when I had been sitting in this very chair. I wondered if that was the night he put them there. I glanced down at the card, which was now sporting a small coffee stain. It didn't say a whole lot, but it had a number and an address under his photo.

'Luciano, is this far away?' I asked, pointing to the address.

He broke into a broad smile, then took the card from me and, without a word, stood up and started towards the front exit. I did a double-take, following his movements and glancing at the clock; was his time up? He stopped at the front door, looking back at me with his brows raised; it was then I realised he wanted me to follow. Leaving my espresso cup, very little of which had actually made it into my mouth, I quickstepped to the door, thinking that Luciano was hailing a taxi to take me to the cryptic address. I came to stand beside him while Luciano quickly lit a cigarette and revelled in the first deep draw. I moved upwind from the smoke.

'There,' he said, pointing somewhere in front of me.

I followed the direction of his finger, wondering what he was pointing at. I couldn't see anything significant and turned back to him, my eyes questioning.

He simply laughed, handing back the card. 'The house on the left with the green door.'

My eyes dipped to the card and then back up to Luciano.

*Surely not.*

'That's where Marcello lives.'

# Chapter Thirty-One

'He lives *there*?'

Luciano had seemed so pleased with himself, until the moment he registered my horror. I could see a moment of regret flicker in his eyes, an awkward shift in his feet.

'Well, yeah, that's how Hotel Luce del Sole became the choice for the tour group to stay; Marcello recommended it to Maria, as she stays with him when she's in Rome.'

I found myself leaving the conversation abruptly, my attention so focused on the green door that I knocked into strangers' shoulders without apology and ignored their shouts. I don't know what made me madder, the fact that he wasn't honest, or that of all the hotels in Rome, he had to choose the worst so that he and Maria could have a comfortable commute? Now I was really mad, madder than hell. I didn't care if he thought I was crazy, because after this morning I wasn't completely convinced I wasn't.

If I were to bang on his door like a mad woman, all wild eyes and flushed cheeks, he'd probably think I had forgone the trip to stay here, hunt him down and offer to bear his children, which I must admit I'd fantasised about in the wee hours of this morning. I had been excited at finding his business card, thinking I had found one person to turn to for help when I needed it most. I had envisioned crying on his shoulder, maybe even for him to rescue me. But after Luciano's insights, I wondered why I thought I could get help from a person whom I couldn't entirely trust, who had kept the most ridiculous secrets. About his sister, about his address?

After bunk beds, bed bugs and cold showers, I was over it. Over Rome, over Bellissimo Tours and over him! As much as I wanted to back away—the memory of how we parted last night fresh and raw—desperate times called for desperate measures. Slamming the side of my fist against the door in a series of unrelenting thuds, I stood and waited, my heart racing, my patience threadbare as I stepped forward and banged again. I glanced back towards the hotel and saw Luciano standing with his hands on his head, watching on as if he couldn't believe what I was doing. His look of terrified wonder did little to deter me, however, and I spun around, ready to knock again, only this time the door opened.

My stomach dropped as I finally began to think through the possible ramifications of my actions; what if he had a wife, a couple of kids? But as the door swung open there was only him standing before me. He didn't look unhappy; surprised, yes, but not as if he'd been caught out. He just looked like Marcello—warm and lovely, a small smile spreading across his beautiful face as he leant against his doorway and those dark eyes drank me in.

'Sammi?' It was like he was seeing things, like I couldn't possibly be standing there, my fists clenched at my side, my brows pinched together, my face unsmiling. And yet, despite what my façade conveyed, my traitorous heart skipped a beat and I could feel my rage simmer down just from witnessing his smile. All the anger that had driven me here dimmed, and for a fleeting moment I simply wanted to forget it all and leap into his arms, have an almighty meltdown and tell him everything that had gone wrong. How I was homeless and trapped, with no idea what to do or where to go. Marcello must have sensed my despair— surely it was rolling off me in waves—but when he stepped out of his doorway and into the street, it was as if he was checking me over for signs of injury. He reached out for me. 'Are you okay?'

I stepped back, out of reach of his touch, wrapping my arms around myself. I shut down any whimsical, romantic thoughts I had about him and instead channelled my reality, which was enough for the anger to rise once more.

'I need to speak to your sister,' I said, my eyes boring into his.

Marcello slowly let his outstretched hand fall. 'What did she do?'

I scoffed. 'What did she do? She left me fucking behind, that's what.'

Marcello's brows rose, as if he couldn't have foreseen a delicate little flower like me using such language. But God, I was mad, so damn mad, even more so when he asked, 'Were you late? I told you she won't wait for anyone.' Instead of simply nodding, being a little empathetic or, God forbid, cursing her on my behalf, he chose to defend her. My vision flashed red.

'Just because you put up with people letting you down and breaking their word doesn't mean it's something that I will let slide. Maria took second-hand information from Jodie, who told her that I had cancelled the second part of my trip to meet up with my sister.'

Marcello remained silent.

'And to be left behind is one thing, but when Jodie takes my passport along for the ride—'

'She what?'

'She took my passport, and now I have no way of getting home, no hotel booking and no way of finding them to tell them I am stranded.' My voice broke—the last thing I wanted to happen. I just wanted to yell at him and then, I don't even know, maybe go and have a bit of a sook in the hotel lounge area.

Still he didn't invite me in, choosing instead to just stand there, his brows knitted together like he hadn't understood a single thing I had said. And just as I was ready to turn and head back to I-don't-know-where, Marcello laughed, forcing my eyes to snap up at him.

Was he serious? Did he actually find this funny?

He rubbed at the stubble on his chin, as if he was taking it all in.

'And all this before lunchtime; you have had one hell of a morning,' he said, looking at me earnestly.

I squared my shoulders. 'Yes, it's been rather . . .'

'Shit?'

'Yes, shit. Really, really shit,' I said, feeling myself falter, because, try as I might, I couldn't stay mad at him, not with the way he was looking at me now. 'How do you say shit in Italian?' I asked.

'*Merda*,' he said, rolling the word on the tip of his tongue.

'You make even that sound pretty. Why does everything sound better when you say it?'

He smiled and, damn him, those dimples were back. That was clearly unfair. I tried to remain focused, clearing my throat and sticking to the business at hand.

'So if you can get Maria to call me . . .' I paused.

*Where? On what number, genius? You have no place to go.*

'I need to tell her what happened, and that she better check with Jodie about my passport; if nothing else, I need that back.'

'She won't have her phone on until tonight.'

*Yeah, because she's so professional*, I thought bitterly.

I sighed. 'Whatever—just get her to call the hotel,' I said, turning away.

'I thought you said you were homeless?' Marcello called out after me.

But I kept walking; this time rage didn't carry me back. All I felt was complete and utter disappointment.

~

The cold, hard facts of life were that you couldn't rely on anyone other than yourself, so as I set up my makeshift office in the lounge area of Hotel Luce del Sole, I drew on an even deeper well of determination—or whatever you call three espressos on an empty stomach.

I had studied the itinerary, phoning each hotel that was listed and leaving a message for Maria at every location. She may have her phone switched off but there would be no avoiding me when the front desk staff handed her a note to call the crazed Aussie tourist at Hotel Luce del Sole as a matter of emergency. I had even left a message at the travel agency, so the first thing they would be hearing Monday morning was a diatribe about the failings of humankind, what were we all doing on this crazy, mixed-up planet, and I how really needed to cut down on the caffeine. Gabriello was kindly going to look after all of my incoming messages, should Maria call after I had left; my next port of call was to find alternative accommodation for however long it took to sort this all out. As much as I hated staying here, I had taken comfort in the kindness of the staff, and in a strange way I had become accustomed to the less-than-glamorous lifestyle: did that make me a true backpacker?

By lunch I was sick with hunger, wired from all the caffeine and calling, yet strangely impressed with myself. I hadn't spoken to my parents once, never alerted anyone back home to the fact that anything was amiss, I was simply getting on with it.

'Sammi, I have booked you a room at the Scalinta di Spagna. It's not far from here and I know Mario, who works there—he will take care of you. Check-in is at two.' Gabriello handed me a folded-up piece of paper.

'*Grazie*, Gabriello—you have been such a lifesaver. I'm sorry I've tied up your phone line.'

'Don't worry about it.' He waved my words away. 'You could probably walk to the hotel but Luciano can take you and your luggage; in the meantime you can stay here as long as you need.'

'Thank you,' I said, trying to not let the emotion flood me as I looked up at the kind man. 'If there's a cancellation, please still let me know.'

Gabriello chuckled. 'Once you check into your new hotel, I don't think you're going to want to come back here.'

'Oh, I don't know, it has its charm,' I said, thinking only of the hospitality.

Regardless, Gabriello straightened with pride. Maybe he didn't hear many nice things from people around here, so seeing his face light up kind of made me feel sorry for the way I had behaved.

'Did you want another coffee?

'Oh, no, *grazie*, I am done,' I said, pushing my empty cup towards him.

He smiled, taking it from me and walking back to his station; this time I swear he had a spring in his step. I, on the other hand, despite all the caffeine, felt utterly spent. I slumped back in my wingback chair, studying the strewn papers covered with the mad scribblings of a woman on a mission. For all my running around I still hadn't got very far, and I didn't feel all that hopeful. What if Jodie had flung my passport out the window somewhere along the Amalfi Coast? I wouldn't put it past her. No, I would not feel at ease until Maria and the group returned to Rome, and a week felt like a lifetime away. I only hoped that I could make the best of a bad situation and last the remaining days. I breathed out a laugh; how ironic that, since arriving, all I had wanted was to be on my own, away from the giggling girls and the woo-hooing boys. Now I had got my wish: I had woken up and they had disappeared.

I guess it's really true what they say.

Be careful what you wish for.

# Chapter Thirty-Two

I closed my eyes for the briefest of moments, pressed back in my comfy wingback chair, thinking that if only I had mastered the art of meditation then I might have stood a chance of blocking out the noise all around me: the footsteps, the chatter, the animated Italian conversations that sounded boisterous at the best of times.

*Block it all out.*

And I did just that until I heard the rather irritating sound of suitcase roller wheels on the marble floor nearing me. Seriously, couldn't they sit somewhere else? Couldn't they see this was the only comfort I had right now?

Gabriello called out, 'It is your funeral, my friend.' And I wasn't sure to what he was referring or to whom he was speaking, but I smiled in answer anyway. A shadow fell over me and, combined with the halting of the roller wheels, I knew that someone was standing before me. I frowned; was it two o'clock already? Had I snoozed? I blinked my eyes open, expecting to see Luciano waiting to transport me to my new accommodation. When I looked up to see Marcello there, towering over me, his face pensive and serious, I straightened, a panic lodging in my chest at the unexpectedness of his presence.

'What are you doing here?' I blurted out.

He had my green cardigan: the very one I had left with my bags was now draped over his arm, which he unhooked and threw on top of me; it was then I realised, my eyes dipping down, that he was holding my suitcase at his side.

*What the . . . ?*

'Let's go!' he said, turning to exit the building as if the request was non-negotiable.

'Whoa! Wait a minute!' I yelled, struggling to get out of my chair. Hobbling after him, I hoped that my leg would wake up sometime soon.

'What are you doing?'

'You need a place to stay,' he said, shrugging one lazy shoulder.

My jaw went slack. 'I have a place to stay.'

'Not anymore: I told Gabriello to cancel the booking.'

'You did what?' This time, despite my anger and state of distraction, I managed to dodge people in my path as we marched down the street.

'Maria is going to contact me first, so it makes sense that you be there when the call comes.'

'I have left a million messages in every possible place she is headed—I don't need you at all.'

He turned to me with a devilish twinkle in his eyes. 'Now, that just hurts my feelings.'

I rolled my eyes, moving to reach for the handle of my luggage, but he pulled it out of reach. 'Look, I know Stockholm syndrome romances are really big right now, but I have no intention of being locked up in your tower.'

Marcello glanced up at his house as if he took exception to my words.

'Seriously, I have booked into a hotel, I have everything sorted. I will be fine.'

Marcello studied my face, as if he didn't quite buy what I was selling, probably because I didn't believe it myself.

'Lunch is ready: do you like cheese?'

I glowered. 'Don't you dare play the cheese card.'

*A totally unfair advantage.*

A smirk formed, like he was dealing me a hand and he knew he had an ace up his sleeve. 'Once you've tasted Rosalia's bruschetta, you are not going to want to leave.'

I curved my brow. 'Oh? And who is Rosalia? Another secret sister? Or a secret wife?'

Marcello laughed. 'Ah, beautiful Rosalia. She is more like an adopted *nonna*—she takes care of me.'

'And now you want to take care of me?' I mused, hoping that he might say yes, but knowing I would probably be mad if he did. *Damned if you do and damned if you don't,* I thought.

Marcello looked at me, weighing up how best to answer. Smart man.

He said nothing, instead stepping closer to me and causing my heart to skip a beat. I was prepared for words, ready with a comeback on the tip of my tongue, but I wasn't prepared for the feeling of support at my back and the warm sensation of Marcello's body pressed up against mine as his dark brown eyes looked at me.

'You must be hungry.' His words were low, deep, and had my mind whirling; was he talking about food or something else? Either way, my mouth watered and I swallowed deeply, my eyes flicking down to his mouth.

'I am a little.'

Marcello smiled, knowing he had me just where he wanted me, then opened the door and pushed it wide with his back.

'*La mia casa è la tua casa*—my house is your house!'

His voice echoed as we walked into the entrance, Marcello pulling my suitcase along behind him on the marble floor. He dumped his keys and sunglasses on a table near the doorway, a totally ordinary thing to do, but this was anything but an ordinary house. We walked past large, ornate columns to a grand curved staircase, but despite the splendour of the surrounds, the first thing that hit me was the mouth-watering smells that filled the home. My belly rumbled its betrayal and, as much as I didn't want to admit it, based on that smell alone there'd be no getting rid of me.

It seemed Marcello had heard the rumblings of my empty stomach, too, as he led me straight up the stairs.

He may not have lived in an actual tower, but it was close: we ascended a tall, winding staircase, flooded with natural light, to the upper levels, where the aroma of food became more intense and the sound of a woman singing made me soften a little.

'Rosalia, c'è qualcuno che vorrei che tu incontri,' Marcello called out as we reached the top level.

'Are you asking her to put a sedative in my food?'

Marcello laughed. 'Of course not, I am asking her to get the shackles ready so I can chain you to your bed.'

I laughed too, something I instantly regretted as my cackle echoed so loudly in the space that I sounded like a mad woman.

Marcello smiled broadly as I slapped my hand over my mouth, mortified as he led me to a door and pushed it open.

I tentatively stepped inside. My feet skimmed along the aged parquetry flooring as I entered the light-flooded room that was ten times the space of my hotel dungeon. Large windows overlooked rooflines of tan-coloured buildings, broken up by potted green plants on neighbouring rooftops. The bed was enormous, tucked tightly with white, crisp sheets that I couldn't stop myself from running my hand over, fantasising about taking a running leap and dive-bombing into the pillow tower.

*Calm down, Sammi, no need to get carried away.*

Marcello opened a beautifully carved, baroque-inspired wardrobe, the kind you might find in Marie Antoinette's boudoir. He placed my suitcase inside and tilted his head in the opposite direction. 'The room has its own bathroom.'

My heart swelled, and I tried to walk casually to where he motioned, barely containing the giddy squeal building inside me. The bathroom was more like a Roman bathhouse, bejewelled with mosaic tiles and featuring a large recessed bath and open shower with a seat. There'd be no worrying about whacking my elbows on the shower door, or shifting piles of dirty towels on the floor as I fought my way to the make-up-trashed vanity; I could almost feel a tear coming, the bathroom was so beautiful.

I caught the reflection of Marcello in the mirror, leaning in the doorway and watching me with a satisfied smile. 'You know you are staying, right?'

I turned to him, leaning against the marble vanity. I regarded him for a long moment, wishing that I was stubborn enough to tell him where to go. Who was I kidding?

'You had me at cheese.'

# Chapter Thirty-Three

Marcello left me to freshen up for lunch: a glorious, long shower, a fresh set of clothes and the promised dive bomb onto my new bed. I was finally allowing myself to revel in my excitement over having a real room, quite the shift in behaviour from this morning's depression, and hardly befitting of someone who had lost her passport. I lifted up onto my elbows, looking around at the space with its lofty, frescoed ceilings and marble mosaic detailing. Everything was light, bright and vast, perhaps all the more so when compared to the dingy accommodation I'd had until now. Had I started off my Italian adventure in such a way, would I have had a completely different outlook? Most definitely.

I opened the enormous panelled door leading me out to the hall, straining my neck to see the curved ceilings and wondering how they swept the cobwebs up there. As big as the apartment was, I wasn't worried about getting lost; I simply had to follow the smells and the singing. Rosalia's rendition of 'Blame It on the Boogie' made me smile as I walked along, exploring the home until I reached a set of large double doors. I wondered where they led to. Was this Marcello's bedroom? A ballroom, maybe? I reached out and touched the carved detailing of the moulding.

'You must be hungry.' Marcello's voice made me jump, and I pulled my hand back as if I had been caught doing something I shouldn't. Despite my intrigue and awe, I had to remind myself that I was a guest, and snooping was probably not a great look.

'What's in there?' I asked, hoping that it might prompt a house tour, but Marcello seemed uncomfortable with the question.

'Nothing. Lunch is ready,' he said, shutting down the inquiry.

*Right. Keep your questions to yourself.*

As he led me away from the doors and towards the kitchen, I couldn't help but hope that he wasn't entirely joking about the shackles. Could a pleasure room lie behind those double doors? I could be convinced to experiment . . .

'Rosalia, this is Sammi, the one I have been telling you about.'

I looked around the kitchen, startled to find that Rosalia was standing right before me, so tiny that I had almost missed her altogether.

'Oh, hello,' I said.

Looking up at me was a weathered face, framed by silver hair tucked neatly in a bun and lit up with sparkling, kind eyes. Thanks to the lessons of various films and TV shows, I expected her to embrace me and then usher me to sit, and start piling up food in front of me while exclaiming how terribly thin I was. Instead she turned her attention to Marcello, unleashing a loud, free-flowing tirade of Italian that had me flinching and looking at Marcello.

Jesus, what had I done now? It didn't sound good. If Marcello turned to me and told me to get my things and get out of his house, I wouldn't be surprised. Instead, I watched his profile as he listened to her intently, giving her his undivided attention. I stood frozen in place, not sure if the twisting sensation at the base of my stomach was hunger pains or fear as I watched the little old lady wave her arms around as she spoke without taking a breath.

'Is everything okay?' I murmured out of the corner of my mouth, trying not to draw attention to myself.

Marcello broke into a broad smile, nodding his head. 'Ah, yes, she said that you are very beautiful.'

I cocked my brow. 'Is that all that she said?'

'Mostly,' he said, leading me to the table, leaving Rosalia to mumble at the stove and cross her heart, as if praying for the strength to get through lunch.

We came to a table, where I expected to see, at most, some crusty bread and minestrone soup dished up for us. Wrong! This wasn't lunch, this was a feast. You couldn't see the surface of the table for food.

'Are you expecting company?' I asked, my ravenous eyes roaming over the dishes.

Marcello laughed. 'No, just us, but you're hungry, right?' he said, pulling a chair out for me.

'Umm, would you judge me if I said I was relieved I don't have to share?'

'Not at all.'

A bowl slammed down onto the table, followed by another verbal onslaught that continued all the way through the kitchen, out of the room and down the hall. I sat, unmoving, remembering to breathe when it seemed the coast was clear.

'So Rosalia is not joining us for lunch, then?'

Marcello shook his head. 'She'll have a nap now, rest up for the next course. She's only small,' he laughed.

'But incredibly feisty.'

'Oh, *si, molto*.'

I loved it when he broke into his language, even if only a word or two; the way he rolled his tongue around the words caused a shiver to run through me; I knew how incredibly clever his tongue could be.

'Sammi?' I blinked back into the here and now, looking blankly at the plate Marcello held out to me.

'Where did you go?'

'Oh, nowhere,' I lied. 'Wow, will you look at all this food, Rosalia does take care of you.'

'She does,' he agreed, spooning a serving of thick spaghetti smothered in a rich tomato sauce and stringy cheese. Marcello couldn't have passed it over quickly enough. 'We may not be blood, but Rosalia is my family.'

There was something rather beautiful in Marcello's words, the way he had said them, meant them. Looking at him from across the table, I had no doubt that in this big, old house, being yelled at, fussed over, cared for by a feisty old lady was something Marcello would love. I saw it in the endearing way he had looked at her, despite her tirade. It was a true insight into his character. I didn't know when or how Rosalia came into his life, but there was one thing for certain: they really were family; it even had me missing my own, which was most unexpected. Despite the lovely aromas and colourful display of mouth-watering dishes, my mood dimmed as I began to run my fork through my pasta.

'Listen, I don't want you to worry about your passport. Maria has her faults but she won't let that kind of thing pass. She is going to feel terrible when she finds out the truth.'

I swallowed a big mouthful of salty, delicious carbs.

*Oh, sure, Maria's a real stand-up gal.*

It's amazing how clean sheets, hot showers and amazing food can make depressing experiences seem like a lifetime away. So enamoured was I with my current situation that I kind of hoped Maria wouldn't call back. The spaghetti was so bloody amazing that I wouldn't mind if my passport was never found.

'I know she didn't mean to leave me behind—it's not her fault.'

'Well, she should have checked with you directly,' he said, breaking a piece of crusty bread.

'Yes, but what is done is done. As long as I get my passport back in one piece, it'll all be okay. But I never want to think about Bellissimo Tours ever again.' I half laughed, trying to spear some pasta with my fork without success. Marcello's silence made me glance up at him; a crease etched across his brow as he examined his glass of water in deep contemplation.

Then I realised the error of my words. 'Oh, hey, look, I didn't mean to bag the tour, I just think that tours in general probably aren't for me. I mean, I'm not exactly worldly, so I think I just need to be eased into things—I'm a bit of a sook like that,' I said, trying to lighten the mood.

'No, you are right. Maria has a lot to learn when it comes to business,' he said darkly, and I knew I had hit a nerve.

We both grew quiet, and after a while I actually wished for Rosalia to come back to yell some more. I didn't know how to restart the conversation; should I comment on the food, the weather? It was going to be a long meal.

'Just to be clear, I actually found your business card at the hotel.'

Marcello's eyes flicked up from his meal.

'You know, just in case you were worried that I might have stalked you. I didn't.'

'Well, that's disappointing,' he said, tucking back into his food.

'I know, it's not nearly as interesting, but what is rather interesting is that you're an artist . . . I never knew that. I felt as subtle as a brick, trying to work in a neat segue to the topic I was most curious about.

He shrugged. 'I didn't mention it.'

Ugh, this was not going to be easy—it was like trying to communicate with a surly teenager. Perhaps it was this closed-off part of him, the one that appeared so cold and professional, that made his career choice so surprising? I glanced at his hands: they were big and strong, and felt amazing against my skin, tipped with perfectly squared, immaculate nails. These were the hands of an artist? There were no telling signs.

'So, what kind of art do you do?' I pressed.

He shifted in his seat, clearly wishing we could be talking about something else.

*Interesting.*

The usually composed, almost perpetually cocky Marcello had a weakness, and it was linked to his passion.

'Buildings, streetscapes, landscapes.' He sounded bored, trying to play it down; it made me even more curious. But then I thought, *What if he wasn't any good? What if the reason Maria was so reluctant to involve her business with his was because he was talentless? Had she told him that? Was that why he was so reluctant to share?*

He sighed. 'Do you want to see?'

I blinked. 'See what?'

'The paintings?'

Did I? If they were really hideous, I didn't know if I'd be able to fake it. I met an ugly baby once—the mother and I were no longer friends. Some things you just couldn't fake.

'Ah, sure, love to!'

Marcello seemed to melt in relief, his shoulders dipping as if he had been tensing them for the whole conversation.

'Okay,' he said, nodding.

'Great!' I lied, digging back into my pasta, the same thought rolling over and over in my mind.

*Oh, please, be good, please, be good.*

# Chapter Thirty-Four

Curiously, we were standing back at the double doors. 'You will have to excuse the mess—I'm not expecting anyone until tomorrow,' he said, rubbing the back of his neck and seemingly stalling for time. He was a fascinating character study in a moment like this; in his home Marcello seemed almost like a small boy, vulnerable and uncertain.

'What's tomorrow?'

'I have a class. A tour group is stopping by.'

'Oh, really? That sounds awesome.'

'Yeah, my friend Giovanni runs some day tours around Rome. He has kindly included me on one of his days.'

We continued standing there, neither one of us moving, until it started to get a little ridiculous. Just as I was about to tell him that he didn't have to show me if he didn't want to, Marcello pushed the giant doors inwards, stepping into the room and revealing what lay beyond.

'Oh, my . . .'

My words fell away; it took me a moment to step forward, to take in the entire space. Dust particles danced in the air in beams of sunlight, momentarily distracting me from the scene. Drop sheets, easels and flecks of paint dotted the aged wooden floors and shelves of paints and brushes, charcoals and pallets overflowed on industrial-style shelving. I could imagine that Marcello was now wishing he kept his things in better order. But aside from the impressive space, the sprawling art supplies and the eclectic energy imbued in every corner of the room, it was nothing compared to what stood on the easel.

'Oh, yeah, that's not finished yet.' Marcello came to stand next to me, scratching his jaw and fidgeting in great discomfort. I tore my eyes away from the canvas to look at him, hoping that he could see the sincerity in my eyes when I said, 'This is incredible.'

Marcello stared at me, his eyes flicking across my face as if looking to see if I was joking. But I was deadly serious.

'So, you like it?'

I turned back to the giant painting, a scenery of oranges and yellows offset with blue and grey skies, broken by green pops of trees that twisted up into the air. It was colourful and textured, structured yet natural; it was like it was breathing, it was the strangest thing.

I shook my head. 'Marcello, you need to change your business card.'

Marcello stared at me, my meaning completely lost on him.

'Why is that?'

'Because it needs to read Marcello Bambozzi: Motherfucking ARTIST!'

I think I shocked him—no, I know I did—his brows disappearing into his hairline. I thought it might have been a step too far, a bit too crass, but then the biggest, broadest, most blinding smile appeared.

'So, how would you say that in Italian?' I grinned, turning fully to him now.

'*Madre cazzo d'artista.*' He almost sang it with pride, and it sounded kind of beautiful. A gasp sounded by the open doorway and we turned to see Rosalia standing with a drink tray, mouth agape and shaking her head, casting us a look so severe it could strip lead paint. She waddled away, the tray clinking all the way to the kitchen.

Marcello winced, then we looked at each other like a couple of naughty schoolkids who had been caught out.

'Oh, dear, I think Rosalia is going to think I am a bad influence on you.'

Marcello burst out laughing. 'Well, I really hope so,' he said, a devious sparkle in his dark eyes.

I could feel myself blush, knowing that when Marcello was on game I never stood a chance against him. Thankfully he saved me from myself, breaking the tension.

'Do you want to see my inspiration?'

I tilted my head, intrigued.

'Sure.'

And although he didn't need to, he grabbed my hand and laced his fingers with mine. It was the strangest sensation, to be touched in such a simple way, yet to be so grounded by it. I didn't want to feel it last night, that connection, knowing I would have to let it go, but now it was back. I lost my breath, and I know he felt it too—I could see it in his face. Gone were all traces of humour; instead, he simply pulled me into step, breaking the trance a little.

'Let's go.'

~

As the elevator door closed behind us, I grinned from ear to ear, my delight apparent when I turned to Marcello.

'What?' he laughed.

'You have an elevator.' I beamed.

Marcello shook his head. 'You are mad.'

'True, but happily mad!' I said, delighted that I had been saved from the ludicrous amount of stairs.

'Still, Rosalia must be grateful for this.'

'You would think so, but she refuses to use it.'

'What?'

'She will use only the stairs—she calls the elevator "*la trappola mortale*".'

The elevator reached the top floor, bouncing to a stop, the doors slowly sliding to the side.

'And what does that mean?'

Marcello stood to the side, placing his hands on the divider to keep the doors open.

'Death trap,' he said with a cheeky wink.

That was all the translation I needed, and I dived out of the elevator. 'Ah, you know what, I think stairs are under-rated. Good exercise and all that.'

Marcello's laugh echoed down the wide, expansive space. I squinted a little, the sun reflecting off the marble floor. My shoes clicked on the floor, so I could only imagine how Maria's would sound. Marcello reached a thick iron door, pushing at it with considerable effort; a cool breeze blasted us, whipping my hair from my shoulders as we stepped through.

'Marcello—' My breath caught. And although I wanted to turn to him, to say something, it just wasn't possible, I was too much in awe of what I was seeing. Before me was Marcello's muse, the same view portrayed in his painting. It was breathtaking, made even more beautiful by his inter-pretation of it.

'It's funny, depending on the cloud, or sun, the colours are always changing; I could paint this view a thousand different ways.'

I shifted my eyes from the view, turning to him. 'You have to paint them all.'

He laughed, but it petered out when he saw my serious expression.

I stepped closer to him: he had to know. 'You have to, Marcello, you have to paint them all. You're so bloody talented, yet you have a business card sitting on the desk of a shitty hotel and the whole world is passing you by. I reckon Maria has done you a favour: you shouldn't be wasting your time on hungover backpackers who are more interested in the next power hour at a nightclub.'

I had probably said too much, getting involved in something that wasn't my business, but the thought of Jodie or Nate slouched in Marcello's studio painting penises on their canvasses made my blood boil.

'You make it sound so simple.'

'It is simple!' I as good as shouted. 'Look at this place, it's amazing; where do you host your classes?'

'In the studio.'

I grabbed his arm. 'Bring them up here.'

Marcello's eyes went from my hand on his arm to the horizon, his focus intense, the cogs in his mind turning.

'Target the right age demographic. Charge them double and offer Roman terrace workshops. You can offer a traditional Italian feast prepared lovingly by Rosalia.'

A small smile curved the corner of his mouth. 'It would stop the waste of our food.'

'Yes! See? Do it!'

'How is it that in the space of one afternoon you have managed to come up with the solution to all of my problems?' He looked at me now like I was some kind of mythical unicorn; it was the kind of look a girl could get addicted to.

'Because sometimes something wonderful can be in front of you the whole time—you just don't see it.'

As stunning as the view was, the ever-impressive panorama of the Eternal City blasted with colour, in that moment nothing compared to the beauty of Marcello's eyes. So soft, yet dark and intense, I swear they were the one thing I would never forget about my trip; the next being the bow shape of his lips or the way it felt when he brushed the back of his knuckles against my cheek as he was now, moving into me and running his fingers down my neck and across my collarbone. His eyes traced the path of his fingers, only to lift and lock with my eyes once more as he leaned into me, his lips oh-so-close to mine, his breath hot against my mouth.

'I see you,' he whispered, and just as he leaned in to close the small distance between us, a loud, jangly tone rang in the air, killing the moment and slicing the serenity of the rooftop terrace. Marcello cursed, drawing back and reaching into his pocket, annoyed until he checked the screen, his eyes flicking up to me. 'It's Maria.'

# Chapter Thirty-Five

I sat in the kitchen, my elbows resting on the spotless table top where Rosalia had cleaned the entire kitchen within an inch of its life; you would never have guessed we'd feasted here just an hour ago. I sat there, my head in my hands, never wanting to show my face again.

I felt warmth at my shoulder as Marcello's hands rubbed calming circles on my back.

'Sammi,' he said gently, trying to coax me to look at him.

'I can't believe I made Maria cry.' My voice was muffled through my hands.

'She's tougher than you think.'

I ran my hands through my hair, sighing. 'Is that a Bambozzi trait, is it?'

'I like to think so.'

'Oh yeah, and who instilled that, your Mama Bambozzi or your Papa Bambozzi?'

It was an innocent enough question, a little tongue in cheek even, or so I had thought, but there was something in Marcello's eyes that looked almost haunted.

My small smile fell away. 'Sorry, you don't have to answer that.'

'No, it's okay.' But he didn't continue; he just sat there with that faraway look in his eyes. The mood had turned my own despair to his, and I really wished that I hadn't said anything. I was all but ready to shift the focus back to me and my seemingly first-world dramas. I went to speak, ready to shatter the silence, but something worse broke through, the unexpected words of an unguarded Marcello.

'Our parents died when we were very young.'

Marcello looked at me, but unusually he didn't hold my stare. I could feel my cheeks burn and my throat tighten.

'I'm so sorry.'

Marcello smiled, but it was small, and sad. 'You didn't honestly think that a struggling artist would be able to live in a place like this?'

It was almost as if I could hear the penny dropping in my brain, spinning and falling and clattering, painfully loud. Marcello had been such a mystery to me—I had never even questioned how he came to be living in the heart of the city, just he and Rosalia and possibly a wayward sister. Now it all made sense.

Inheritance.

Sensing my unease, Marcello moved to stand, in part distracting me with a glass he retrieved from a top cupboard. He filled it with water from the fridge and held it out to me.

'And don't be too concerned by Maria's tears: she will channel her embarrassment into determination. You heard her, she is going to get to the bottom of this and will bring back your passport.'

I had no doubt she would; even if she had to hold Jodie's head under water in a Venetian canal, she would get to the bottom of this.

'So, just allow her to make amends: bringing the passport and refunding you your money will make her feel a little better about what has happened.'

I knew all these things, but I still felt bad. My intention wasn't to make Maria feel like she had failed, I just wanted ... well, I wasn't so sure anymore. I was beyond exhausted. I ran my hands through my hair, breathing out a long, weary breath.

'Why don't you go lie down—I'll wake you when dinner is ready.' Marcello rubbed the back of my neck and it was like he flicked a switch: my eyes closed briefly and I felt instantly fatigued.

'To be honest, I don't think I will be able to eat for days. I think I'll just slip into a food coma, if that's alright?'

'Rosalia's cooking has taken down full-grown men, I understand.' He shifted his hand to squeeze my knee before moving from the table to refill my glass.

'*Grazie mille,*' I said, holding the cool glass next to my burning cheeks.

'Listen to you—you sound like a local. You'd fit in well here.'

'Ha! Sure, just as long as you could guide me around so I don't get lost.'

'I could do that,' he said, unfazed.

'Yeah, well.' I pushed my chair out and stood, feeling the fatigue of a stressful day seeping into my bones. 'You'd soon get sick of me.'

Marcello grinned cheekily. 'Probably.'

I punched him playfully in the arm. 'Well, the sooner Maria gets back with my passport, the better,' I said, swaggering out of the kitchen; it was only when I was well down the hall that my smile slipped away, thinking about that very reality. As I turned into my room, I was so lost in my thoughts that I didn't notice Rosalia until she coughed, making me jump.

'Jesus, Rosalia, you scared me.'

She looked rather pleased about it; it was an unnerving thing, having a little old lady laying in wait for me, surveying me with distrust. She was clearly no fan of mine. I wondered if she was here to yell at me again, until I realised the real reason for her visit.

Rosalia had turned down my sheets and placed fresh towels and a bar of soap on the end of my bed. My life had done a complete one-eighty, going from bed bugs to five-star service in less than a day. I could feel my eyes getting a little misty.

'Aww, *grazie*, Rosalia,' I said, my hand on my heart, watching her waddle slowly from the bed towards the door. She paused next to me, looking up at me with her soulful eyes, assessing. I realised then that Rosalia didn't hate me—she was just taking my measure. She was a smart lady.

I smiled, nodding my head in appreciation.

Only then did a little smile form and I felt mildly victorious, until she spoke, pointing a crooked finger up at me. 'You hurt him, I hurt you.'

My brows rose, and I felt both shocked and terrified. I simply nodded my head, and she shuffled out of my room without a backward glance. It was perhaps the quickest lesson I had learned since being in Rome: whatever you do, don't mess with Rosalia.

# Chapter Thirty-Six

I thought the sun might have woken me up—a foreign concept of late—but it was the voices that did it. The laughter and the slide of furniture across floorboards had me sitting up and looking around, trying to get my bearings. I could have stayed in bed all day. The mattress was like a giant sedative, so insanely plush and cosy; it took an immense amount of willpower to peel back the sheets and pad my way to the wardrobe.

It wasn't until I opened it that I realised all my things had been unpacked, either hanging or folded neatly and placed in drawers. Oh, God, I even had my own little knicker drawer. I cringed. Rosalia had seen all my unmentionables, including the French knickers I had packed 'in case'. Having climbed straight into bed after my pow-wow with her, I hadn't realised her turndown service had gone to the next level. Even my toiletries in the bathroom were lined up like perfect little soldiers; it would have been a little disturbing if it wasn't so sweet.

Showering with no thought for time, and free from the paranoia of being barged in on by a hungover back-packer needing to take a leak, I savoured every droplet, lathering myself into a frenzy and filling the entire room with steam.

As I got dressed I could still hear the voices, and I wondered if I should venture out of my room. Though Marcello had told me to treat his place like a home away from home, it was still strange and new. With only the sun for reference, I knew that it was day, but not what time, and the timelessness combined with the restorative effects of sleep and a shower had me feeling reborn.

Without thinking too much about why, I put partic-ular effort into making myself look nice, but not too nice; something told me that Rosalia would be watching me like a hawk in her attempt to safeguard her adoptive grandson's heart. So I kept well away from the red dress, opting for the casual, sun-kissed tourist look, with shorts, sandals and my tan leather shoulder bag. Dabbing on some berry lip gloss and the last dribble of Calvin Klein perfume, I was ready to venture out for the day, wherever it might take me.

I opened my door just enough to peer through, and to better hear the conversation happening below. The laughter settled and I could only make out Marcello's unmistak-able voice. I opened the door and slowly stepped along the hall, seeing the light spill through the opened doors to Marcello's studio, where the voices were coming from. I had no way of walking to the kitchen without being seen, and I paused for a moment, torn between walking past without making eye contact, pretending I was unaware of the room's occupants, or doubling back to my room and waiting until the guests had left, however long that took. I chose the former, taking in a breath, lifting my chin and walking as lightly as I could, trying to channel the ghost-like presence of Rosalia.

*I'm not here, I'm not here, I'm not here . . .*

'Sammi!' Marcello's voice sounded from behind me.

*Crap!*

I turned on my heel, feigning surprise. 'Morning,' I said, turning to face Marcello at the door of his studio, and seeing we had a captive audience.

'Sleep well?' he asked, drying one of his brushes with a paint-speckled towel slung over his shoulder.

'Amazing.'

'*Magnifico.*' He beamed. 'Come, I want you to meet some people.'

'Oh, I don't want to intrude . . .' I protested, but it was no use. Marcello took me by the hand and dragged me into the studio. Suddenly seven sets of eyes were upon me.

'Everyone, this is Sammi from Australia.' I waved, wanting nothing more than to slink away.

'Well, ain't she a doll; hey, Marcello, do you think we can paint your friend?' a big-bellied man with a Texan drawl chuckled.

The woman to his side, who I assumed was his wife, gave him a playful tap. 'Eddie, shush. Look, you've turned her all red now.'

'Oh, no, don't mind me, I am perpetually sunburnt.'

Everyone laughed, tilting their heads like I was simply adorable. What an easy crowd to please.

A man from the back slid from his stool and came over to me. 'Giovanni,' he said, offering his hand. 'It is nice to meet you, Sammi.'

'Oh, Giovanni, you're the tour guide?'

'*Si*, someone has to keep the rabble in check.'

'He's the worst of us all,' interjected another lady, wearing a pink sun visor paired interestingly with a pearl necklace.

Once again the laughter that had pierced through my sleep sounded again; they were most definitely a different kind of clientele than Maria would have brought along. You could just tell that Marcello would have them eating out of the palm of his hand. A group of, mostly, women in their twilight years, and one lone husband who had no doubt tagged along to humour his wife, they all sported matching white T-shirts that read 'Golden Slumbers Tours', and had the image of a sun setting over the ocean. It sounded more like a retirement home, but the matching T-shirts was a nice touch, and probably prevented them from getting lost in one of the world's busiest cities. Giovanni was sure to have his hands full.

Marcello turned to me, lowering his voice. 'Are you doing anything today?'

'Um, I don't have anything planned.' I felt my heart rate increase a little, hoping that he might have something in mind.

'Well, do you want to stick around? There's something I want to give you, but I won't be finished here for about an hour—is that okay?'

*Give me something?*

'Sure, I can wait.'

Marcello smiled. 'Good.'

'Hey, lover boy, we're on the clock, you know.'

Marcello turned. 'Shall we all head up?'

Excitement rippled through the group as they moved into motion, grabbing their packs and canvasses. Marcello walked with me out of the studio, reading the question on my face.

Marcello smiled. '*Sì*, I am taking them to the roof terrace.'

I wanted to throw my arms around him, glad he was listening to my suggestion, but instead stepped to the side to let the group of laughing Americans through.

'Come on, son, give her a kiss and tell her you'll see her later.' The Texan whacked Marcello on the shoulder, and I could have sworn I saw him blush, but he didn't move; instead, he stood there looking more intent.

'See you in a bit,' I said, wishing the minutes away so I could see what it was he had to give me.

Marcello nodded before turning from me to catch up to the group. Glancing quickly back to me, his eyes made a silent promise. It made the butterflies in my stomach dance, or it could have been hunger. I wandered into the kitchen, amazed that I could eat again after yesterday. On the table sat a basket of breads and pastries, and a bowl of fresh fruit. My mouth watered in anticipation. Alongside the spread sat a note:

*Sammi, use the phone and call home if you want; let your family know you're okay.*
    *M*

*P.S. Juice is in the fridge.*

I shook my head—he really had thought of everything. As far as my family knew, I was heading for a gondola ride in Venice today. Although I had never been there, and I was sure it would have been lovely, there was something seriously lovely about sitting in Marcello's kitchen, eating baked goods and drinking freshly squeezed orange juice. I might have been missing out on being serenaded while cruising along the canals, but I didn't feel too bad at all. In fact, as I plucked a grape from the basket and popped it into my mouth, I realised I had never felt so bloody content.

# Chapter Thirty-Seven

It was rather comical speaking to my mum, knowing that we were both hiding the truth from each other. I had no doubt that my sister was sitting in the background, miming questions to her; I could tell from the uneasy, wooden conversation.

'And is the weather nice?' she asked.

'Yeah, you already asked me that, Mum—it's lovely.'

'Oh, right. So what's been your favourite part of the tour so far?'

My mind flashed to an image of Marcello's head between my legs. I cleared my throat and pushed that out of my mind.

'Oh, um, the, ah, Pantheon was pretty amazing,' I stammered. I could only hope that I wasn't on loudspeaker; Claire would be picking up on my weirdness with her older sister's intuition.

'Ah, anyway, Mum, I better go. We've got another jam-packed day planned.'

'Oh, yes, of course, you best hurry. Don't want to get left behind.'

I bit my lip trying to contain myself.

*If only she knew.*

'Okay, well, give my love to Dad.'

*And Claire and Louis.*

'I will—love you, be safe.'

'Love you too.'

By the time our call ended I think it was safe to say we were both equally relieved; living a lie was exhausting. Though I wanted to be honest, to tell her I had been abandoned in Rome and was now stranded in a gorgeous Italian man's apartment with no passport, I knew that no matter how much I assured her I was safe, she wouldn't believe it. The important thing was that I knew I was safe; I mean, there was a *nonna* keeping an eye on me, for God's sake. Could there be a better bodyguard? I think not.

I wasn't sure where Rosalia was at this point—possibly restocking the cavernous pantry for lunch—but she could be lurking around the corner at any given moment. So I stayed in the sunny kitchen, flipping through a newspaper, looking at the pictures instead of trying to decipher the words; it was something to pass the time, and I sorely needed distraction as Marcello's class was taking forever. Finally, I heard the approach of cackling laughter once more, and I straightened from my slumped position at the table.

I leapt out of my seat and made my way towards the voices. I walked out into the hall, and out from the elevator stepped a group of smiling, flushed faces sporting rather windswept hairdos; it was enough to tell me the roof-terrace session had been a success.

'Simply stunning. I'm telling you, young man, hit me up with some more of that local wine and I'll be back again and again,' said a tall lady with dyed black hair and thick plum lipliner that didn't quite blend with her lipstick.

'Now, our canvasses will be ready to pick up when?' asked a delicate little lady with hot-pink nail polish who had her arm linked with Marcello's.

'Tomorrow. I will have them all wrapped for you,' he assured her.

'And we won't have any trouble at Customs, will we?' asked big Tex.

'Not at all; there are no materials used that will pose any problems for Customs.'

'Oh, super! I am going to hang my Roman masterpiece above the fireplace,' announced his wife.

'Very well,' Giovanni called. 'Best we get a move on.'

It was then that Marcello's eyes landed on me, hovering near the kitchen doorway.

'Hold up, Giovanni!' he said, moving to skim through the group and come directly towards me.

'Looks like you got some happy customers there,' I said.

Marcello's face was lit up in a way I had never seen before; he looked energised and impassioned, and it was contagious. He pulled a sheet of folded paper from his back pocket and handed it to me.

'Here.'

I looked at his outstretched hand rather sceptically. 'What's this?'

I took it from him, but before I had a chance to unfold it, Marcello, like an excited child, started telling me, 'It's a ticket to the Colosseum—Giovanni will take you. It's a "Skip the Line" pass so you don't have to wait all day.'

I laughed. 'Skip the line?'

A woman squeezed in between us. 'Oh, honey, at our stage in life we don't have time to waste on lining up! Some of us would be dead by the time we got to the front of the queue,' she said, breaking away and moving to be ushered out by Giovanni, who appeared to have the patience of a saint.

I turned back to Marcello, who was still looking at me. 'I know you didn't get to see it last time so . . .' He shrugged.

Grinning like a mad thing didn't really convey what I was feeling in that moment, and although we had an audience—a loud, boisterous one at that—I did the only thing that could truly express my gratitude. I stepped forward, cupping the sides of his face and kissing him so passionately that the entire apartment was drowned out with wolf whistles and cheers. I thought Marcello might have pulled away, embarrassed, but he kissed me back, circling his arms around me and tilting me backwards like in the movies, putting on a real show. He lifted me up and we laughed like teenagers at the commotion.

One of the ladies was fanning herself with a booklet. 'Does everyone get a goodbye like that?'

Marcello jokingly went to step towards Giovanni, his hands outstretched, but Giovanni quickly bolted to the stairs. 'Let's go! *Avanti! Avanti!*'

The cackles rolled down the stairs, delighting at Giovanni's embarrassment. We lingered at the top. 'You don't want to come?'

'I've got to clean up, organise their paintings.'

The kiss had turned more slapstick than I intended, so I stepped forward again, kissing him gently on the lips, wanting him to know I meant it when I said, 'Thank you for this.'

Marcello smiled. 'Thank me when you survive the Golden Slumbers experience.'

'Good point.' I giggled, heading down the stairs to where Giovanni held the door open.

'Are you ready for this?' Giovanni asked.

'As ready as I will ever be.'

~

I was on a rickety bus with a driver who continually ground the gears. After each crunch of the gear box, without fail, big Tex said 'Excuse me' as if suffering from a severe case of flatulence, to a chorus of giggles. I, too, found myself laughing, even when the joke got really, really old. I was clearly in a jolly mood, indeed. It was an unexpected delight to be heading back to see the

Colosseum, a place so old yet so alive, which in retrospect summed up my newfound travel companions rather perfectly. On this tour, the pace was slower, the laughs were louder and my spirit had completely changed as we lined up with our elitist 'Skip the Line' passes. I was even presented with a Golden Slumbers T-shirt, which I wore with pride, even if it was three sizes too large. I tucked it into the front of my shorts; wow, if only the other group could see me now.

The last time I had left the Colosseum I had been sick and sorry, with unsatisfied curiosity, speeding away on Marcello's Vespa. Now, I stood in front of the large stone mass, awe-struck and ready to discover the layers of its history. Our tour explored not only the main arena but the dungeons and upper tiers that were closed to the general public, revealing the deepest, darkest secrets of the arena. It was a sobering exploration: long gone were the giggles and jokes; instead, a quiet reflectiveness came over the group. It would take more than one afternoon to truly unpack this ancient wonder, but it was a mighty good way to start ticking off my Rome wish list. I couldn't have hoped for a better experience, with a better bunch of people. When Nora's little blue-rinsed head rested on my shoulder on the journey home, and a light snore filtered through my ear, I didn't mind, and I was a little sad bidding the Golden Slumbers crew goodbye from Marcello's doorstep.

With my new T-shirt and a spring in my step, I knocked on the big green door. To my surprise, it opened straight-away, but no one stood there to greet me. I pushed it slowly open, peering inside to see Rosalia.

'*Ciao!*' I said; I was in such a great mood that I was happy to see her, even if the feeling wasn't mutual. Mumbling under her breath, she scooped up the sunglasses and set of keys that Marcello had dumped on the side table, then headed for the stairs.

'Busy day?' I pressed.

Rosalia stopped on the stairs, turning to look down at me. 'He is like a snake, shedding his clothes by the door, things here and there.'

I tried to contain myself; it was the most English I had ever heard her speak.

'Boys, huh, always so messy.'

She hmmphed, rolling her eyes and starting up the stairs; once again the house was filled with the most deli-cious aroma.

I followed Rosalia into the kitchen, where her main focus was the pot on the stove. I was caught between the lure of the smell and finding out where Marcello was.

As if reading my mind, Rosalia pointed up. '*Di sopra.*'

'Upstairs?'

'*Si, la trappola mortale.*'

I laughed. 'Roof terrace, huh?'

Rosalia nodded, retrieving the spoon from the pot, blowing it before holding it out to me, '*Gusta,*' she said.

'Oh, okay.' I leaned down, slurping the tomato sauce from the spoon. An explosion of flavours burst in my mouth, causing my eyes to widen as I looked at her.

'Good?' she asked.

I said the only word that really fit the feeling, *'Bellissimo!'* and gave her a thumbs up. A satisfied smirk lined her weathered face as she looked at me as if I were a little mad. Still, I saw that smile for what it was.

*Another little victory.*

~

Braving the lone ride in the 'death trap', I made my way up to the roof terrace, pushing through the heavy door. I kind of expected to see Marcello at work, painting one of the thousands of shades of light; instead, he was walking towards me, having heard me come through the door. Seeing his face was enough of a welcome, but seeing the terrace lit with dozens of tea light candles was something else.

'What's all this?'

'You can't come to Rome and not have a dinner on a terrace.'

'I won't argue with that,' I said, moving towards a table set for two, covered in white linen. I picked up the single rose that was set on my folded napkin and smelt its perfume, watching as Marcello uncorked some wine.

'I had such a great day,' I said.

'Me too,' he said, glancing up from pouring my glass.

As I picked up my wine and admired the view, my heart swelled so big I had no words to fill the space, nothing would fit. I couldn't express my feelings in Italian or English—it was all too much. I glanced down at the table setting, my brows pinching together.

'Marcello, how is Rosalia going to—'

'Ah,' he cut me off, 'I knew you would ask me that.' He took a sip from his glass, then placed it back down before moving to the opposite side of the terrace. I watched, intrigued, as he lifted a hutch to reveal a small alcove inside. 'A mini death trap for food,' he said, reaching over to pick up the rose, holding it up to me, asking if I minded.

'Go ahead.'

He placed the rose inside, closing the hutch and pushing the button, sending it downstairs.

'You didn't think I would make her carry it up the stairs, did you?'

I laughed. 'No, but I know she would; she'd do anything for you—even clean up your mess at the front door,' I said, looking at him pointedly, sipping on my big glass of red.

He winced, knowing exactly what I was talking about. '*Si*, old habits die hard.'

He motioned for me to sit, pulling the chair out for me before taking the seat opposite.

Straightening my cutlery, I was just about to ask Marcello how the rooftop class went when I noticed him flicking over the screen of his phone, looking lost.

'What is it?'

'Maria left a message, said she would call in the morning.'

'Do you think she's found my passport?'

'I dare say that's why she is calling. If it was anything bad, she would have called back tonight.'

'Maybe, but she might not have found out anything yet. She may just have been calling for an update.'

'Well, if I know Maria she will get to the bottom of it soon, I wouldn't worry,' he said, switching off his phone and pocketing it, giving me his full attention. 'Now, how was your day?'

I broke into a winning smile. 'That's what I was going to say.'

# Chapter Thirty-Eight

'Let's take the stairs!' My voice echoed as I pulled Marcello along the hall.

'Are you serious?'

'Come on, we need to walk off this food.'

'And wine?'

'That too.'

'You know wine and stairs can be a deadly combination.'

'Well, to be honest, being enclosed in a small, intimate space with you right now is also probably not the best idea,' I said, leaning against the wall near the elevator, my eyes burning into Marcello's.

'Oh, and why is that?' he asked, feigning innocence.

*You bloody well know why.*

The way his leg brushed against mine under the table, or the slide of his spoon on my tongue as I sampled the sweetest panna cotta. I wasn't sure if it was the setting of the sun, the twinkling of candlelight or the warm summer night, but there was something brewing between us, and it was definitely a dangerous thing.

I stepped forward, pressing my lips to his ear. 'Why do you think?'

And just as the elevator chimed and the doors opened, I took off, running for the stairs.

'Sammi, wait!'

I swung around the bannister, my hand skimming all the way down as I tried to steady myself while flying down the stairs, It was an unwise thing to do, but I didn't care much about anything other than the sound of Marcello's steps closing in on me as he called out for me to stop, which only urged me on. Out of breath from laughter and sheer excitement, I swooped around, ready to descend the next flight, but Marcello reached out and grabbed me by the waist, spinning me around to the wall, my breathing heavy, my cheek resting on the cool surface of the plaster. I could feel his breath at my neck, blowing strands of my hair across my other cheek, both our hearts thundering in unison.

'Trust you to stop on this floor,' he breathed.

I slowly turned myself around to face him, his hands splayed on the wall on either side of my head, caging me in.

'I didn't exactly stop by choice—you caught me.'

Marcello laughed. 'And so I did.'

Something intense burned in Marcello's eyes. I had seen it before, and I felt the same pull now as I had the night I invited him up to my room. As amazing as it had been, I really didn't want to think about that night. The way I had behaved, as if I had used him. Christ, I had even looked to Jodie as an example. I was embarrassed, ashamed. Marcello had every right to slam the door in my face but instead he had opened his home to me. Fed me, put a roof over my head, shared with me the most intimate part of him, his art. One brick at a time, his barricade was falling, and I was seeing the deeper side to him. Beyond the gorgeous smile and the self-assured way he carried himself, there was so much more to this man, and I really wanted him to know that there was so much more to me than that horrible version I had showed him.

'Marcello, about the other night, I just—'

'It's okay,' he said, cutting off my words.

'Well, no, it's not.'

Something shifted in him, as if we were headed somewhere he wasn't comfortable going. The wall was back up.

'I just want you to know that I'm not the kind of girl who brings men into my bed and kicks them out come sun-up. In fact, it never happens, and certainly not with someone like you . . . so, yeah, I guess I just panicked, and I wanted you to know that, in case what I did or how I behaved made you think less of me.'

I winced; I really needed to just stop talking. I could see the darkness in Marcello's eyes, as if he was drinking in everything I had said, rolling it around in his head, unpacking it. He looked confused, which only made me feel worse.

*Will I ever learn to shut the hell up?*

Was now the right time to slink back to my room?

But instead of giving me reassuring words, he did something far simpler, and far more effective. He smiled, big and brilliant, and pushed off the wall, pointing to the door behind him.

'You coming?'

I glanced up the hall. I had never been on this level before. I leaned over the bannister to get my bearings.

'What floor are we on?'

'My floor,' he said, looking at me intently.

And just like that, I was sober. I cleared my throat. 'Oh, right.'

All amusement drained away from us and now we simply stood there, our breaths the only thing filling the space. It was such a strange feeling. It wasn't like we hadn't been in this position before: we'd fooled around before, so why was this time so different? Why was there so much more weight to this moment?

Marcello voiced the very reason. 'If you come into my room, I am not going to be able to stop this time.'

I smiled, stepping closer to him, trying to break his stony façade. 'Are you saying you want to go all the way with me, Marcello?' I joked, but he didn't seem to be in the laughing mood, not anymore. Instead, he slid his hand down my arm, causing a shiver to run through my body, lacing his fingers through mine as he backed against his door, pulling me with him. He never answered my question but the way his eyes burned into mine, I think I knew my answer.

Marcello opened the door to his bedroom, which was more of an apartment. The warm tones of his bedding and dark furniture were a stark contrast to the marbled greys and whites of the main house. This room was all Marcello; he had put his stamp on it. I let go of Marcello's hand in order to explore the room as he shut the door behind us, the thud making my heart jump. Marcello crossed his arms and leant against the door, watching me move along the expansive fireplace, under a large, macabre streetscape.

'Did you do this?'

'*Sì*, a long time ago.'

'How long have you been painting?'

'Since I was a boy.'

'It makes you happy?'

'Not always. It can be . . . frustrating.'

'Well, nothing worthwhile was ever easy.'

He moved to stand by my side, the two of us looking up at the painting like we were standing in a gallery—except what I was about to do, well, it probably wouldn't be socially acceptable in a public place. I pressed into him, kissing his neck, basking in the warmth of him, the smell of his skin and the way his chest expanded when I touched him, my hands sliding over his chest and feeling the soft fabric of his shirt as I linked my hands behind his neck, looking up at him with a small smile.

'What?'

I shook my head. 'I can't believe you let me take you back to my squalid, bug-infested bedroom when you have this literally a stone's throw away.'

Marcello's chest vibrated against me. 'Well, you know what they say?'

'You do it with your eyes closed?'

Marcello shook his head. 'No. Nothing worthwhile was ever easy. Also, I couldn't wait any longer.'

'Aha! So that's why you wanted to take the elevator tonight.'

'What can I say? I'm an impatient man.'

And with that he scooped me up from the floor, lifting me into his arms and spinning me around towards his bed, dumping me on the mattress in a fit of giggles. Collapsing on top of me, he caged me in with his arms.

'Stop laughing, I am trying to seduce you,' he said, struggling to keep a straight face.

'Oh, sorry,' I said, trying to breathe as I wiped the tears from my cheeks.

Marcello rolled on his back, rubbing his hands over his face as if giving up on me; the harder I tried to stop laughing the more hysterical I got, the mattress vibrating as I clamped my hands over my mouth.

'Okay, okay, I'll stop now,' I said, sitting up and taking in a deep, steadying breath. Marcello looked up at me, his hands linked behind his head, his eyes alight with mischief, looking at me as if to say, 'Are you quite done?' And I was, because if there was anything that was going to calm me, it was those eyes, near on hypnotising, looking into my soul and making me burn in places that begged to be touched. Never taking my eyes from him, I shifted, moving to slide my leg over his hips, straddling him as he lay there watching my every slow, deliberate move. His eyes dipped to my hands moving to his shirt buttons. A sure long line downwards, popping them apart one by one. I wouldn't be so kind to his belt buckle, I could promise him that.

Marcello sat up, grabbing the fabric of my Golden Slumbers T-shirt, frowning at it and yanking it over my head. 'That's definitely got to go,' he said, kissing my mouth and nipping at my lower lip.

'What, you don't find my T-shirt sexy?' I breathed against his mouth, but he was too distracted to answer. His breaths were heavy, his hands too fast and clever, working their way into my unbuttoned shorts, sliding inside, beyond the damp, thin fabric of my knickers. My hands dug into his shoulders, rocking against his fingers, first one then another sliding in and out, working me up for what was to come. I pulled the fabric of his shirt backwards, biting into his neck as he rocked me harder, faster, yanking my bra down and exposing me to him, his eyes watching as my breasts moved with every rock, lowering his head to take my nipple in his mouth, moaning into my skin.

Unlike the last time, there was the faintest light in our room, casting a rich, low, warm glow around the space. And this time I was glad because I wanted to see every curve of his body, every expression twist on his face as I freed him from his pants.

'Marcello.' I swallowed, my voice uneven, a simple one word spoken in a plea and he knew exactly what it meant. He shifted and I fell back onto the mattress. He hooked his fingers into my shorts and in one swift motion they were gone, followed by his shirt, which he threw aside as he pressed down on me, his broad shoulders engulfing me as he took my mouth, hot and heavy. He had filled me with fingers and now his tongue but I wanted more. Reading my mind, my body, he reached for his drawer to grab a condom. My mind was suddenly reeling.

*Oh, God.*

He sheathed himself—apparently there were condoms that big. I swallowed, feeling my chest rise and fall heavily as Marcello positioned himself between my legs, splaying his hands on my thighs and pushing them wider, opening me to him. He ran his hard length along my dampened seam, looking down between us then up at me, smiling as he teased me, edging his way in slowly while my hands twisted in the bed sheets.

*There's no way . . . there's no room.*

But he made room. With one deep push he was inside me and I gasped into his shoulder. Marcello stayed still, allowing me to adjust to the feel of him, looking at me intently, then kissing my mouth.

'Are you okay?'

I nodded, because I had no breath to speak. My only reality was the feel of him inside me, filling me so completely it was almost too much. But when I looked up into his eyes, I could see his tenderness, the light of the moon casting a glow over his beautiful face, and I leant up on my elbows, taking his mouth and kissing his lips oh so softly, telling him I was okay, giving him the reassurance he needed. As he kissed me back, his once tense body melted into me and I started rocking my hips into him, slowly at first, encouraging him to move with me.

Each stroke led to another, each one faster, deeper, more needed than the last as our fucking became frenzied and sweaty, sheets twisting and my screams echoing in the room. Marcello didn't tell me to be quiet; if anything, he encouraged me, whispering wicked-sounding things in my ear that, despite not knowing their translation, made me even hungrier for him.

Marcello rolled onto his back, taking me with him. My hands splayed on his chest, he grabbed my hips, guiding my pace, urging me to ride him faster and faster until his groans told me what I needed to hear, allowing me to let myself go. I came, so hard, unable to give any more as the sensation became too much, too raw, while Marcello thrust into me one final time and then came, clamping me in place and giving everything he had to give.

I fell over him, breathless and utterly consumed, my damp hair plastered to his chest, my temple feeling the racing of his heart as the aftershocks twitched through our bodies. I closed my eyes, shivering at the feel of his arms sweeping over my sensitive skin as he held me. He held me for so long, still inside me, one being as our breathing slowed, Marcello running his fingers through my hair. Finally I lifted my face to his, smiling broadly and resting my head on my hand.

I blew out a breath, parting the strands of hair that fell over my face. 'Well, I never saw that on the itinerary.'

Marcello simply shook his head, pulling me into his arms and kissing my giggles into silence.

# Chapter Thirty-Nine

I sat up quickly, the twisted sheets wedged under my arms as I brushed the hair from my eyes. 'Marcello, what is it? What's wrong?'

Marcello's face was sombre as he came to sit on the edge of the bed and hung up his phone, the call having woken us up from deep and dreamless sleep.

'Jodie doesn't have your passport.'

'What? That was Maria?'

Marcello nodded.

'Well, is she sure? Jodie is probably lying.'

'She is sure. Jodie admitted to lying about you meeting up with your sister, but she said she would never have taken your passport.'

'And we're going to trust a liar?'

'Sammi, Maria got the police involved.'

'Oh, my God.'

'Yes, I told you Maria doesn't muck around.'

I sat there, stunned. I had never even entertained the thought that someone else might have taken my passport—Jodie had been the most obvious suspect. I had sat right next to her at dinner, my bag looped on the chair near her, it was far too easy. And as for my suitcases, they hadn't magically made their own way to the baggage area of the hotel. I was sure she was behind it; she had crossed the line on more than one occasion. I tried not to think too much about the foundation and perfume I pilfered from Kylie and Harper. Besides, that was different.

'Marcello, what if someone stole it? They could be using my alias as a forged identity for a drug cartel by now.'

Marcello clamped his hand over mine. 'Don't worry; now we know, we can do what we need to do. We'll go to the embassy in the morning.'

I chewed on my thumbnail. 'I should have reported it straightaway.' I felt like kicking myself.

'Come, it's not like it means you have to stay here forever,' Marcello reasoned, getting up from the bed.

I watched his broad, bare shoulders flex as he opened his cupboard, picking out his clothes for the day. Watching him from the bed as he went about his morning routine made me realise how temporary it all was; despite our amazing night together, or even the past few days, this was just a fleeting moment. Maybe I hadn't reported the loss of my passport because a part of me had never wanted it to be found. Somehow, I had gone from swearing never to return to his city to never wanting to leave, largely due to the man in front of me. Despite his good intentions, Marcello's reassurance that everything would be alright felt like a knife to the heart. What had I expected—for him to beg me to stay, to tell me to forget about the passport and enjoy more time together? I was so deluded.

I scooted to the edge of the bed, picking up my clothes and quickly dressing while Marcello ran the water in his bathroom. It was a mistake to come here last night, to get caught up with the view and the candles, and those eyes. So bloody stupid. The best thing I could do was report my passport missing and face the inevitable. It was time to end this fantasy and head home.

'You jumping in?' Marcello called from the shower.

However tempting that was, I knew better in the light of day. 'I'm just going to grab some clean clothes,' I called back.

'Use the elevator.'

I know he suggested it because it was quicker to get back, but I wasn't coming back. The only reason I was going to *la trappola mortale* was because I could bloody hardly walk, every step a stark reminder of all the sordid things we had done last night. The memories only made me even more depressed, because I knew it would never be happening again.

～

I showered and dressed in my own room in record time, grabbing my handbag and heading down the hall, my hair dampening my collar. There was no time for make-up—I was on a mission. I scribbled a note—'Gone to get coffee!'—and placed it on the kitchen table, then headed back towards the stairs, only to spin around and come crashing straight into Marcello's chest.

'Whoa, slow down!'

'Oh, sorry I was just . . .'

'You've showered?'

'Oh, yeah, I was just going out to get us some coffee.'

*And secretly book into Hotel Luce del Sole.*

'Are you okay?' Marcello ran his hands down my arms and, damn him, it felt so good.

'Yeah, of course. I think I just have an addiction to coffee.'

*Among other things.*

There was a quickening in my chest, but I reminded myself to focus, to keep to my plans. I was freaking out for a very specific reason: I was losing myself—to this place, this city, to Marcello—and if I didn't get out now, who knew how much of me would be left when it came time to return home? I brushed past him to head down the stairs, almost making it to the front door.

'Sammi?'

*Shit.*

I turned, my eyes lifting to Marcello standing above me on the stairs, smiling until he saw my face.

'What's wrong?' he said, descending the steps and reaching out to me, but I moved away. I didn't want him to touch me; I didn't think I could bear it.

'What are we doing?' I blurted out.

'What do you mean?'

'Like, seriously, what are we doing, Marcello?'

'Well, breakfast.'

I sighed deeply. 'And then?'

'Report your passport?' Marcello answered tentatively, like he was a little frightened to guess the wrong answer.

I breathed out a small, sad laugh, shaking my head. 'I'm going to see if the Hotel Luce del Sole has any rooms available.'

There was a flash of pained confusion in Marcello's face. 'Why?'

'Why? Because what is the point, Marcello, to any of this? I live on the other side of the world, and this is just a summer fling, forgotten as soon as you change the sheets.'

'What has brought all this on?'

I couldn't voice the reason—it seemed too ridiculous. Like a child having a tantrum at not being able to have the things she wanted. Maybe it was last night, lying in his arms, listening to his heart, knowing I was the reason it was beating so fast, or the way his eyes had lit up taking his class up to the terrace, knowing he was doing it because I had suggested it. All the little victories, and heated looks, stolen kisses and in-jokes: it was all leading to nothing.

'I can't stay, Marcello, it's too much.'

'I don't understand.'

Marcello stepped forward, cupping my face, forcing me to look into his eyes, shaking his head. 'It will be too much, if you go.'

'Why prolong it?'

'Why rush it?' There was rawness in his words; I could feel it run through his body. He didn't want me to go; it should have fed my soul but it only made me feel more hopeless.

I gripped his hands on my face.

'Look,' he coaxed, 'let's grab some coffee—there's a place down the road called Gino's, it's the best coffee in Rome. If you still feel the same after breakfast I will roll you back to the dungeon myself. Deal?'

I looked at him for a long moment, knowing I should be comforted by the fact that he didn't want me to walk out the door, but I was no less terrified by the feelings swirling around inside my head.

I had joked to my parents that there was no chance of me finding love here. I'd been so confident, so cocky. Well, look at me now.

'Okay,' I relented, and saw a glimmer of hope in Marcello's eyes; the very thing I had been lacking since Maria's call. I didn't know if a cup of coffee would fix it, but I at least owed it to Marcello to try. He opened the door and stood to the side.

'After you.'

~

Maybe it was the Italian sunshine, or the insanely good coffee, or Marcello walking beside me in comfortable silence, but with each step back to the apartment I felt calmer, a little less manic. If anything, I felt a little foolish. I'd had a mini breakdown—it was the only explanation. Seriously, threatening to check back into Hotel Luce del Sole? I must have been mad. I glanced at the grimy exterior of the hotel as we walked by, earning an animated wave from Luciano.

'Eh, Marcello, Sammi, *ciao.*'

We both laughed, waving back, the first sign of the ice being broken and a lightness coming back between us. Marcello must have felt it too as he reached out to take my hand, the connection giving me a shot of pure joy. I smiled.

*Just live in the moment, Sammi, live in the moment.*

We reached the door, pushing beyond the green barrier into the cool, grand entry, leaving the white noise of the street behind. Marcello dumped his possessions on the table without so much as a thought, then kissed me on the forehead and headed to the stairs, coffee in hand. I watched him go, feeling a warmth swell my heart at this beautiful, yet messy man.

'Marcello, Rosalia is going to murder you!' I laughed, walking to the side table, where his jacket, keys and wallet sat in a pile. Shaking my head, I flicked out the jacket, hooking it up on the coat rack; jiggling the keys and pulling a pair of glasses from the pocket, I opened the table drawer to put them away.

'Oops, okay, so that's not going to work,' I mumbled, seeing the drawer jammed full of letters, and shoving it closed again. I moved over to the next drawer, and was about to place the keys inside when I froze.

The keys fell from my hand as I stared down. The crash of them against the marble floor echoed through the entire space, but it was a muted sound, as was Marcello's voice, calling from above.

'Sammi, are you okay?'

I blinked, twice, his words rolling through me, slowly registering, connecting.

*Was I alright? No, no, I most definitely wasn't.*

I slowly reached out my shaking hand, delving into the recess of the side table, barely able to breathe as I opened the booklet. With a whimper I lifted it up to the light, my blurry vision struggling to focus on what I held in my hand.

*My passport.*

# Chapter Forty

The passport slid across the kitchen table, until it hit Marcello's newspaper.

His eyes flicked from the blue rectangle up to me with a bemused smile. 'Where did you find it?'

*Was he for real?*

'Are you serious right now? Where do you think I found it?'

Marcello studied the passport, looking up at me as if I had lost my mind.

'I FOUND IT IN YOUR FUCKING DRAWER!'

All the colour drained from his face as he slowly stood, looking at me.

'That's not possible.'

'*Si*, very fucking possible, Marcello. The question is: how did it get there? No, no, don't answer that. I think we both know.'

'No, we don't know, but I would sure like to.' His voice was raised, his face cast into thunder.

I scoffed. 'I should have known better than to trust you—you were so cagey about even the smallest things,' I said, pacing the kitchen.

'Sammi, I am telling you I don't know anything about your passport.'

'Well, excuse me if I don't believe you,' I said, walking over and snatching it from his hand.

I stormed out of the kitchen, heading down the stairs—so many fucking stairs. I skipped two at a time, knowing he was behind me but praying he would just leave me alone.

'Samantha, wait!'

I stopped near the door, spinning around, fire in my eyes. 'No! No one calls me that, especially not you. You don't get to call me that—you don't get to call me anything, anymore, ever again. Just stay away from me.'

Emotion welled in Marcello's eyes, his hands moving to his head as if in denial, powerless to stop what was happening.

Pain wrenched Marcello's face. 'Don't go, not like this.'

I shook my head. 'You don't get a choice.' And with that I turned to leave; with my passport back in my possession, there was nothing left to stop me. I stepped outside and slammed the door behind me.

~

Once again, I sat in a wingbacked chair in the lounge area of Hotel Luce del Sole, reeling from the words that echoed through my mind, over and over again. The bottom of my world had dropped away the moment I had opened that drawer. I shut my eyes.

*Oh, God, I feel ill.*

I wrapped my arms around my stomach, leaning over, wishing it all away. I heard the sound of wheels against marble like I had done before; the last time it had been Marcello coming towards me. I straightened in my chair, only to see a lone traveller passing through reception. I knew if anyone would be bringing my suitcase it would be Luciano, who had kindly agreed to pick up my things from Marcello's. He knew better than to ask questions; he just had to see the look on my face to know.

It was all so simple now. Flight booked, all I had to do was wait for Luciano, who had also agreed to take me to the airport. I would not be spending another night in Rome.

'He shouldn't be too much longer.' Gabriello took my empty coffee cup from me—no doubt my last one of those, too.

I smiled. 'Thanks, Gabriello. I'm going to give your customer service a five-star rating when I get home.'

Gabriello didn't know what to say; instead, he simply took my hand and kissed the back of it.

'Safe travels, *signora*.' And right on cue, the infamous sound of roller wheels heralded Luciano's arrival with my things.

'I think this is everything,' he said, juggling my belongings.

I didn't really care if it wasn't—I was ready to go. Hooking my bag over my shoulder and clenching my passport in my hand, refusing to let it go, I followed Luciano out to the waiting car. I stood near the boot, staring off into the distance, numb and waiting for my possessions to be locked away; the thud of the boot pulling me out of my trance. Moving towards the passenger door, I was careful not to look down the street, not entirely sure what I would do if I laid eyes on that green door again.

I slid into the passenger seat of Luciano's car; with an overflowing ashtray and bags of junk food at my feet, it seemed like a poetic way to be leaving.

'Oh, *scusi* for the mess, Sammi.'

I honestly couldn't have cared less. 'Let's just go,' I said, grabbing for my seatbelt. A loud tap at my window caused me to jump, my eyes locking with that of a steely-faced nonna. I quickly unwound my window to see just how angry she was, staring down at me and shaking her head.

'Rosalia?'

'You broke him.' She pointed in my face.

I scoffed. 'Yeah, well, he broke me first.' I looked away. The last thing I needed was a parting lecture from Rosalia; I had been the villain in her eyes from day one.

'Come on, Luciano, let's go,' I said, wanting nothing more than to put distance between myself and this place.

But before Luciano could even shift into gear, Rosalia shouted, 'No!' and snatched the passport from my hand, her eyes wild.

'Hey!' I yelled, opening the car door and grabbing for my passport. The day had officially hit a new low; I was now wrestling with an old lady who was half my size. Managing to pull it from her gnarled grasp, I moved back to the door, only for her to block my path.

'*Si, si, passaporto!*' Rosalia shouted, pointing.

'*Si,* Marcello took it,' I snapped, thinking it was time she learnt a few home truths. Horror registered in Rosalia's eyes. I knew the feeling; the truth was shocking. All she could do was clasp her cheeks and shake her head.

'*No, no,*' she repeated.

'*Si, si,*' I said, hoping now she would simply leave me to my misery, to get in the car and drive away. But she was still unmoving, and my patience was wearing thinner by the second. Grabbing for the handle, I was no longer ready to play nice, brushing past her and opening the door. I was about to slide in, when her words hit me.

'I found it!'

I froze, turning to see Rosalia's teary face. She stood there, twisting her hands.

'W-what?'

'*Si, si,* it fell from messy jacket.'

'What are you talking about—what jacket?'

'Eh, blue jacket, on hallstand.'

My heart stopped.

'Rosalia, when did you pick the jacket up?'

She thought for a moment, her eyes sorrowful. 'The night before you came.'

I stood still, not saying a word, only letting the sickness twist in the pit of my stomach.

My mind cast back to that night in my room, how Marcello had dumped his jacket on top of my bag, how I had knocked the chair over in the dark, my things strewn all over the floor, of Marcello scooping up his jacket and wedging it under his arm, the memory of that very jacket hanging in the hall.

*Oh, God.*

My widened eyes shifted back to Rosalia. 'And you never told Marcello . . . about the passport?'

She shrugged. '*No.*'

I blinked.

*Marcello didn't steal my passport.*

My face was on fire, the truth shaming me to my soul. I cupped my burning cheeks as the tears welled in my eyes.

'Oh, Rosalia, what have I done?'

Rosalia beat her chest, like the full realisation was almost too much to bear.

'*No, è colpa mia, è colpa mia.*'

I looked at the frail old lady, the very life and soul of Marcello's house, cooking, cleaning and caring for every aspect of his life. I imagined her easily shoving keys and letters into drawers without thinking, her mind on the many other tasks she had to attend to.

I reached for her withered hand and held it while I looked down at her. 'This is not your fault, do you understand?'

Something sparked within her misty eyes: the sudden look of hope. 'Come, come, see Marcello—we will tell him.'

She pulled at my arm, but I was unmoving. Instead, all I could do was stare off into the distance, looking at the green door; the door that had been my saviour, the very same one I had slammed on Marcello, so hard the sound haunted me still. Closing my eyes, I shook my head. How could I face him? The vision of me throwing my passport across the table came to me again, the things I had said; I hadn't even given him the right of reply. It was better for me to simply go.

'Goodbye, Rosalia,' I said.

Rosalia stilled, realising I meant what I said when I looked into her eyes.

'Thank you for everything.' My voice broke and I knew that if I didn't get into the car right that very second I would let her drag me back to Marcello, and beg for him to forgive me, but I knew there was no point. Leaving now was going to be easier, yet still so incredibly hard. I slid into the passenger seat next to Luciano.

'Ah, do you want to—'

'Just go!' I sobbed, not daring to look out my window. Luciano didn't have to be told twice; we drove off, with the green door at my back and Rosalia's eyes seared into my memory.

*What have I done?*

# Chapter Forty-One

*Remember, Sammi, act surprised!*

I didn't have to fake it. Seeing Claire and Louis in the distance, a surge of sheer joy had me running so fast that I crashed into Claire, hugging her fiercely and bursting into—quite hysterical—tears. Louis simply stood to the side, not knowing what to do.

'How long has she been away?' he asked.

Claire cut him a dark look. 'It's not just that. I have this effect on everybody. Who wouldn't miss me? Isn't that right, Sammi?' Claire looked at me, assessing, and I knew she knew that there was more going on with me than jet lag and a bad case of missing her sister; she saw straight through me in her usual unnerving way. But she stayed quiet for now, and for that I was extremely grateful.

'Exactly,' I said, rubbing at my eyes and sniffing, imagining how hideous I looked.

Claire cupped my face. 'Oh, my God, you are so tanned!'

'And about five kilos heavier.'

'You look amazing—that Italian sunshine served you well.'

I knew she was lying—I looked like a bag lady; there was no other way to put it. The poor woman next to me on the plane was a witness to my sobbing, as I cried until the tears came no more. I think I had exhausted my tear ducts—the well had run dry.

Claire hooked her arm in mine. 'I want you to tell me all about Rome!' It took every effort for me not to visibly recoil at the question—the first of many, no doubt.

'It was . . . life-changing.' Was there any other way to describe it?

'Louis and I have thought about Rome, you know. Something new for the show, plus I really just want to go to Italy,' she confessed.

I walked along in a daze, relying on Claire's guidance as I became lost in my thoughts. Claire and Louis had met in Paris, rather controversially through Louis' famed show *Restoration or Detonation*. With his platform as a famed celebrity chef, Louis would go into failing hotels, tear everything and everyone apart and then give the hotel the mother of all makeovers.

'Have you really thought about Rome, as in for the show, I mean?'

We stopped near the baggage collection.

'Sure, why not?' said Claire.

'There's mine, there!' I pointed to the silver roller bag with scuffmarks and a hot-pink nametag.

Louis moved past the hordes, grabbing it with ease. 'Why—do you have some place in mind?' he mused.

And for the first time in a long time a smile broke out across my face, a really bloody big one. 'Louis, I have the perfect project for you!'

Claire and Louis stood before me, looking intrigued, if a little disturbed at the now-smiling nutter before them. My hair a mess and wearing my baggy Golden Slumbers T-shirt, which I had changed into mid-flight for comfort, I must have looked quite the sight.

'Oh, do tell,' he pressed.

'Absolutely—we're always up for a challenge.' Claire beamed, excitement radiating through her.

I pulled my roller bag into line. 'Well, if you want a challenge, Hotel Luce del Sole is the place for you!'

~

Having Claire and Louis at home was a godsend; they were the perfect buffer, holding back Mum and Dad and their tirade of questions. I wasn't quite sure how I was going to explain the lack of photographic evidence of me jokingly holding up the Leaning Tower of Pisa, and why I didn't have the promised gift of Venetian glass for Mum; they were already rather confused about why I was home so early. I didn't have the answers; all I knew was I wanted to go to my room, draw the curtains, crash into bed and never leave home again.

I don't know how I would have survived without Claire force-feeding me—of course, it did help that Louis had taken over the kitchen. She was incredibly patient, and when the time came for me to talk, she listened, staying silent until the climax of the story.

'Oh, no, you didn't.' She shook her head, her eyes wide.

'Yep, I accused him of stealing my passport,' I said, hugging my pillow to my chest.

The look of sheer devastation on Claire's face said it all. 'Oh, Sammi.'

I shook my head. 'I didn't even say I was sorry—I was too much of a coward.'

'Well, do you think he knows you know the truth now?'

I scoffed. 'Oh, I am certain Rosalia would have told him.'

'And he hasn't contacted you in any way?'

'I'm sure, now that some time has passed, he is thanking his lucky stars that I live far, far away.'

Claire blew out a long breath. 'Loving a foreign man is never easy, especially when they are this gorgeous,' she said, lifting up his business card from my mattress. My eyes snapped up at her, her words resonating with me deeper than she could have realised.

*Loving.*

Without saying as much to Claire, I knew that was my biggest problem, my biggest fear. I had fallen for the very person I couldn't have. The discovery had me unwittingly self-sabotaging us the moment Maria had called. I knew that, now; I'd had hours upon hours of unpacking it all.

'So, what now?' asked Claire.

'Well,' I breathed out, 'I get on with my life.'

Claire looked sad—she was always the hopeless romantic. I knew she wanted more from this. I did too, but sometimes the fairytale ending doesn't come true.

'I just wish there was some way I could make it up to him. He was so good to me: he put a roof over my head, fed me, showed me the most amazing places.'

*Any plenty of other things.*

I blinked, squeezing the pillow tightly.

'And he's an artist, you say?'

'An amazing artist! Claire, you should see his work, and he's locked away, schooling seniors on how to paint sunsets and working as a tour guide—it's insane.'

Claire's head tilted in that scary way she had when an idea was brewing.

'What? What are you thinking?'

'Well, I will be forever grateful to a man who saved my sister from certain peril.'

'Claire.' I said her name as warning.

'Oh, don't worry, you can still mope and sook over the one that got away, but we seriously need to pay him back some way. Louis!' Claire called out down the hall.

It didn't take him long to appear, his eyes alight anytime he set them on Claire. It was the way a woman longed to be looked at—I knew because I had seen it for myself.

*Yeah, let's not think about that, Sammi.*

'Louis, you're an art lover,' Claire chimed.

Louis folded his arms and leant in the frame of the door. 'I am?'

'You are! So, I think we need to retweet a little recommendation for a soon-to-be-discovered Roman artist.' Claire held up Marcello's business card to him.

I sat up straight. 'Oh, my God, Louis, would you?' I asked, fearing to hope.

One recommendation from the likes of Louis Delarue, world-renowned Michelin-star chef, and your life was destined to change forever. There'd be no more need for Marcus to drag filthy rich westerners up to his terrace and show them a good time.

Louis sighed. 'This won't affect my brand, will it?'

Claire laughed. 'Oh, please, you didn't even care about a brand or know what it was before me. Now you're a Twitter addict, and you even post food pics on Instagram.'

Louis smirked knowingly. 'I don't know who I am anymore,' he said, taking out his phone and snapping a picture of the business card. 'Leave it with me; if I am going to make a recommendation, it has to be done right.' Typical Louis—a stickler for the details.

Having made one wrong in the world a tiny bit right, I leapt out of my bed and wrapped my arms around him.

'Thank you, Louis, thank you, thank you, thank you!'

# Chapter Forty-Two

Four months later . . .

So fate had other ideas for me. And don't judge me, but somehow going back to the place it all began felt kind of poetic in some really messed-up way. I'm not talking Rome, of course, no-no-no. I'm talking about sitting at a desk, with an irritating-as-all-hell neck scarf and a stiff, ill-fitting jacket that made working on the keyboard really tricky.

After taking my still-wounded soul bursting through the doors of Jan and John Buzzo's travel agency, unleashing my tirade of the complete and utter shambles of my Italian adventure (minus the hot, sordid details of Marcello), I took great pleasure in telling them that their 'no regrets' philosophy had left me with nothing but regrets! I thought that was a rather killer line; I know because I had practised it over and over again on the car ride over to their office.

That was three months ago, and I never imagined that I would have received not only a written apology and a phone call, but a job offer. Jan was planning to retire Mr Buzzo to the golf course and fill his well-indented seat with someone who actually had a clue. The thought of another year of binge-watching Netflix at Mum and Dad's was all the inspiration I needed: I was only too happy to accept Jan's offer. The next thing I knew, I had my own headset and was booking other people's dream holidays.

*I had found my calling!*

As much as I liked a challenge, and it was definitely a challenge, I actually enjoyed the job, especially on the odd occasion when I knew what I was talking about; that is, giving recommendations for Rome. Whether it be a little lunch place with a view of the Pantheon, or the famous gelato they simply had to try, or, if they were up for it, the power hour at Rome's hottest nightclub. It kind of made it fun, too, that Louis was shooting his next TV series at Hotel Luce del Sole, the worst hotel he had ever seen, which made for great television. I was now in a position to recommend the hotel to travellers and feel confident about it. The location was excellent, the staff were A plus, and now it was entirely bedbug free!

And I never failed to recommend Bellissimo Tours. I had Googled Maria often enough to know that her business was booming, with no joint venture with Marcello in sight; he didn't need it. Since Louis had tweeted his 'discovery' of the Roman artist Marcello Bambozzi, my former flame's career took off. I tried desperately not to Google him, which was tough with a computer at my fingertips most days of the week, but last I heard he had his own gallery opening, showcasing his art. I'm not going to lie: I cried. Cried like a newborn baby, I was so happy for him; it was exactly what he deserved.

It all seemed like a distant memory now. Despite the rather disastrous parting of ways with my fellow travellers, I still kept in touch with the Gold Coast besties, who often sent me updates of all things Jodie and Bookworm Gary – engaged, buying a puppy, heading back to Rome! I guess they threw their coins in the fountain successfully. I tried not to let the bitterness eat away at me. At least Nate would send me the odd humorous YouTube clip to take the edge off, and Johnny liked my status updates on Facebook. In some weird way we were all still connected; we probably always would be. I certainly wasn't expecting an invite to Jodie and Gary's wedding, and she was never going to make it onto my Christmas card list, but hey, I was a-okay with that.

I glanced at the clock, my head shaking at my calculations: another two-hour lunch for Jan. I didn't mind, though, as it offered me a reprieve from her constant chattering.

I sighed, checking over the details for the Berrymans' annual trip to Bali, then pressed print in a fury of clicks until a symbol flashed up on my screen.

'Oh, great!'

I swivelled in my chair, making the long trek to the ancient printer, doing my usual pull tray, slam, bang, jiggle routine that usually brought the old beast to life. I was so focused on my task that I didn't see the thread of my bracelet get caught in the door, snapping the accessory off my wrist.

'Oh, shit.' I slammed the top of the printer in frustration, my vision instantly blurring as I pulled the green, white and red strip from the door in despair. It was the bracelet Marcello bought me in Rome from a dodgy vendor, promising good luck if it broke. I closed the door, staring at it, my heart aching as I held the limp strand.

'Yeah, well, I need all the bloody luck I can get.'

And just as if the universe was listening to me, the machine began functioning again, shooting out sheets of perfectly printed paper. I burst out laughing, sniffing and wiping at my eyes.

'It's a miracle!' I shouted to the sky, grabbing the papers and walking back to my desk. I head the telltale groan of the shopfront door, announcing Jan's return.

*About bloody time.*

'Hey, Jan, the printer's on the fritz again. Do you want me to call Tony?' I sat down in my chair, swivelling around to see the cause of her lack of reply, ready to repeat the question.

I glanced up, then froze. My grip clenched on the papers so tightly that I could feel them crinkling in my hands. I slowly stood, shaking my head in utter disbelief.

'What are you doing here?'

There he stood, tall, tanned and eyes as dark as I remembered, standing next to a plastic pot plant, holding a very real rose. He slowly stepped forward, a twinkle in his eyes.

'I need to book some tickets.'

'What?' I couldn't breathe, couldn't register what he was saying.

'H-how did you know . . .'

'Where to find you?'

I nodded, because that's all I could manage.

'Louis is a great man, and an interesting neighbour.'

The penny dropped. Claire and Louis at Hotel Luce del Sole. I should have known.

I could feel my legs shaking, watching him make his way around the desk, coming closer to me.

'He could probably learn a recipe or two from Rosalia.' I swallowed; why was it getting harder to breathe? It was as if all the oxygen had been sucked from the room. He smiled, and there was no escape, those bloody dimples were weapons of mass destruction. Standing before me, he handed me the rose.

'This one is yours to keep this time . . . if you want it?'

I shook my head, tears welling in my eyes, my heart beating so fast I didn't think I could take it.

The door opened, letting a blast of cool air into the office. Jan shrugged her coat off and looped it over the back of her chair.

'Sorry I'm late, love, I had to zip to the bank and the lines were mental . . .' Jan came up short. 'Oh, hello,' she said, touching her neck and smiling. 'Sorry, I didn't mean to interrupt.'

I tore my eyes from Marcello's, desperately needing the reprieve, knowing it was the only chance I stood to think clearly.

'It's okay, Jan. I was just helping Mr Bambozzi with a booking.'

'Oh, fab—where to?' she asked, plunking herself back behind her desk, grabbing a nail file and listening intently as she filed her talons.

I turned back to Marcello's solemn, serious gaze. He looked lost, hanging on for the very next moment, his eyes ticking across my face.

The heart was a ridiculous thing.

I lifted my hand, placing my fingers around the stem of the rose.

*No thorns.*

Bringing it close to me, I smelled its perfume, the memory making me smile as I lifted my eyes to look at him, really look at him. Stepping closer to Marcello, I spoke to him and only him, finally able to voice what I wanted—the only thing I ever truly wanted.

'Two tickets to Rome!'

# Acknowledgements

To my loving husband, Michael, thank you for making me eat, drink and sleep, even when I say, 'Just one more chapter!' Living with a tortured artist mustn't be easy but you do it with a smile and a shake of the head, and I love you for that.

Thank you to my wonderful publisher, Hachette (the A Team); Kate, you are my editing spirit animal, I adore you!

To Anita, Keary, Jess and Lilliana, thank you for always pushing me and helping me to the finish line even when it seems impossible. Your friendships, patience and smarts are what help govern my success; I cherish each and every one of you.

Thank you to my amazing family and friends for putting up with my lockdowns and neverending deadlines and for constantly reminding me of things I tend to forget; you remind me to live and be balanced. Your love is the best anchor I could wish for.

To all the bloggers and readers and reviewers of my stories, thank you for taking something away from my words, for loving and embracing the characters, and for wanting to read Australian voices, no matter what city they may stand in.

I also need to convey the most difficult acknowledgement of all. Five years ago, I connected with a fellow author, a kind, creative, lovely soul who encouraged me to 'own what I do', four little words that changed my life. Fifteen books later, there isn't a day that goes by when I don't appreciate your words, knowing how very different my life could have been without them. Now you are gone, and far too soon. It is hard to process. Thank you, Ednah, for your gentle reassurance, your fierce determination and, above all, your beautiful friendship. You will be sorely missed in the book community. My thoughts are with all the people who were lucky enough to call you their friend, and with your wonderful family – I know you loved them dearly.

RIP Ednah Walters
October 18, 1965 – September 16, 2017
(And know I am still owning what I do.)

IF YOU LOVED *WHEN IN ROME*
YOU WILL ADORE *HOLLYWOOD HEARTBREAK*

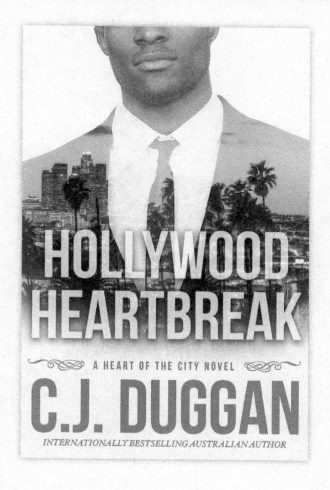

COMING 2018

READ THE OTHER
STANDALONE TITLES
IN C.J. DUGGAN'S
HEART OF THE CITY SERIES:

READ ON FOR A PREVIEW

# NEW YORK NIGHTS

A HEART OF THE CITY NOVEL

## C.J. DUGGAN

INTERNATIONALLY BESTSELLING AUSTRALIAN AUTHOR

# Chapter One

et's get one thing clear. Being an au pair is nothing like in *The Sound of Music*. To start with, I'm certainly not a nun, I have zero musical abilities, and I failed sewing in high school. There's no handsome Captain von Trapp and there's definitely no choreographed frolicking.

All that aside, it had sounded appealing. The plan was I would sacrifice x amount of hours caring for someone else's children, then stroll through a foreign city during my downtime, immerse myself in some culture, learn another language, study maybe, truly find myself, all before falling in love with a wealthy fisherman called Pascal who enjoyed crafting small objects out of wood with his bare hands. Come nightfall, we'd make an incredible paella with the freshest seafood while we sipped wine, arms interlinked as we toasted to us. I mean, we all have to have goals, right?

The reality was somewhat different. For one, I landed a job in my painfully small hometown in Australia, so the chances of meeting a handsome fisherman called Pascal were pretty slim. Instead, my days consisted of shampooing a toddler's hair or wiping the bottom of a five-year-old, and defrosting meat for an early dinner. It was hard to feel like an adult when sitting at a tiny table with my knees around my ears, trying to convince the children how delicious each mouthful was. 'Look, they're little trees, eat your little trees,' I'd say, coaxing them to eat broccoli.

And as much as my employers made me a part of their family, there was never that feeling of freedom, the kind that let me wander into the lounge to flake out on the sofa and idly channel-surf, or to fling open the fridge for an impromptu snack. There was no inviting friends over for dinner and definitely no bringing guys around. It wasn't all bad, but it had been my whole life for the past three years, and I had needed a change.

Now, seemingly a million miles from home, I sat on a plush white sofa, shoulders squared, surrounded by white walls and fresh white flowers. Everything was white, save the glass-and-gold coffee table dividing me from them: Penny Worthington and her equally cold daughter, Emily Mayfair. Like her mother, Emily's smile didn't reach her eyes; there was no warmth there. She swept her blonde bob from her face and looked down at the paper she was holding, no doubt a background check they'd organised through a private detective. I wouldn't have put it past them.

'Won't be long now—we're just waiting on one other,' said Emily. Even her name sounded like she had married into money: Lord Mayfair or something equally distinguished. So distinguished I had been rather taken aback. The Worthingtons' driver—yes, they had a driver—had picked me up from the Park Central Hotel and driven me to a beautiful brownstone in Turtle Bay Gardens. I'm not sure what I had expected; I'd always thought of New York as cramped apartments with fire escapes and air-conditioner boxes hanging out of the windows. Instead I saw an enclave of row houses, gardens arranged to form a common space with a stone path down the centre and a fountain modelled after the Villa Medici in Rome, or so Dave the driver informed me.

'Oh, Emily, I think we'll just begin. You know what Dominique is like.'

*Dominique?* Who was she? Was Emily the mother of the children I was meant to be caring for, or the less-punctual Dominique? And more importantly, why was I about to be interviewed by three women? I took a sip of the water I was holding, kindly provided by the maid. A driver and a maid; they made my previous employers, the rather self-sufficient Liebenbergs, look middle-class. I chose to hold onto my glass of water for fear of leaving a condensation ring on the coffee table. I was certain that act alone would mean instant dismissal.

'So, Miss Williams, tell us a bit about yourself,' Emily said, skimming the pages before looking at me expectantly.

Oh, God, how had I not prepared for perhaps the most obvious question of all? Somehow I'd thought I could simply wing it, turn on a bright and cheerful—not ditsy—façade and fake some confidence. I started by making eye contact with the maid, who promptly came forward and took away my empty glass. But before I could begin the Sarah Williams story there was a distant commotion; doors were slamming and a voice spoke loudly out in the entrance.

Penny Worthington closed her eyes, apparently silently summoning the strength to remain calm. Emily sighed deeply. The maid prepared to throw herself into the path of the impending cyclone.

'Hello, Frieda, my love, how's that gorgeous man of yours?' A loud and heavily pregnant blonde woman burst into the room. She shimmied out of her jacket and handed it, and her purse, to a mortified-looking Frieda.

'He is well, thank you, Miss Dominique.'

'Frieda, how many times do I have to tell you? Call me Nikki; every time you say Dominique it's like you're running fingers down a blackboard.' Dominique, or rather Nikki, brushed wisps of hair out of her face. She had none of Penny's and Emily's poise or elegance, but as soon as Nikki turned I saw the same perfect nose and blue-grey eyes. There was no mistaking that she was Penny's daughter.

'Hello, Mother.' She pecked Penny on the top of the head. 'Sorry I'm late.' She waddled around the couch and sat beside Emily.

'You're always late,' said Emily through pursed lips.

'Well, you're always in a bad mood, so neither one of us can win. Ugh, Frieda, my love, can you please get me a water? I am so fat.' She sighed, turning to look at me with a big smile. 'And you must be Sarah?'

I knew within an instant of her turning that smile on me that I loved her. Warmth and authenticity just radiated from her.

I stood, leaning over to shake her hand so she didn't have to bend over her belly. 'And you must be Nikki?'

Her smile broadened as she looked at her sister and then at me. 'Oh, I like you, you don't miss a beat.'

I was flooded with relief, inwardly saying a prayer that it was Nikki's children I would be caring for and not Emily's. My eyes skimmed her belly, thinking maybe this was the reason I had been called here so quickly; maybe Nikki, clearly the black sheep of the family, needed help with her soon-to-be-here baby.

'We haven't begun as yet, Dominique. We had just asked Sarah to tell us about herself.'

Something told me that there would be no way in hell Penny would resort to calling Dominique 'Nikki'.

'Oh, come on,' Nikki said, rolling her eyes, 'don't you know enough about the poor girl? How many more hurdles must she jump before you give her the job?'

Penny and Emily had matching glares, and it wasn't just because they had the same eyes, although that probably helped.

'Let me ask a question,' Nikki said, propping herself on a cushion that looked like it was more for show than actual use. 'What brought you here, Sarah?'

It was a question that was not easy to answer. Being dumped from the Liebenbergs' employment had not exactly been part of the plan, but neither had following them to Slovenia, where they were opening a remote medical practice. Admitting as much, however, might make me seem unreliable, and an au pair is nothing if not reliable; I would have to think of something better.

Nikki looked at me as if trying to tell me that she wanted my answer to be perfect, so I responded honestly.

'I've dreamed of New York City all my life. I am so grateful to Dr Liebenberg for setting up this interview for me—I know he is a very good friend of your family.'

Penny stared at me; there was a long, uncomfortable silence as I waited for her to say something, but she was giving me nothing. I cleared my throat and glanced at Nikki, who smiled and nodded, encouraging me to continue.

'The moment I stepped off the plane I knew I'd made the right move. I feel I'm more than ready for this new chapter of my life.'

'And you believe you can handle a challenge?' Emily asked, her perfectly sculpted eyebrows raised in interest.

'I'm the eldest of four from a working-class family so I've been surrounded by children all my life, in times when it wasn't easy. But my family worked hard, banded together and pulled through. I don't shy away from anything – my stomach doesn't turn, and the tears don't flow. I mean, I'm not a robot or anything, but I come from tough stock. I will love the children and I will care for them, something that was never more apparent to me than when working for the Liebenbergs. I cared for their boys, Alex and Oscar, since they were babies, which was a challenge, but I loved my time there.'

'Dennis did provide a rather impressive recommendation for you,' Penny said finally. 'And I am going to be completely honest with you: if it wasn't for that recommendation, I seriously doubt I would have let you through that door.'

*Okay, ouch.*

'You see, I don't much care how many brothers and sisters you have or how hard it was for your father to put food on the table – that doesn't affect me one way or the other. Nor do I care for any girlish fantasies you have about traipsing around New York City. What I care about is you being fully present; in your mind, in your heart. That your dedication is solely to my grandchild.

'You are to ask no questions, you are to simply do what is required and nothing more. If you are successful, you will be given a full induction on what is expected of you. You will sign a non-disclosure form.'

'And how am I to know if I am successful?' I asked, perhaps not as confidently as I would have liked.

'Well, we have a fair few questions to go through first,' said Emily in a no-nonsense tone.

'And another interview,' said Penny.

'Another?' Nikki and Emily both looked at Penny, confusion creasing their foreheads. Well, creasing Nikki's, anyway; something told me Botox was keeping the wrinkles at bay for Emily.

Penny gave her daughters a pointed look. 'Yes, another.'

'You don't mean—'

'Are you sure that's a good idea?' said Nikki, cutting off Emily's question.

Penny sighed, the first proof of her having any human emotion. 'We can't hold off any longer—we have to get him involved.'

The three women looked grim, like they were about to encounter the bogeyman. Their dread was palpable, and although I had just banged on about being able to handle anything, now I wasn't so sure.

'Get who involved?' I asked tentatively.

Penny's eyes cut sharply to mine, and I regretted my words immediately.

'First lesson, Miss Williams: ask no questions.'

I glanced at Nikki, hoping to find some comfort in an eye roll or a wink, but I saw nothing more than her sad, worried expression.

I swallowed, nodding my understanding even as I thought, *What the hell have I got myself into?*

# Chapter Two

I knew I'd screwed up the interview. I would be hearing 'if you are successful' for the rest of my days. I went down the steps of the brownstone and made my way back to the car, feeling deflated despite the VIP experience. The driver was holding the car door open. Such a different world, I thought, as I smiled my thanks to him. Not really knowing the rules, I had tipped him on the way here, and I supposed I had to tip him again. I was seriously going to run out of money at this rate. Maybe there was something in my NYC guide about tipping etiquette for private chauffeurs. I flipped through the pocket guide, wondering how this could be my biggest drama right now.

Then the door opened. 'Slide over, sweetie.'

Juggling my book, I did as the voice said, too shocked to think. Then I recognised the body of Dominique as she got in beside me.

'Where are you staying?' she asked, holding her belly and catching her breath.

'Park Central Hotel,' I said, looking at her, slightly worried we might be taking a detour to the hospital.

'Oh, nice. Hey, Dave, drop Sarah off first, then drag me home. I know how much you love going to Brooklyn.'

A smiling pair of brown eyes flicked up in the rear-view mirror. 'I would drive to the ends of the earth for you, Nikki Fitzgerald.'

'Aw,' she said, tilting her head and offering a high-wattage smile.

'You live in Brooklyn?' I asked.

'Much to my mother's disgust.' She laughed.

Silence fell as Dave indicated to pull out into the street.

'Hey, don't worry about that interview, it's just a process my mother and sister like to go through to ensure they are in control, when they're actually not. The job is yours.'

'You really think so?'

'They haven't even interviewed anyone else, and if the recommendation came from Dennis Liebenberg, you could be an axe murderer and they would be hard-pressed to go against it.'

'Well, I'm not an axe murderer, so hopefully that would go in my favour, too.'

'I should think so,' she said, examining me. 'I would pack my bags if I were you; I don't think you'll be staying at Park Central too much longer.' She turned away to look out her tinted window.

I was afraid to hope, but then I thought, *If I am going to be the au pair to her baby, shouldn't she have a say?*

'When are you due?'

Nikki sighed, her hand going to her belly. 'Never. I am never, ever having this baby. I feel like I've been pregnant for twelve months already.'

'Your first?'

Nikki burst out laughing. 'Oh, no, but definitely my last; I have four more rugrats waiting for me back in Brooklyn. As much as my mother complains about my location, I am sure a big part of her is relieved that I don't visit with the grubby-fingered little munchkins often. I mean, you've seen how white that place is—that couch would be smashed within seconds.'

If not for the physical resemblance, I'd have sworn Nikki was adopted. She had a warm, genuine aura about her; she had alleviated the thick tension when she entered the room. I liked her, but I couldn't help but swallow at the thought of five children. Was I destined to become the au pair for them? Was this what the cryptic interview was about? Capture my interest and then hit me with the big reveal?

I cleared my throat. I knew I wasn't meant to ask questions but I wouldn't sleep tonight unless I had some more clarity. 'So have you had au pairs before or is this your first time?'

Nikki looked at me and frowned. Now she resembled her mother. Then her face lightened as she broke into laughter. 'Oh, God, no, I'm not hiring an au pair. No, no, no, I would never subject any poor soul to my brood. Oh, you poor thing, is that what you thought? No wonder you've gone white.' She continued to laugh, which didn't make me feel any better because that left a far worse alternative: I was going to be an au pair for Emily Mayfair, ice queen. I felt sick.

'Oh, okay, so how many children does Mrs Mayfair have?' I asked gingerly.

'Emily?'

I nodded.

'Emily has a boy and a girl, precious little poppets who have been sent away to the best boarding school that money can buy. Don't stress, my sister's au pair days are well and truly over.'

Now I was confused. Why was I even here? Who could I possibly be employed by? I knew they were being cryptic but this was just getting ridiculous. The no-questions rule be damned—I had to know.

'So, why are you here?'

'Exactly.'

Nikki smiled. 'Well, you're about to find out. Dave, can we take a detour to Lafayette, please?'

'Are you sure?' Dave asked.

'Oh, it's okay, he's not there today,' Nikki said, waving dismissively as she tapped away on her phone.

'And Mrs Worthington—'

'It will be our little secret.'

Dave mumbled under his breath.

'Don't worry, Dave, she hasn't put a tracking device on your car . . . yet.'

As much as I was looking forward to the mystery being solved, I didn't want to get Dave fired. I leant across the leather seat. 'You know, I think I'll just wait until tomorrow's interview. I mean, what's one more day anyway?'

'Absolutely not, I don't want anyone else for the job, and I certainly don't want you having a night to think about it and change your mind.'

'Why would I change my mind?'

Dave's eyes flicked up again, meeting Nikki's briefly before she looked out to the streetscape again. 'Oh, no reason,' she said unconvincingly.

Now I was worried. From the moment Dr Liebenberg had spoken of helping with a 'situation' it was obvious that I was signing up for something strange. What was this place on Lafayette? If I woke in a bathtub of ice without my kidneys, I was going to be seriously pissed.

# Chapter Three

I wish I could say the beauty of the rustic building made me feel more optimistic about things, but I was tired, hungry and over it as we rode the elevator to the ninth floor. It opened directly opposite a set of rich mahogany doors with a gold 9A in the centre. Nikki walked towards the doors while I stood in place, widened eyes taking in the luxurious space. The white and grey marble floors gleamed, reflecting my totally inappropriate outfit choice back to me. The click of Nikki's low heels bounced off the ornate high ceilings. I tried not to let my mouth gape, because, well, that would just be embarrassing.

Then I remembered: whatever the feeling churning inside me, I was in New York fucking City!

Nikki had already announced herself via the video intercom and now she confidently pushed the unlocked door and made her way through, leaving it open for me. She grinned as I followed her, sensing that I was rather taken aback by the scale of the apartment.

'Three and a half thousand square feet, Brazilian hardwood flooring, twenty-six-foot ceilings, roof garden.'

'Wow!' I said.

'If you think this is impressive, wait until you see the star attraction,' she said, gesturing for me to climb the sweeping stairs that wrapped around the wall. As I ascended, my attention was diverted to the massive windows with their sweeping city views. I misstepped a few times and made sure to grip the balustrade to make the climb without serious injury. With a view like that I didn't begrudge the detour anymore—I could sightsee from the apartment. The whole day had been a bit of a magical mystery tour; from Seventh Avenue and Park Central Hotel to a Turtle Bay Gardens brownstone to a Manhattan penthouse. Yeah, just another Monday.

On the landing of the second floor we were greeted by an older lady, the penthouse equivalent of the brownstone's Frieda, except this woman seemed a little more guarded as her eyes swept over me.

Nikki slid off her scarf and handed it to the woman. 'How is she?' Nikki whispered, not an easy feat when she was trying her best to recover her breath from the ascent.

'You shouldn't be climbing those stairs, Miss Nikki. I will not be mopping up if your waters break. I could have come down to you.'

'No, don't wake her.'

'She's awake.' The woman waved her words away as she went to the closest door.

Nikki's eyes were alight when she looked at me. 'Come,' she said, and stepped into a nursery bigger than my parents' lounge, dining, kitchen and bathroom combined. A light grey shaded the walls and was highlighted by white furniture and pink fabrics, and another giant window that overlooked the city. A rocking chair next to the window made for the most out-of-this-world nursing corner. I stood in the middle of the room, taking it all in, hardly believing that people could be born into such places. It was such a far cry from my world.

Nikki crept forward, peering into the white cot that had pride of place in the centre of the room. As she tucked her hair behind her ears, a beaming smile spread across her face. 'Hello, beautiful,' she crooned. 'Look who's awake.'

I walked closer, but before I could cover much distance, Nikki reached in and carefully lifted the baby from the cot. Bigger than a newborn and far more alert, at a guess the baby was three or four months old.

Nikki shifted her into her arms with well-practised ease. 'Did you have a good sleep, Gracie girl?'

And almost as if on cue, the crinkled little pink face yawned. We all smiled, even the cranky maid, who watched from over Nikki's shoulder.

Nikki looked at me, as if seeing me for the first time. 'Now, Grace, I want you to meet someone very special.'

She came over to me, rocking the baby ever so gently.

'This is Sarah. Don't tell anyone, but she's going to be your new au pair. You are going to be hanging out with her a lot, and she's new to New York, so you're going to have to take care of her, okay?'

Grace's wild, roaming gaze shifted around the room, flitting from Nikki to the ceiling, and then my way – I could almost feel my heart tighten. A jet-black mop of hair and those blue-grey eyes I had seen before: the worldly, distinctive gaze of a Worthington.

I held out my hand, placing it in the little curve of her soft, wrinkled fingers. 'Nice to meet you, Grace. I hope you can keep a secret.' I smiled, admiring the perfect bow of her lips, and her button nose.

Nikki laughed. 'Don't worry, she won't tell anyone.'

'What? Not even me?'

A deep voice pulled our attention to the nursery door, where a man watched with interest. It wasn't the shock of his voice or that he'd appeared out of nowhere that caused my breath to hitch in my throat. It was that his unnerving blue-grey eyes were looking right at me.

'Hello, Ben,' Nikki said, turning her attention back to Grace. 'I thought you weren't going to be in today.'

'No such luck,' the man said as he walked to the other side of the cot. His demeanour made Penny Worthington seem like Mary Poppins. He scooped a soft teddy from the mattress and looked at it thoughtfully.

'You say that like you don't want to see me,' Nikki teased.

'Just how often do you use this place as a drop-in centre?'

'Can't an aunty come see her favorite niece?'

My eyes shifted to Ben with a new interest as the penny finally dropped: this was Nikki's brother, Ben Worthington. I quickly turned away when he looked at me, focusing on Grace, now fully awake and squirming in Nikki's arms.

'Don't let Emily hear you say that,' he said, his hardened eyes changing as he regarded his daughter. Love softened his face, transforming him, making him more human and no less handsome. His hair was dark, as were the circles under his eyes, and there was stubble along his jawline. His tall, lean frame was encased in an immaculate business suit, but his look was tempered by something unkempt. I tried to stop them, but my eyes kept straying back to him. I had never felt more awkward, but then it suddenly hit me: Grace was the 'situation', and I was to be the au pair for this little baby. Ben Worthington was my potential, rather intimidating, new boss; the one I was meant to meet tomorrow. He probably had no idea.

Until Nikki let the cat out of the bag.

'Ben, this is Sarah, the one Mother has been grilling about the au pair position for Gracie.'

Ben's eyes went from soft and lovely to harsh, flicking to me and then to his sister.

Nikki read the change, and handed Grace over to the maid. 'Ruth, can you take Gracie, please?'

Perhaps I should have been grateful that Nikki was on the receiving end of those eyes, but I felt even more uncomfortable when the siblings continued to speak as if I wasn't there.

'A little young, don't you think?' he said.

'Don't start; she is more than qualified. You read the profile.'

'It's just paper.'

'Well, what are you going to do then, Ben? Because you can't keep up what you're doing; it's ridiculous. Ruth may be a wonderful housekeeper but she can't be your nanny, too. Have you even held your daughter today?'

His rage was palpable. If looks could kill I would have been seriously concerned for Nikki's safety. But she refused to back down, ignoring the vein that bulged in his neck.

'Go home, Nikki, and worry about your own brood.'

Nikki breathed out a laugh. 'You are just as selfish as Dad. Come on, Sarah. I'm sorry you had to witness this.'

I was more than happy to follow her out and get away from him. At least I had clarity once and for all: come Thursday, I would fly home and write this off as an experience.

We had barely made it to the stairs when Ben's voice stilled us.

'I didn't ask Sarah to go, just you.'

Nikki looked at me from the step below; she appeared as shocked as I was. 'What?' she asked.

Ben leant casually on the doorframe, sighing wearily and rubbing the stubble on his jawline. 'Might as well get this over with, saves having Mother and Emily on my doorstep tomorrow.'

'Yeah, well, nobody wants that,' agreed Nikki. She stepped up to be level with my terrified expression. 'I'll wait for you downstairs, and then Dave can drive you back to the hotel,' she told me.

'I'll make sure she gets home.'

'It's no trouble; I'll wait,' Nikki said adamantly.

'I don't know how long this will take.'

How long could it take for him to say I wasn't suitable for the position? I could tell Nikki was thinking the same.

'I'll wait,' she said pointedly.

Ben shook his head. 'You're stubborn as a mule.'

'I could think of worse traits.' Nikki turned to me. 'Go on. I'll be downstairs.' She spoke like I was about to go off to war. Maybe I was.

As she started to descend the stairs, leaving me alone with Ben Worthington on the landing of his penthouse suite, I switched into another mode. Adopting a new bravery, I turned and met his expectant stare, ready to hold out my hand and properly introduce myself, but I was curtly cut off.

'This way,' he said, pushing off the doorframe and stalking down the hall.

All I had to do was follow.

I really didn't want to.

C.J. Duggan is the internationally bestselling author of the Summer, Paradise and Heart of the City series. She lives with her husband in a rural border town of New South Wales. When she isn't writing books about swoon-worthy men, you'll find her renovating her hundred-year-old Victorian homestead or annoying her local travel agent for a quote to escape the chaos.

CJDugganbooks.com
twitter.com/CJ_Duggan
facebook.com/CJDugganAuthor

## ALSO BY C.J. DUGGAN:

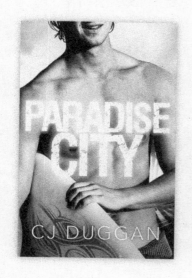 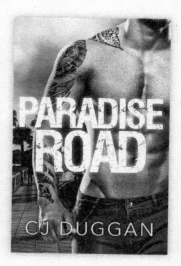

THE PARADISE SERIES – SEXY AUSTRALIAN
NEW-ADULT ROMANCE FULL OF SUN, SURF
AND STEAMY SUMMER NIGHTS

**THERE'S BOUND TO BE
TROUBLE IN PARADISE . . .**

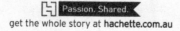